Dead Man Manor

Valentine Williams

Originally published 1936
London, U.K.

This edition published 2023 by

OREON

an imprint of

The Oleander Press
16 Orchard Street
Cambridge
CB1 1JT

www.oleanderpress.com

ISBN: 9781915475237

Sign up to our infrequent newsletter
to receive a free ePub of
Fatality in Fleet Street
by Christopher St John Sprigg and get
news of new titles, discounts and give-aways!

www.oleanderpress.com/golden-age-crime

A CIP catalogue record for the book
is available from the British Library.

Cover design, typesetting & ebook: neorelix

The language and views expressed herein are those of a
bygone era and, whilst probably obvious, it should still
be noted that they are not shared by this publisher.

Dead Man Manor

Chapter 1

THE PEACE OF THE warm July afternoon rested over the fishing camp like a benediction. Under a sky of peerless blue the lake, girdled with firs, was a sheet of glass. On its bank half a dozen log cabins, strung in a wide arc about the central mess hut, showed shingles deep red against the pale green leaves and white trunks of the birches. The air was drenched with the resinous fragrance of balsam and spruce and from time to time, with a quiet plop a trout leaped in the lake.

The portly, pink-faced man in plus fours who, on the verandah of the hut inscribed 'Number 3', was studying a piece of paper, paid no heed to the beauty of his environment. It was a single line of writing, scribbled on the notepaper of a New York club, and, since crossing the frontier into French Canada, he had had the paper out of his wallet at least a dozen times. As he scanned it now, so rapt was his *mien*, one would have said he had never seen it before.

He was a well-groomed individual, past middle age, whose height – above the medium – set off a certain tendency to overweight. Iron-grey hair lent him dignity, stressing his air of mild benevolence. He had a pair of singularly shrewd, very bright blue eyes which just then were veiled in thought. While his material presence – two hundred and forty pounds of it – was indubitably earthbound at the St. Florentin fishing camp, his spirit was far off among the cloud-capped towers of Manhattan, back in the club smoking room giving ear to Dudley Hunter recounting his bizarre experience.

Fixedly he stared at the paper and the four words it contained. *Joseph Ruffier, St. Florentin* – at the sight of the writing his nostrils seemed to dilate with excitement, his blue eyes glittered. So deeply sunk in thought was he that he failed to hear a footstep on the duckboards of the path below. Then a brisk 'Hello, there!' broke in upon his meditations. Looking up with a start, he thrust the paper quickly into his pocket.

A trim figure in well-worn tweeds, a tweed hat garnished with sundry trout flies in one hand, a fishing rod in the other, stood at the foot of the verandah steps. It was a lean, wiry man, with close-cropped, grizzled hair and a tanned face radiating energy and determination. He was smiling agreeably. 'I'm Adams,' he announced imperturbably. 'I have the hut next to yours. I saw you drive up as I was finishing a late lunch, so thought it only friendly to drop round and say "hello," as we're neighbours.'

'My name's Treadgold,' the other replied. 'Come in, won't you?'

'I can't stop more than a minute,' said Adams, going inside the hut. 'I'm taking young Rees out – he's a nice kid and a grand little fisherman. He's here with his father, a retired British General. Why don't you come along, too?'

Mr. Treadgold reddened. 'You're awfully kind,' he said rather hastily, 'but the fact is, I've one or two things to attend to.'

'Some other time, then. You're a fisherman, of course?'

The other coughed nervously. 'Of a sort!'

Adams laughed. 'Like the rest of us!' He had a very easy way with him, his voice well-bred and pleasantly pitched, his smile charming. 'Quebecker, are you?'

Mr. Treadgold shook his head. 'I'm from New York!'

His companion elevated a polite eyebrow. 'How on earth did you happen to strike this remote spot of all places? Most Americans go to the salmon clubs or the Government camps. Or are you a friend of old Forgeron?'

Mr. Treadgold shook his head again. 'I just chanced to hear that he took in paying guests,' he observed airily, 'and the idea of a private camp appealed to me. The place struck me as being suitably off the map, so, as I wanted a complete rest and change.'

The other's musical laugh cut him off. 'You've come to the right spot for that, Mr. Treadgold. Ever been in French Canada before?'

Mr. Treadgold confessed that it was his first visit.

'It'll surprise you. They've put the clock back two hundred years – one might be in eighteenth-century France before the French Revolution. I've spoken French ever since I was able to talk and I've known these people all my life, but I never return to French Canada without a curious feeling as though I were entering through a door opening on the past, as one does in a dream. Nothing ever changes here, you know!'

His companion's eyes sparkled – suddenly he looked strangely elated. One hand thrust deep in his pocket tightly clutched the address he had been scrutinising. 'I'm greatly looking forward to seeing something of the country and its people,' he declared with considerable earnestness.

Adams smiled indulgently – he was fingering a row of books which were neatly arranged on the dressing table behind Mr. Treadgold's hair brushes and shaving tackle. 'They're a rum lot,' he said briefly. 'Speak French, do you?'

'I used to be fairly fluent...'

'That'll help. I don't suppose there are more than a dozen people in the village of St. Florentin who know any English.'

'Are you a French Canadian?'

'Me? No, I'm from Toronto – a lawyer, if you're interested. But we always had French servants at home – my stepmother was a French Canadian.' He had drawn a book from the row. 'Tristram Shandy, eh?' he said, reading the title on the back.

Mr. Treadgold's face lit up. 'You know it?'

'I haven't read it since I was a student at McGill.' He replaced the book and leaned forward to scan another title. 'Universal Stamp Catalogue,' he read out. 'You collect stamps?'

Mr. Treadgold looked slightly flustered. 'Just a hobby of mine,' he murmured.

'Manuel de Police Scientifique,' Adams read out. He gave his companion a quizzing glance. 'Crime, too?'

The other blushed. 'Purely in an amateur way!'

Adams nodded. 'Very interesting. Crime has always fascinated me. We must have some talks. Well, I suppose I mustn't keep my young friend waiting.' He moved towards the door. 'Hello,' he added, as they went out on the verandah, 'here's the Angel coming to see if you're all snug.'

A bulky figure in a uniform cap came plodding along the duckboards that were laid along the path.

'It's the caretaker, or whatever they call him, isn't it?' said Mr. Treadgold. 'But why "The Angel"?'

The other smiled. 'Tremblay, his name is. But as his first name is "Ange" and he's the gardien or caretaker, Montgomery – that's an American who's stopping here – calls him "The Angel Guardian" – "Angel" for short...' He chuckled silently. 'We're all very French up here!' A shrill voice calling at this moment, 'Ahoy, Mr. Adams!' he bestowed a friendly nod on Mr. Treadgold and, fishing rod at the trail, strolled off towards the little landing stage where a small boy in white flannels was waving to him frantically.

The gardien puffed up. 'I come see you got ev'yt'ing you want, Mis' Treadgol',' he announced importantly. He was a solemn man with an elongated face like a horse's. A mouth unusually small and a trick he had of pursing it after speaking invested him with a perpetual air of mild disapproval. With his steel spectacles and cap trimmed with tarnished gold lace he suggested a German bandsman.

'I'm very comfortable, thanks,' said Mr. Treadgold. 'Didn't you say I was sharing this hut with somebody?'

'Correct. With Doctor Wood. He come by auto from New York. He don' arrive yet, but he come pretty soon. You lak' to feesh tomorrow, you tell me, I arrange canoe, guide, ev'yt'ing.'

'I don't believe I'll make any plans for the moment,' Mr. Treadgold broke in rather quickly. 'How do I get to the village?'

The gardien extended his hand. 'You have telegram, letter, no? I take heem after supper on my motocyclette.'

'Thanks, but I'd rather go myself. I want a walk.'

'Walk?' Ange Tremblay's smile was compassionate. 'But, Mis' Treadgol', it ees eight mile!'

'You mean by the road? I thought I'd go by the woods.'

A singular change came over the gardien's heavy and rather stupid countenance. Shaking his head with owlish solemnity he said, 'By the woods? It ees impossible!'

'Why? There's a trail, isn't there?'

The man's face was a blank. 'Better you take your auto and go by road, I t'ink,' he replied stubbornly.

'I prefer to walk, I tell you. The trail's shown on my map – it leads through those woods on the other side of the lake straight down to the village. It can't be more than three miles at the outside!'

The Angel only shook his head. 'Vair' bad trell! You lose yourself in the woods, mebbe. You tell me what you want in the village and I go there now on my motocyclette, hein?'

The gardien was palpably ill at ease. He shuffled from one foot to the other, casting apprehensive glances sidelong through his glasses at the determined face at his side. It was apparent to Mr. Treadgold that, for some obscure reason, Tremblay was determined he should not take the path through the woods. Opposition always made him stubborn, and without more ado he said firmly: 'I'm going to walk and I'm going through the woods. How do I get across the lake? There's a boat, I suppose?'

There was a boat, the gardien admitted sulkily, but no one available to row the gentleman.

'And what's wrong with my rowing myself?' Mr. Treadgold demanded crisply. 'I'm not so young as I was, but at least I can still pull a pair of sculls. I've been sitting in a car for the past three days and a bout of rowing exercise is the very thing to loosen me up!'

A quarter of an hour later he was tying up the boat on the far side of the lake. Following the Angel's reluctant directions he crossed a trestle bridge that spanned a river flowing into the lake and saw the trail before him. An instant later he was in the woods.

The trail was narrow but clearly marked – too deeply rutted for a car, maybe, but quite practical for a farm cart. Fringed with a vivid mass of wild flowers, it wound its way ever deeper among the trees. Notwithstanding the heat of the afternoon, Mr. Treadgold advanced at a swinging pace. Dudley Hunter's half-sheet of paper was in his pocket, and every time he thought of it, he instinctively lengthened his stride, itching as he was to probe to the bottom Hunter's story. The woods seemed endless and the trail ran on without the slightest obstacle – he asked himself what motive the gardien could have had in trying to dissuade him from using it. Bah! The fellow was probably paid for running messages on his motorbike to the village and was only angling for a tip. He shut the incident from his mind, his whole attention focussed on the quest which from New York, more than seven hundred miles away, had plunged him into the heart of French Canada.

His watch told him he had been walking for some twenty minutes when the trail emerged upon a narrow, stony road which presently dropped downhill to woods again with branches overhanging so that he moved in a greenish half-light. He was reflecting that he had come a good two miles without encountering a living soul or any sign of human habitation when he discerned, bathed in sunshine, at the end of the leafy tunnel he was threading, the roof of a building rising above a cluster of trees.

Chapter 2

EVEN BEFORE HE WAS clear of the trees the sound of rushing water was loud in his ears and he saw that, past the building he was approaching, a white-railed culvert carried the road over a torrent which tumbled gurgling from the hillside. The building, two storeys high and solidly constructed of rough-cast masonry, with a slate roof, stood in a dip below the road. At first he thought it was a barn; but then he caught sight of the great water wheel enclosed in a cage overhanging the torrent and knew it was a mill.

There was no sign of life about it. Under the broad stone lintel the door was padlocked, the windows were blank and dusty, while the wheel, trailing streamers of moss, stood idle. Yet the mill was in good repair. The roof was intact and the upturned shafts of a cart were to be seen above the trelliswork enclosing a yard at the side. If abandoned, the place had not been abandoned long. The depression, Mr. Treadgold told himself, and passed on.

He crossed the culvert and, behind the mill, the swirling pool from which the stream, to turn the wheel, was diverted came into view, rushing through a deep crevice strewn with boulders and overhung with willows and alders. Raising his eyes from it, Mr. Treadgold caught the gleam of a long white façade among the trees. Somewhere beyond was evidently a private house, standing in its own grounds. But how silent everything was! He listened – not a sound save the sharp, metallic note of some bird and the gurgle of the water.

A little way along the road, where a rusty front gate tied up with wire broke the line of a high stone wall, he had a glimpse of the house. It crowned a low eminence which, screened by trees, formed a compact mass at the junction of two roads. One – that which Mr. Treadgold had been following – led down a sharply curving gradient towards where a distant spire, rising from a cluster of grey roofs, marked the site of the village of St. Florentin: the other circled the outer wall of the property. From the gate an ill-kept drive lined with some fine old walnut trees crossed the stream by a log bridge and disappeared in the direction of the house.

It was clearly an old house. Time had weathered the shingles of its immensely broad, steep roof to a rich madder brown and a row of dormer windows that marked the upper storey brought to Mr. Treadgold's mind the old-world mansions of the Cours La Reine and other streets abutting upon the Palace of Versailles, where the Court officials used to live. From the circumstance that the front gate was wired up, he inferred that the house was unoccupied. So, to obtain a better view, he climbed over the gate and set off up the drive.

Once inside the property, he perceived that the place had not been inhabited for some considerable time. On either side of the avenue the park was a jungle of long grass which had begun to invade the roadway at the sides. The land in front of the house, traversed by the stream, had evidently, at some distant epoch, been carefully landscaped. Paths planted with bushes and flowers zigzagged their way in and out of the boulders and rocks, there was a rustic bridge, and a bench crowning a knoll. But now the garden was a wilderness, the paths half obliterated by the tangle of undergrowth, the bridge in ruins, the bench crumbling.

The house itself was in better shape, but in appearance no less forlorn. The broad platform, with its elegant balustrade that ran its length before it, like a verandah without a roof, was deep in mud and leaves. Every window was shuttered. One of the panes in the graceful, conch-shaped fanlight above the curiously wide front door was broken and a leaking gutter had dripped a slimy green blot athwart the dull cream of the façade. Boasting but a single floor, if you did not reckon the attic storey above, the house was unpretentious, but, snuggled under the deep eaves of that tremendous roof, it looked spacious and warm and comfortable. 'A grand old house,' Mr. Treadgold murmured to himself. A stone above the front door was inscribed with the date '1799', and he could picture those hardy French settlers of more than a century since, when the first snowfall heralded the advent of the long Canadian winter, installing themselves cosily behind those massive walls, under that spreading roof-tree, to wait resignedly for spring. He wondered what the history of the old house might be and why it had been suffered to fall into abandonment and neglect.

He had turned to regain the road when a slight rustle in the bushes caught his ear. Startled, he swung about sharply. But the forsaken gardens lay quiet and silent in the sunlight – there was not so much as the swaying of a leaf to betray the presence of any living creature. He laughed to himself and with his finger eased his collar. The unrelieved solitude of the place was getting on his nerves, he decided – anyway, it was high time he was pushing on to the village. It was only at the foot of the hill – in a very few minutes now he'd know whether Dudley Hunter had sent him on a wild-goose chase or not.

At that moment he was aware of a face looking out at him through the foliage, a face, dark as an Indian's and framed in matted hair, with a single, savage eye that glared at him and a mouth that slavered through black and broken teeth. It was visible only for the fraction of a second, then it vanished as noiselessly as it had appeared, and Mr. Treadgold found himself regarding the trembling tangle of greenery.

He sprang towards the tree, forcing his way through the underbrush. 'Hey, you there!' he called peremptorily, 'come out of that, d'you hear?' But not a twig stirred – once more brooding silence had descended upon the grounds. In a voice made harsh by the fright he had received, he repeated the summons. His cry, echoed back from the house, fell dead, and with a baffled shrug, he disentangled a thistle from his stocking and made briskly for the gate.

Ten minutes later he was passing the first houses of St. Florentin. The village street, with its bleak frame dwellings, each with its small platform supported on struts before it, was deserted, except for the swarms of black-haired, barefoot little children squatted on almost every porch – he had already discovered that French Canada is the land of large families. The whole colour scheme of the village was russet – russet-gravelled roadway, russet fences, russet houses – and there was a characteristic odour in the air as of charred wood. He was chilled by a sense of isolation. The houses, each with its rounded clay bake-oven at the side, were so primitive, hoisted on low stilts like the huts of some native village: the silhouettes of the men in the fields so unfamiliar – broad-brimmed straw hats, pale yellow corduroy breeches, woollen socks and boots reaching halfway up the calf: the names over the shops so quaint – why, they were pure Balzac! Euclide Fortin, Druggist: Evariste Laliberté, Butcher: Narcisse Laframboise, Baker.

Ruffier's store, Mr. Treadgold knew, was at the far end of the village, with a petrol pump before it – Dudley Hunter had been coming from Trois-Ponts and had stopped at the store for petrol: he had said that Ruffier's was the first pump he had encountered on entering St. Florentin. Several of the village shops boasted pumps, Mr. Treadgold noticed – there was even one outside a somewhat flyblown sweet-stuff shop styling itself, rather pathetically, 'Restaurant de la Gaieté.'

Then with a thrill he saw a faded blue signboard inscribed *Joseph Ruffier, Marchand Général.*

Chapter 3

THE STORE WAS A dusty, twilight place, crammed to the rafters with a bewildering jumble of merchandise, from canned goods to wooden hay forks, from bolts of cloth and bedding to storm lanterns and stovepipes. High under the roof a row of women's dresses swaying eerily on a wire might have been Bluebeard's wives strung up in their forbidden chamber, and in the dim background a suit of cotton jeans dangling from a hook suggested a farmhand who has hanged himself in a barn.

A pallid woman in a blue and white frock appeared behind one of the counters as Mr. Treadgold entered. 'Is Mr. Joseph Ruffier in?' he asked in English and, perceiving that she had not understood, repeated the question in French.

'Un petit instant, Monsieur!' Noiseless in felt slippers she glided to the back of the shop.

A moment later a man, who might have been in his late forties, came out enquiringly from behind a stack of packing cases. A pen was behind his ear and he had a ledger in his hand, as though he were taking an inventory. He wore a cloth cap and had discarded coat and vest. His blue shirt and dark trousers belted at the waist were neat – in station he looked distinctly superior to the general run of villager.

'Mr. Ruffier?' said the visitor.

The storekeeper shot him a quick, appraising glance. His eyes were small and lively. 'C'est moi-même, Monsieur,' he replied guardedly, and added rather thickly, 'No onderstan' English!'

Mr. Treadgold was so excited that he could scarcely speak. With an effort he pulled himself together. 'Then I'll try to explain myself in French,' he said in that language. 'I've come on rather a curious mission. About a month ago an American gentleman, a friend of mine in New York, stopped here to buy some petrol.'

He spoke slowly, framing his sentences in his mind ahead as was his custom when speaking French. His measured diction seemed to make the storekeeper restless. 'That may well be,' he broke in rather impatiently.

'On that occasion,' said Mr. Treadgold, looking at Ruffier sharply, 'you showed my friend an envelope of old stamps, and asked him if he'd care to buy them. But my friend isn't interested in such things – besides, he was in a hurry and wouldn't stop. On his return to New York, however, he mentioned the incident to me and, as I happened to be in your neighbourhood on a fishing holiday, I thought I'd run over and ask you to let me look at them.'

All this, Mr. Treadgold got off very glibly. He was warming to his task and his French was going well. He glanced up hopefully to see to his dismay the storekeeper solemnly shaking his head.

'There's some mistake,' he protested stolidly. 'I've no stamps to sell!' His arm described a wide arc. 'You see what I am, a general merchant. I sell almost everything. But not old stamps. I regret!' He turned away and began to arrange a shelf.

'Yet my friend was quite specific,' the other persisted. 'Is there anyone here to whom he could have spoken except yourself?'

'Nobody but my wife. Your friend may have bought his petrol elsewhere. My name is not uncommon.'

'Is there another Joseph Ruffier in the village?'

The man shrugged. 'For that, no! But the gentleman may have got the name of the village wrong?'

'Out of the question! My friend is a most accurate-minded person. He couldn't be mistaken about a thing like that!'

With an indifferent air Ruffier hoisted his shoulders once more and fell silent.

But Mr. Treadgold was not so easily beaten. He had no doubt that the stamps were there. The only thing was, he had been too eager – he had shown his hand too soon: the fellow was merely stalling, to put up the price. The time had come to talk straight, he decided.

'My friend,' he said, putting his hands on the counter and leaning forward to look the other in the eye, 'I'm going to be frank with you. I'm a collector of old stamps and I'm prepared to pay a reasonable price for any you have for sale!'

Ruffier's face darkened. 'But I tell you I have no stamps!' he cried angrily.

Mr. Treadgold smiled amiably and, producing his wallet, extracted a five dollar bill, which he laid on the counter. 'You play poker, Monsieur Ruffier?'

The storekeeper frowned – he was puzzled. 'Yes,' he said dubiously.

'Eh bien, I'll see you – for five dollars!'

Ruffier stared at him hard, then at the note. Thinking that the man had not grasped his meaning, Mr. Treadgold elucidated further.

'There's five dollars! It's yours for the sight of any old stamps you happen to have in your possession. And,' he added, 'I won't deduct it from the price, if we come to terms!'

In a tense silence the storekeeper continued to regard Mr. Treadgold and the money in turn. The visitor made no sign – he knew from experience that, in such an impasse as this, there are few arguments more persuasive than the display of hard cash, however little.

At length the man shrugged. 'If you must know it,' he muttered reluctantly, 'there are a few old stamps in the cash desk which I may have shown to your friend – if I did I don't recall it...'

He paused, scanning the back of his hairy hand. 'Voyez-vous, Monsieur, I'm not over-anxious to dispose of them, for, properly speaking, they belong to my wife, or rather to her family – she found some old letters among her mother's things when the old lady died. I'm not on the best of terms with my wife's family and if they should find out that I'd disposed of these stamps, sapri! I should never hear the end of it. But, Monsieur, I perceive, is a person of discretion, and since he's so insistent...'

He broke off and walked composedly to the high cash desk. Raising the lid he burrowed for an instant within. When he came back he held in his hand a large, used envelope. He placed the envelope silently on the counter and, picking up the bill, carefully folded it and put it away in his pocket.

The visitor fairly pounced upon the envelope, spilling its contents out upon the counter. A jumble of stamps lay there. Each had been squarely clipped, with great exactness, from its envelope. Mr. Treadgold suppressed a groan. 'What on earth possessed you to cut them from their covers?' he cried.

Ruffier moved his shoulders. 'It was on account of Madame Ruffier – I don't wish to risk her finding out: it would only lead to unpleasantness with her brothers!' Then, as there was the sound of a door opening in the rear of the store, he quickly cast a newspaper over the stamps. 'Psst!' he whispered. 'Here she comes now!'

The woman Mr. Treadgold had seen before came from the back of the shop. This time she was wearing an old-fashioned hat with a bird on it. At the sight of the stranger standing there, she fired a quick remark at her husband. She spoke so rapidly that Mr. Treadgold failed to catch the sense; but her eyes were unfriendly, her lips compressed, and he divined that it was a reproach. Ruffier rapped out an equally unintelligible reply and the woman, with a formal inclination of the head to the customer, went out through the street door.

With a whimsical air the storekeeper regarded his visitor. 'Ah, les femmes!' he murmured, shaking his head. 'They double our joys and triple our expenses. Monsieur is married?'

'I'm a widower!' With a rapt air Mr. Treadgold was raking the stamps over with his finger.

'Monsieur will appreciate, then,' Ruffier proceeded waggishly, 'that, even in the happiest marriages, there are matters which the most loyal husband, if he value his peace and quiet, must keep from his wife. Madame Ruffier is conscientious and full of scruples – were she to tumble on the fact that I had disposed of these stamps, she would insist on her good-for-nothing brothers having their share and I should reap nothing but trouble, maudit!'

Mr. Treadgold turned but an absent ear to him. The stamps claimed his whole attention. They were mainly Canadian, United States, and French, with a few specimens from other countries, chiefly England and the British Dominions. And none was of later date than the seventies – he was thrilled. Many of them, it is true, were common: but there were some early United States stamps, some Confederates, and a number of old French stamps, at the sight of which his eyes shone.

'What do you want for this lot?' he asked, looking up at last.

The storekeeper squeezed his palms together. 'A nice little collection, eh?' he said jovially. 'A big chap like that, now' – he picked out a large United States excise stamp which Mr. Treadgold had passed over as of small interest – 'it's worth something to a collector, hein, mon bon Monsieur?' His eyes were mere slits. 'Shall we say – fifty dollars?'

Until he should have had the opportunity to examine the stamps with the aid of lens and catalogue, Mr. Treadgold had a very uncertain idea of their actual value. But, having in his mind that the stamps before him might represent only a small part of the find he had unearthed, he resolved on the instant not to haggle. Let him play his cards rightly now and, if the storekeeper had other stamps he was holding back, they would surely be forthcoming! Without speaking Mr. Treadgold drew forth his wallet again and counted the money out in American bills. Then, scooping up the stamps into their envelope, he thrust it into his pocket.

Ruffier picked up the bills. 'If Monsieur will agree that the matter remain between us,' he remarked slowly, 'in the interest of the conjugal peace, that is,' he added, with a delicately ironical air, 'I might take a look around at home and see if I can't unearth some more old stamps!'

Mr. Treadgold exulted – his strategy was triumphantly justified. He felt that he and Monsieur Ruffier understood one another perfectly. That was one good thing about doing business with a Frenchman – the French were always quick to size up a situation, without the need for embarrassing explanations. To cover his elation he brought out his pipe and began to fill it from his capacious oilskin pouch.

'Good!' he rejoined as calmly as he could. 'I'm stopping at the camp on the lake. My name is Treadgold, if you want to let me know when to come again. Or I could look in about this time tomorrow if you liked.'

The man shook his head. 'No. Better I send you word. In the meantime –' With a flick of the hand, lightning-quick, he wet the tip of his finger with his tongue and drew the finger across his throat. Mr. Treadgold recognised the characteristically French gesture for imposing absolute discretion and smiled. 'On account of—' Ruffier broke off again and, with an indescribably droll expression on his mobile face, jerked his head towards the rear of the store.

Mr. Treadgold laughed – Ruffier amused him. Like most Frenchmen he was good company, well-mannered and suave, with a fund of high spirits upon which he did not hesitate to draw on occasion. At present his transaction appeared to have put him in excellent humour.

'As one with twenty-two years of married life to his record,' the visitor replied gravely, 'you may rely upon my silence!'

A distant bell, tolling thrice, cut across his words. Ruffier whipped off his cap. 'It's the Angelus!' he announced.

Mr. Treadgold hauled out an old-fashioned gold half-hunter. 'Six o'clock!' he exclaimed. 'I must go. Supper is at half-past and I've a long road home!'

'If Monsieur wouldn't mind waiting five minutes while I pay a call in the village, I could run him back! The car is there!'

'If it isn't giving you too much trouble.'

'Not in the least!' The storekeeper removed the pen from his ear, donned cap and coat, and, taking a cardboard sign from the desk, ushered his visitor to the door. He locked the door behind him and hung the sign on the handle. 'Retour en 5 minutes,' it read in rough hand-lettering.

A sedan was parked in the runway of a yard beside the store. Ruffier went to it and opened the door. It was a car of one of the better American makes and recent date which, with the duty added, must have cost at least twenty-five hundred dollars Canadian, Mr. Treadgold, who had a fondness for pricing things, figured. He felt rather impressed. Clearly the storekeeper was a man of substance.

Chapter 4

They stopped outside a white house near the church, Ruffier explaining that he wanted a word with Maître Boucheron, the village notary, who lived there. Getting out of the car Mr. Treadgold strolled as far as the church and, noticing the date '1753' on a stone over the porch, went inside. After the hot sunshine of the square, the interior, faintly permeated with the lingering fragrance of incense, was dim and cool. Before a statue of the Madonna, at an altar ablaze with candles, a woman knelt in prayer, her lips moving silently. She wore a blue and white dress, a hat with a bird on it – it was Madame Ruffier. Except for the solitary suppliant Mr. Treadgold had the church to himself.

It was admirably proportioned, with an elegant rococo pulpit and high altar sumptuously carved and gilded. A mural tablet was affixed to the wall of the sanctuary. It was dedicated in French to 'Ignace Antoine Hector Charles Ferdinand de St. Rémy, Seigneur de Mort Homme,' who, to judge by the somewhat flowery epitaph, had been a pattern of all the Christian virtues and had passed away at St. Florentin, fortified by the rites of Holy Church, on the 21st of March, 1858. As Mr. Treadgold was reading the inscription, a figure in a long black cassock came through the sanctuary. It was a priest, grey-haired and keen-eyed, the amply skirted soutane encircling a respectable girth – evidently the curé.

From his reading Mr. Treadgold was aware that the parish priest is the most important figure in a French Canadian village. He made up his mind to address him.

'A fine old church, Monsieur le Curé,' he said politely in French.

The priest bowed. 'It dates from before the English conquest,' he replied gravely. Then he pointed at the sanctuary lamp which glowed ruby red before the altar. 'For a hundred and eighty years that lamp has never gone out. An ancient parish, Monsieur!' He pointed at the wall. 'That tablet commemorates the last of the seigneurs of St. Florentin under the old order. The seigneuries were abolished in 1855. The old Manoir de Mort Homme, the seigneurial mansion, rebuilt in 1799, is still standing on the outskirts of the village.'

Mr. Treadgold was instantly interested. 'An old house with a stream running through the grounds? I saw it as I came along. It's uninhabited at present, isn't it?'

The curé nodded. 'The present Seigneur lives abroad,' he said rather coldly.

'I thought you said that the seigneurs had been abolished?'

Only their rights, not the title, the cleric explained in his precise French, and the tenants still paid the Seigneur rent for their land, albeit a very nominal sum. The seigneuries were a relic of the feudal system. To encourage colonisation the kings of France granted leading settlers, for the most part officers who had served with the army in Canada, large tracts of land coupled with specific rights over their tenants, such as the right of *la corvée* or forced labour, and contributions in kind. 'One valuable prerogative,' he added, 'was the right to grind the tenants' corn. Where the old manors survive, you will still sometimes find the seigneurial mill adjoining, the community mill, as it was called. The Mort Homme mill is still extant, although it no longer belongs to the St. Rémy family. You must have seen it if you passed the Manor.'

'I did,' said Mr. Treadgold. 'But it doesn't seem to be working.'

A shadow crossed the curé's face. 'The miller died,' he explained shortly, 'and in the present difficult times no one has found it worthwhile to take his place.'

'And why do they call it the Manoir de Mort Homme?' Mr. Treadgold wanted to know.

The priest shrugged his shoulders. 'It's said that a settler was killed by Indians at those crossroads. Who knows? The name also occurs in France, they tell me...'

Manoir de Mort Homme – Dead Man Manor! The name had a sinister ring in Mr. Treadgold's ears.

'I see,' he observed. 'I thought, perhaps, there was some legend attaching to the house, some ghost story, maybe.'

The curé gave Mr. Treadgold an odd look. He did not speak. Vaguely aware that he had said the wrong thing, the other put in hastily: 'You see, the gardien at the fishing camp where I'm staying was most insistent that I should not go to the village through the woods. He tried to tell me that the trail was impassable, which is sheer nonsense, so I can't help wondering whether he wasn't trying to keep me away from the Manor. It's a pretty creepy place, isn't it? And then, while I was in the grounds...'

The priest interrupted him very sharply. 'Ange Tremblay would do better to attend to his trout,' he declared acidly.

Mr. Treadgold subsided. He had been leading up to his adventure in the Manor gardens, intending to sound the curé about the face that had peered out at him through the foliage. But the uncompromising severity of the priest's regard told him he had blundered again and he quickly proceeded to change the subject by questioning the curé about the early history of the parish. There was something disarming about Mr. Treadgold's personality. Whether it was his frank and open countenance flushed with health, or his agreeably modulated voice, people were seldom brusque with him for long. So successfully did he practise his wiles upon the curé that before he left the church they had exchanged cards and he found himself invited to call upon the Abbé Bazin at the presbytery beside the church that same evening after dinner to inspect some of the old parish records.

But, back in the car with Ruffier, on their way to the camp, his thoughts kept returning to Dead Man Manor, silent and shuttered amid its neglected gardens. It occurred to him that the storekeeper, who was clearly a person of prominence in the village, should be able to explain the enigma of the gardien's behaviour.

Ruffier had none of the curé's reticence. With a short laugh he said, 'Queer things have happened at the Manor since Seigneur Hector went away!'

'What sort of things?' his companion demanded bluntly.

The other shrugged. 'Our people are superstitious, Monsieur. They believe that the spirit of old Seigneur Ignace, the one who has the tablet in the church, walks the empty rooms at night. No villager, it is certain, will go near the Manor after dark, or even in the daytime, if he can avoid it, especially since the miller's death.'

'What happened to the miller?'

'They found him in the stream with his neck broken and a bruise on his head. The police came from Quebec to investigate and brought it in as an accident and so did the coroner's jury – it's thought he slipped from a boulder in the dark. But every man, woman, and child in St. Florentin believes that Télésphore Gagnon met his death at the hands of the evil spirit that haunts the Manor. I don't ask Monsieur to credit these ghost stories, but if he's wise he'll do like the rest of us and give the Manor a wide berth.'

'But why?'

'Voilà! There's a drunken poacher who has a shack on the riverbank nearby. He's appointed himself a sort of guardian of the place, roaming about the grounds at all hours of the day and night.'

'But I saw him there myself this afternoon,' Mr. Treadgold cried in high excitement. And he proceeded to relate his adventure.

Ruffier looked grave. 'You were in considerable danger. This fellow – One-Eye, they call him in the village' – he used the French expression 'Le Borgne' – 'is obsessed by the belief that anybody who approaches the Manor comes to steal it away from the St. Rémys. It's my conviction that it was he who surprised this poor Gagnon going to take a trout from the pool for supper, and killed him. Indeed, the coroner had him arrested on suspicion. But there was no proof and we had to let him go.'

'And you mean to tell me that a homicidal maniac like this man is allowed to remain at large? I never heard of such a thing!'

The other hoisted his broad shoulders. 'He does no harm where he is, since no one enters the Manor grounds any more, now that the miller is dead. But let it be a warning to you, Monsieur, and the other guests at the camp, to steer clear of the Manor in future!'

Mr. Treadgold shuddered. 'I don't have to be told twice!' he affirmed with much emphasis.

The next moment a turn of the narrow forest road they were following showed the roofs of the camp among the trees.

Chapter 5

Mr. Treadgold made his way to his hut in a sobered mood. That face in the tree dwelt unpleasantly in his memory. He was a modern-minded man, but still under the influence of that sombre house, sunk in the silence of slow decay, he found himself thinking of the face he had seen as the incarnation of the evil spirit reputedly haunting the Manor. But then his collector's enthusiasm came to his rescue. With a delicious thrill he remembered the parcel of stamps in his pocket. He would sit down forthwith with lens and catalogue, he promised himself, and examine his treasure trove.

But on reaching the log cabin his hopes were dashed by the discovery that it already had an occupant. A hot and dusty young man stood there, gazing about him with every evidence of frank approval. With its grass-green curtains and matting, its furniture and walls of unstained pine, and its big open fireplace, the hut was very attractive, boasting, too, such luxuries as a bathroom and electric light – from the distance the cough of a Diesel engine pulsated rhythmically over the quiet evening air. The young man had apparently just arrived, for his baggage was draped about his feet and he grasped the canvas-covered sections of a fishing rod strapped together.

Mr. Treadgold had forgotten all about his roommate. The stamps would have to wait, he told himself with a sigh.

'Dr. Wood?' he enquired politely.

'The old physician himself,' the other retorted, and added, 'Mr. Treadgold, I presume?' He chuckled to himself. 'Like Stanley and Livingstone, isn't it? Only for Darkest Africa, read Darkest Quebec!' He doffed his battered felt and mopped his brow. 'Gosh, what a day this has been!'

He was a strapping young man, broad of shoulder and lean of hip, with a merry eye and the nonchalant, good-humoured air which is frequently found in association with freckles and a snub nose.

'What about a small drink?' said Mr. Treadgold.

'Will a duck swim?' the other declared with feeling.

With the calm deliberation which marked his every movement, his companion went to an open suitcase on one of the beds, slipped his parcel of stamps out of sight under a shirt and came back with a bottle of whisky and a corkscrew. Glasses, a bowl of ice, and a siphon were on the table. He drew the cork, measured out two drinks, and silently handed the doctor his tumbler.

'Here's good fishing!' Wood exclaimed, throwing himself full length in a chair and raising his glass. A staid nod acknowledged the toast and in a silence broken only by the chatter of the birds and the faint grunt of the Diesel engine the two men drank.

Mr. Treadgold put down his glass and, drawing up a chair to the table, seated himself and let his glance range unobtrusively over the new arrival.

'So your car broke down?' he observed urbanely.

The young man groaned. 'Wouldn't it happen to me? The ignition coil burnt out. The gardien's gone to try and raise a team of horses to pull it clear of the road, as it's blocking the traffic.'

'The road was clear when I came through the woods just now,' said Mr. Treadgold, 'so I fancy they've towed it away. It's a bad place to be stalled in.'

'You're telling me!' Wood declared with great emphasis. 'Didn't I carry those darn bags of mine about a mile into camp? But how did you hear about it?'

His companion laughed. 'I didn't. I merely inferred it.'

'You inferred it?' The doctor was puzzled.

Mr. Treadgold smiled. 'As the immortal author of Tristram Shandy remarks, "Give me credit for a little more wisdom than appears upon my outside!" It's really very simple. You've obviously had a hot and dusty tramp and I perceive marks of black engine grease, not only on your hands, but also high up on the right sleeve of your coat, suggesting that you've been exploring under the bonnet. I knew that you were arriving by car, so I naturally reasoned that your car had broken down.'

The young man was blankly surveying his grimy hands. 'That's all right as far as it goes,' he remarked. 'But you said I was stalled in the woods. How did you know that?'

Mr. Treadgold laughed. 'Well, you have a leaf caught in the turn-up of your right trouser leg and your shoes are covered with red dust, which tells me that you walked in, not from the main road, where the dust is white, but from that trail through the woods, which is of red sand!'

Wood guffawed. 'Swell!' he chortled. 'Gosh, you ought to be a detective. Or perhaps you are?'

The other shook his head, smiling. 'Nothing so exciting, I'm afraid.'

Wood grinned. 'I didn't think so myself. You look more like a businessman.'

'I hope so.'

The doctor cocked his head on one side, dandling his glass. 'Advertising?'

'Not enough imagination!'

'Manufacturer?'

'Let's say a simple tradesman!'

'You mean you have a shop?'

'Yes, indeed!'

The young man ran an appraising eye over the blue pullover, the well-cut Harris tweeds, the neat stockings and brogues. 'I bet it's a swagger joint?' he hazarded.

Mr. Treadgold chuckled. 'It's not bad!'

'New York? Fifth Avenue?'

'Near enough to the Avenue to be fashionable!'

The young man sat up abruptly. 'It isn't a speak, or what do they call 'em since Repeal, a club?'

His companion shouted with laughter. 'That's good, that's devilish good. I must tell that to Henry. Henry's my partner. He can see all sides of a question except the funny side. Oh, dear me!' He held his hands to his ribs and laughed until the tears stood in his eyes. 'A speak, indeed! I believe Henry would call you out for that! No, young man, I don't keep a speakeasy, whatever my appearance suggests. I ply a trade which is every bit as essential to the welfare of the community as yours. And like yours it fulfils a Biblical precept. You visit the sick, I clothe the naked!'

The doctor stared. 'I'm a tailor,' said Mr. Treadgold and drank.

'Treadgold?' exclaimed the young man suddenly. 'Not of Bowl, Treadgold and Flack, is it?'

'I'm the senior partner. Why? You're not a customer of ours, are you?' He looked at him keenly. 'I don't want to be personal, but surely that suit didn't come from our place?'

'Lord, I can't afford your prices,' was the cheerful answer. 'Ready-for-wear with an extra pair of pants is all poor old Doc Wood can manage, yes, by crikey! But I've heard of your firm all my life. My granddad, Dr. Caleb Wood, who was quite a headliner in the New York of his days, used to get his clothes at your place when it was on Lower Broadway.'

'So you're Caleb Wood's grandson, eh?' said Mr. Treadgold with approval. 'I remember the old gentleman well. A great character, as you say.'

'He was full of stories of the old guy who ran your outfit. A crusty old devil called Oliver Bowl, as British as the Bank of England and a regular sketch!'

'My cousin,' returned the other, not without dignity. 'Ours is an old-established business, young man. It has been a going concern in London since the year 1807 and since 1857 in New York, and there's never been a time, since my great-grandfather, the first Treadgold, joined Josiah Bowl, the founder, as his cutter, that there hasn't been a Treadgold connected with it. My old guv'nor, dead these twenty years, bless him, joined Cousin Oliver at the New York branch 'way back in '75 when I was still in short trousers. My second name commemorates the founder – my full name is Horace Bowl Treadgold and I represent the fifth generation in the one business. Not so bad, eh?'

The doctor wagged his head, impressed. 'I should say not. So you're a fisherman?'

Mr. Treadgold coughed. 'Why, yes!'

'It's a grand hobby, don't you think?'

'Of course. Although, mind you, a fellow can have other hobbies besides.'

'Have you? What, for instance?'

'Stamps!'

The snub nose wrinkled disapproval. 'Pretty staid, isn't it?'

Mr. Treadgold's laugh was quite good-humoured. 'To quote Tristram Shandy again, which I must warn you I do fairly often, as it's my favourite book, "So long as a man rides his hobby-horse peaceably and quietly along the King's highway, and neither compels you or me to get up behind him – pray, sir, what have either you or I to do with it?"' He chuckled. 'But let that go. I'm also interested, albeit in quite an amateur way, in criminology. Does that meet with your commendation?'

'It's a bit more red-blooded, anyway,' said the young man more graciously. 'So you were trying out your what-do-you-call-it – your inductive reasoning on me, eh?'

'Deductive,' Mr. Treadgold amended, and sighed. 'It's a bad habit of mine, I'm afraid!'

Wood laughed. 'Well, I give you fair warning, Mr. Treadgold, you're going to have the sudden death of a number of fine trout to investigate. By the way, what fly did you think of using?'

The other seemed slightly taken aback. 'Fly?' he murmured vaguely.

'They use a Montreal or a Silver Doctor mostly round here, the gardien says,' Wood rattled on. 'But take my tip and stick to a Brown Hackle!'

Mr. Treadgold bit his moustache. 'It's rather a long time since I did any fishing and I'm probably a bit rusty,' he observed tentatively. 'Perhaps you wouldn't mind my going along with you once or twice until I get the hang of it again.'

'Sure. Any time you say. By the way, my French isn't so hot. How's yours?'

'I can make myself understood.'

'Then you're hereby appointed interpreter to this outfit. Gosh, is that the supper bell already? I've got to clean up.'

There was no formality about the evening meal. People sat down anywhere at the long table in their fishing-clothes. Madeleine, the Angel's bespectacled and bustling daughter, was already serving the soup when Mr. Treadgold and the doctor arrived. Tisserand, Monsieur Forgeron's head clerk from Quebec, who was spending his summer vacation at the camp, rose up from the head of the table to greet them. Then he introduced them in turn to his wife and two plain daughters and to their fellow guests – General Rees, a rather irascible-looking Englishman, and his wife, Lady Gwendolen, parents of the small boy, whom everybody called Shiner; the Montgomerys, a middle-aged American married couple; and lastly Adams, who, holding out a welcoming hand, made room for Mr. Treadgold beside him.

Mr. Treadgold found himself instinctively drawn to Adams. The man had natural charm. He seemed to possess an effortless knack of drawing people out, of making them like him. The whole conversation at table centred about him. In faultless French he chatted with the Tisserands, making gallant remarks to the drab daughters, chaffing old Tisserand on his fishing prowess, and, dropping into English, talked fish with the General or Wall Street prices with Montgomery. Polished and highly intelligent, he was an excellent conversationalist and appeared to know everyone and to have been everywhere. The small Rees boy was obviously devoted to him and Mr. Treadgold was quite touched to see the trouble Adams took to interest the youngster and put him at his ease. Shiner rattled away to him freely – Adams and Batisse, the guide who usually accompanied them on their fishing excursions, seemed to be his two great heroes.

'And what did you do with yourself all the afternoon?' Adams took advantage of a lull in the conversation to ask Mr. Treadgold.

The latter explained that he had strolled as far as the village – he was careful not to allude to his business with Ruffier. 'And, by the by,' he went on, 'I had a curious adventure...'

His opening secured immediate silence in which he told his story. 'I gather I had a narrow escape from closer acquaintance with a homicidal lunatic,' he concluded.

Adams laughed rather contemptuously. 'He's no more a lunatic than you are, unless you call an habitual drunkard a lunatic!'

'You know this man?' Mr. Treadgold asked, in surprise.

'Sure. I used to visit at the Manor when the old seigneur was alive – that's more than twenty years ago. Even then this ruffian – Le Borgne, as they call him – was the village ne'er-do-well, a poacher and what have you, and half the time soused to the eyeballs with whisky blanc, if you know what that is!'

'It's spirit made from corn,' Shiner piped up. 'Batisse drinks it.'

'I thought he'd died of drink years ago,' Adams continued to Mr. Treadgold. 'I'm very interested by what you tell me – very interested!' He fell silent, staring at his plate.

'It seems a crime that such a fine old house should fall into ruin,' Mr. Treadgold remarked. 'The present seigneur lives abroad, they tell me.'

His neighbour nodded. 'Yes. In Paris.' And he added rather grimly, 'If he's wise, he'll stop there!'

Mr. Treadgold elevated his eyebrows. 'What's the trouble?'

Adams shrugged. 'One of those cases of a gentleman leaving his country for his country's good, shall we say?' He relapsed into silence.

The General's metallic voice rang out. 'Whether this Le Borgne, or whatever his name is, is mad or sane, it's a pretty state of things, I must say, to have a drunken savage roving round the camp. A poacher, too, by the Lord Harry! Shiner,' he cried to his son, 'don't let me catch you going near this house, do you hear?'

'Okay, Dad,' said the boy composedly.

'I'm told that the villagers believe the Manor's haunted,' Mr. Treadgold observed mildly.

Shiner caught his breath. 'Haunted?' he echoed, saucer-eyed.

'I think that old what's-his-name is the ghost, myself,' Mr. Treadgold opined shrewdly. 'But the story is that the spirit of one of the old seigneurs walks the empty rooms at night...'

Adams looked up quickly. 'Do you mean to say that footsteps have actually been heard in the Manor?' he demanded.

Mr. Treadgold laughed. 'That's the gossip. I don't know anything about it, and as things are I certainly don't propose to find out!'

The lawyer did not echo his laugh. It appeared to Mr. Treadgold that there were lines on either side of the cleanly-chiselled mouth which he had not observed there before, as though the smooth-shaven face had suddenly hardened. Their further conversation was broken off by the company rising from the table. Joyfully Mr. Treadgold skipped off to his stamps.

Chapter 6

BUT HE HAD RECKONED without the rather primitive lighting arrangements at the camp. On reaching his hut and seating himself at the table, the stamps spread out before him, lens, perforation gauge, and catalogue within reach, he soon discovered that the electric light was much too feeble for his purpose. He noted, however, that the three Confederates included a five-cent green-and-carmine Bâton Rouge issue which was new to him, and that among the Canadians was the seventeen-cent blue with the Jacques Cartier head – an issue of the sixties – which was missing from his very comprehensive British Empire collection.

Locking the stamps away again, he took from its hook his old brown Inverness cape, which he had purchased on a shooting holiday in Scotland a good fifteen years before, and throwing it about his shoulders, went out into the cool, bright evening. It was not yet eight o'clock and still daylight. He strolled out on the landing-stage, smoking his cigar and watching the sun sink behind the lake.

He was presently joined by Wood. The Tisserands had settled down to pinochle, the doctor announced, and the others were playing bridge. 'The Rees woman wanted to rope me in,' he remarked rather ruefully. 'But that husband of hers handed me a dirty look, you know, like a traffic cop that's going to give you a ticket – Montgomery told me that his wife and Adams and the

Reeses have made a four for the last two nights – so I scrammed. Don't you play bridge?'

Mr. Treadgold shook his head warily. 'Not with retired British Generals!'

The doctor laughed and shrugged. 'There's not much else to do in the evenings, is there?'

'I'm going down to the village presently to call on the curé. He's promised to show me some of the old registers. Want to come along?'

'Will it mean talking French?'

'I shall be surprised if the Abbé Bazin knows any English!'

The young man's head-shake was exceedingly positive. 'Not me! But I don't mind walking with you as far as the village!'

'It's eight miles by the road. By the woods it's a lot shorter, but you don't catch me going near the Manor again. I shall take my car.'

'Okay.' The doctor paused. 'Just where is this haunted house of yours, anyway?'

Mr. Treadgold stopped dead in his tracks. 'You don't propose to go there, I trust?' he said gravely.

His companion laughed. 'Why not?'

'And risk running into this dangerous lunatic?'

'Oh, shoot! The fellow's probably perfectly harmless. You heard what Adams said?'

With his casual, jesting air he began cross-examining Mr. Treadgold about his encounter.

The big, grey coupé slid to a halt before the presbytery. The hands of the church clock pointed to twenty minutes to nine. Mr. Treadgold switched off the lights, stepped sedately to the ground and tugged the iron bell-pull under the porch.

'You may as well come in, old man,' he encouraged his companion, who stood at the foot of the steps. 'I'll do the talking. We needn't stay long, you know!'

But the American was not to be persuaded. 'I'll hang around for a bit. If you don't see me when you come out, don't wait!'

The door opening at that instant, Mr. Treadgold's attention was momentarily diverted. When he turned round to look for his friend, the latter had disappeared.

The Abbé Bazin was in his study. It was a little room, smelling of wax polish, with a bookcase of religious books and crudely coloured pictures of sacred subjects on the walls. Above the littered writing desk was a large portrait of Pope Pius XI, his hand raised in blessing: below it, an eighteenth century print of St. Florentin, showing the church.

The priest presented the visitor to the woman who had ushered him in: 'My sister, Mademoiselle Bazin, who keeps house for me! Perhaps, my dear Agathe,' he went on, 'these gentlemen will take a glass of whisky, unless they would prefer to try your cherry wine!'

Mr. Treadgold now perceived that the curé had another caller, a jerky, rather corpulent, little man in black, who with his restless black eyes and silky moustache had a vaguely swashbuckling air. He proved to be Maître Boucheron, the village notary. Maître Boucheron declining a drink, Mr. Treadgold agreed to sample the cherry wine which he found not dissimilar to the ginger and cowslip wines made by the cottagers in the England of his youth. He and the curé had a glass apiece, served very genteelly by Mademoiselle Bazin on a tray with a view of Lourdes, flanked by a plate of sweet biscuits.

Both the priest and the notary seemed well versed in the history of the parish, from its earliest beginnings in the seventeenth century, when Governor de Lauzon, on His Most Christian Majesty's behalf, granted the seigneurie of Mort Homme to Charles Ferdinand de St. Rémy, officer in the Carignan Regiment. Maître Boucheron, who had obviously been bidden there to help entertain the English visitor, had brought some documents of interest with him in his shabby portfolio – an old treaty with a local Indian chief, some ancient parchment deeds. The curé, warming to his subject, went repeatedly to the shelf where the oldest registers were kept, to come back with a tattered volume and show an entry in the fine, spidery hand of the parish clerk on the age-yellowed paper.

The Englishman was too interested in his surroundings to be bored; but he found his attention frequently wandering. Here, he mused, was a civilisation which in its fundamentals had been static for centuries – it made things like the tailoring business, the stock market, taxes, bad debts, seem of little account. He saw St. Florentin as the type of hundreds of other tiny French Canadian parishes – a self-contained community with its own little niche in the history of the country which its forefathers had hewed for it, just as with their axes they had hewed the original settlement out of the virgin forest. Nothing ever happened at St. Florentin and so its inhabitants were supremely unconcerned with what took place elsewhere. Empires might rise and fall, but these people went on. It made Mr. Treadgold feel very far from home.

It was ten o'clock when he finally took out his watch. His conscience smote him at the thought that Wood might have been waiting all that time and he rose to take his leave. Maître Boucheron did likewise. The notary refused a lift, saying that he lived only just down the street, the white house next to Euclide Fortin's, the druggist. Gravely saluting his companion, he departed. In his black felt hat, as he walked away in the moonlight, he looked more of a swashbuckler than ever, Mr. Treadgold decided.

Wood was not outside. He was not at the car, and the square, with its dramatic figure of the Christ, lay empty and still under the moon. Mr. Treadgold shrugged and got into the car. Wood had told him not to wait – he couldn't blame the other for taking him at his word. Nevertheless, as he drove through the sleeping village, he could not help remembering that Wood had spoken of going to the Manor – he hoped nothing had happened to the young idiot!

It was ten-twenty when he got in. The doctor was not at the camp. The main hut was dark as Mr. Treadgold put his car away and so was Camp Number 3 when he reached it. He had just switched on the light when he heard a step on the duckboards and, glancing out, beheld Adams strolling up from the direction of the landing-stage.

He had not seen the doctor since dinner, Adams said. The rest of the party had gone to bed: he had been for a row on the lake – he hadn't been sleeping very well and he thought the exercise might help. With that he bade the other good night and went on up the duckboards – he had Number 4, the camp adjoining, about fifty yards along the path.

Back in his cabin Mr. Treadgold hung up his hat and cloak and, going to his suitcase, fetched the whisky bottle to pour himself the nightcap which it was his invariable habit to take before retiring. He had the bottle in his hand when he heard, from somewhere close at hand, a raucous, muffled cry, followed by the sounds of a scuffle.

He put the bottle down and went quickly to the door. As he looked out, there was a crash as the screen door of the adjoining cabin was hurled back and Adams burst onto the verandah, lugging a supine, unresisting figure. He hauled his captive to where, halfway between the two cabins, an electric bulb affixed to a tree illuminated the path and jerked the other's head back so as to see the face in the light, at the same time exploding in a volley of French.

'Sacrée canaille!' he cried. 'Eh, salaud, je t'attrappe bien!' And with that he banged his prisoner's head against the tree-trunk, not once, but again and again.

Horrified, Mr. Treadgold rushed forward. 'Stop!' he called out. 'Mr. Adams, for Heaven's sake! You'll kill him!'

In the pale rays of the solitary bulb the lawyer's face was convulsed with anger. But on Mr. Treadgold's shout he desisted and, with a contemptuous snort, flung his captive from him. The victim lurched sprawling against the tree, but with considerable agility regained his feet and stood there with head lowered, like an animal at bay. To his amazement Mr. Treadgold recognised the face that had peered out at him in the Manor grounds.

Le Borgne was a wild-looking apparition. He was burnt almost black by exposure to sun and wind, with a tangle of coarse, dark hair standing out round his head and an empty socket where his right eye should have been, explaining his nickname. He wore a tattered cardigan buttoned across his grimy, naked chest and patched corduroy trousers reaching only to the ankle to display sockless feet thrust into hide shoes. His remaining eye had a fitful, unstable gleam, and forehead and chin, sloping sharply back, set the whole face at a curiously vulpine angle. He paused but an instant, pawing clumsily at his head and glaring defiance about him, then, whipping round, shambled swiftly off into the darkness.

Adams did not attempt to follow. He gave Mr. Treadgold a penitent look.

'Sorry! I'm afraid I lost my temper. I caught him in my cabin – he tried to hide in the bathroom when he heard me coming!'

'Did he take anything?'

Reassuringly the lawyer shook his head.

'We'd better notify the gardien, hadn't we? He may have robbed other camps!'

Adams laughed. 'Not he. I know what he wanted.' He laughed again. 'Never mind, I've given that gentleman something to remember me by. He won't come snooping round after me again, I guess! And now,' he added composedly, 'I think I'll turn in!' He nodded to the other and re-entered his hut.

Adams had not seen fit to mention just what it was One-Eye was after, the Englishman mentally noted. He remembered the lawyer's scathing condemnation of the man as a drunkard and a wastrel at dinner – One-Eye's surreptitious visit to Adams's hut, he conjectured, had probably to do with some old friction dating back to the attorney's former visits to the Manor. It was none of his affair, anyway, Mr. Treadgold reflected. After convincing himself by a rapid survey that his camp had not been visited, he switched off the light and, climbing into bed, promptly dropped off to sleep.

He was roused by the turning up of the light. He opened sleepy eyes to find Wood standing by the table.

'Whatever time is it?' Mr. Treadgold demanded.

'Close on midnight. May one take a drink?'

'Help yourself!' The other smothered a yawn. 'Where on earth have you been?'

The doctor did not answer – with a happy, musing air he was slowly splashing whisky into a tumbler. He tossed off three fingers neat, set down the glass, rumpled his obstreperous hair and laughed aloud.

'What's the joke?' his roommate demanded drowsily.

The young man started from a reverie. 'Nothing!' He began to peel off his clothes. 'Treadgold, old man,' he asked suddenly, pausing with one leg out of his trousers, 'what colour would you say eyes were that are grey one minute and blue the next?'

Mr. Treadgold yawned again. 'Oh, dear! I don't know! Plaid, I should think!' With a vast heave, he turned his face to the wall. The doctor cast him a pitying look and, perceiving that his companion was already asleep again, went on with his undressing.

Chapter 7

IT WAS YOUNG REES, really, who first gave Wood his great idea. He happened to glance at the lad while Mr. Treadgold was telling his story at dinner. The look of gloating awe on the youngster's face, the ecstatic thrill in his voice as he echoed 'Haunted?' after Mr. Treadgold, brought back to Wood's mind vivid memories of his own youth – of a certain dime novel, dog-eared with much clandestine thumbing, entitled *The Phantom of the Moated Grange*, of nocturnal excursions in Greenwich Village, where his childhood was spent, to a deserted stable, reputedly stalked by a spectre with clanking chain.

A haunted house! He'd have to see that! Boy, was this the real stuff? To Mr. Treadgold's tale of the face in the leaves he paid scant heed – why spoil a perfectly good ghost story by dragging in a one-eyed poacher? His roommate having plainly indicated his disapproval, the doctor said no more about his plan. But no sooner had his companion turned away to speak to the curé's housekeeper than Wood slipped round the corner of the square and made off down the village street. He had extracted from the other a clear description of the location of the Manor, and, leaving the main road through the village where it swung off to follow the river to the camp, he was soon mounting the stony slope which Mr. Treadgold had descended that afternoon.

It was dusk and already the bats were skimming between the trees. Away from the evening coolness of the camp, the air was balmy and sweet with the scent of the dog roses. It was early yet for seeing ghosts, the young man reflected as he strode along. But the light was fading fast; and he could wait.

There it was, the high saddle of a roof, clear-cut and black against the faint shell-pink of the sky! He was conscious of a tingle of excitement. There was the crossroads which, Mr. Treadgold had told him, had given the Manor its name; there the rusty gate Mr. Treadgold had climbed; beyond it the walnut avenue, and at the end, the long, white shape of a house. He vaulted the gate and plunged into the obscurity of the drive, his feet in their rubber-soled deck shoes noiseless on the mossy roadway. A moment later, his heart beating rather fast, he stood before the Manor.

He wasted no time in admiration of its architecture, but, mounting upon the platform that ran before it, attempted to peer through a shutter. But the slats were set at a downward angle and he could see nothing: moreover, every shutter – and he tried them all – was firmly fastened on the inside.

He descended from the platform and at hazard went round the side of the house, following a path that seemed to lead to the rear of the premises. It brought him to a back porch with a few steps mounting up and a door. No light was visible anywhere. He softly tried the door. It opened to a turn of the handle.

At that moment he heard a light step behind him.

He was horribly scared. He whirled about, letting the screen door clatter to behind him. A girl, young and slim and dressed in black without a hat, stood at the foot of the steps, staring up at him. His gaze was held by her eyes. They were dilated with fear, wide open and glassy, so that her face in the dusk was like the mask of Tragedy.

He had no hat to doff, but he smiled encouragingly and said in his airy way: 'Don't be scared. I was only having a look round. I'd no idea that anybody was living here!'

She vouchsafed no answer, but, darting past him, plucked open the two doors and called in a low, agonised voice into the darkened room beyond, 'Jacques! Jacques!' When all remained silent within, she called again, raising her voice cautiously as though fearful of being overheard, 'Jacques, où êtes-vous?' Still there was no reply, and now, veering about, she said to Wood, who was silently observing her, 'Someone is ill down there' – she pointed away from the house. 'He must be brought in and I can't carry him alone. Will you help me?' She spoke, without any accent, in English.

'Of course,' the young man answered promptly, and added, 'By the way, I'm a doctor!'

She gasped. 'A doctor? Come quickly!' Without waiting to see if he followed, she sped swift-footed by the way he had come, back to the front of the house and thence down a path which wound its way along the brink of the stream. So fast did she run that, in the gathering darkness, Wood had difficulty in keeping up with her. He liked the delicate grace with which she moved.

In the shadow of a great boulder at the water's edge an old man sat huddled on a bench. His hat had fallen to the ground, showing his abundant, silvered hair. He was bent nearly double, clutching at his chest and groaning feebly.

The girl dropped to her knees and put her arms tenderly about him. 'Grandpère,' she said in French, 'this gentleman is a doctor. We are going to take you indoors!'

Wood had seated himself beside the old man.

'What happened?' he asked gently, leaning forward to scan the livid face in the twilight.

The old man groaned. 'I walk with my granddaughter,' he panted weakly – he spoke in English, but as a foreigner speaks it. 'Suddenly I feel like a blow in the chest and this terrible pain begin – here!' He drew a thin hand across his breast. Then his bluish lips were contracted in a sudden spasm. 'Ah, mon Dieu, que je souffre!' he gasped.

Alert and professional, the doctor spoke across him to the girl.

'Did you know he suffered from his heart?' he asked in an undertone.

She nodded, grave-eyed.

'What has he been taking for it, do you know?'

'A German drug – metaphylin, it's called!'

'Metaphylin, eh?' He pursed his lips. 'Just as I thought!' He stood up, gazing down at the sufferer who had closed his eyes and was rocking himself silently to and fro. 'We'll have to get him to bed. Have you any coffee?'

'There's some on the kitchen stove. I don't know if it's still warm!'

'Go on ahead and heat it. And wait, fill a hot-water bag – two, if you have 'em. I can manage him alone!'

With an understanding nod the girl hurried away. Stooping, the doctor gathered up the old man in his stalwart arms – fragile and small of build, he was no great weight.

As the American lifted him, he opened his eyes. They were shadowed with fear.

'This sensation of approaching death,' he whispered, 'it makes me so afraid!'

'You've got a dicky heart, my friend,' said the young man composedly. 'But don't worry – you're not going to die this time!'

At the sound of his tread on the back porch, the girl appeared at the door. Beyond her was a big kitchen where a candle burned on the table. Without speaking she took the candle and led the way through a narrow passage to a little bare lobby or hall, with doors opening off it. One of these was ajar; they entered, and in the light of the candle the American saw what appeared to be an office, with a desk in the centre of the floor and empty shelves all round. There was an open fireplace where some logs glowed and of furniture little else save a narrow truckle-bed against the wall. While he laid the old man down, the girl lit an oil lamp that stood on the desk, then whispering, 'I'll fetch the coffee,' silently vanished.

By the time she returned, bearing a tray in one hand and two hot-water bags in the other, her grandfather, robed in his white nightshirt, was already in bed. He was still moaning with pain. The doctor had set the lamp on a packing-case that stood beside the bed. Now he put the hot-water bags to the patient's feet and, turning, showed the girl a small bottle.

'Did you know he had these tablets? This bottle fell out of his waistcoat when I was undressing him.'

She shook her head blankly. 'No. What are they?'

'Morphine. We'll give him a couple to ease him. Pour out some of that coffee, like a good girl, will you?'

Submissively the old man let the doctor administer the tablets and drank some coffee, then lay back, with eyes closed, upon the pillow. Wood drew up a chair to the bed and sat down to observe the patient. He looked very distinguished with his snowy hair and strongly marked, jet-black eyebrows jutting out above a high-bridged, patrician nose. With a puzzled air the American glanced surreptitiously round the bare chamber. What were these two doing, living in these improvised quarters in that deserted house?

From time to time, as he waited for the drug to do its work, he stole a glance at the girl. She had withdrawn from the circle of lamplight and her black frock melted into the shadows, leaving only her face discernible. Now that he had leisure to scan her more closely, he was aware of her beauty. It was a beauty rather of expression than of features, for she had her grandfather's proud, aquiline air and a mouth too wide and full, a chin a tad too firm, for mere prettiness. With her rather broad shoulders and lean hips and clean-cut, vital face she might have been a handsome boy. But, as she stared down with a sort of tremulous compassion at the motionless figure in the bed, there was a softness in her eyes that hinted at unplumbed depths of tenderness. She looked so brave and lonely standing there that the young American felt a quick stirring of sympathy for her in her predicament. How serious this predicament was, none realised so well as he.

At length the old man dozed and the doctor stood up. 'I'd like a word with you,' he said, and added, with a glance at the bed, 'but not here!'

The girl nodded and picked up the candle. 'Come with me!'

She brought him through the lobby into a room lined with cupboards. In the middle was a table set for meals and a few books and fashion magazines were scattered about – the place seemed to be a linen room or something of the sort which the old man and his granddaughter were using as a sitting room. The air was fresher here and he noticed that a window was partly open.

He closed the door behind them and looked at his companion gravely.

'You may as well know it,' he said. 'Your grandfather's a very sick man. How long has he had this heart trouble?'

Her eyes had clouded over. 'For about a year. He went to a doctor in Paris, where he lives. I didn't know it was serious. Please be frank with me. Is it?'

'Coronary thrombosis is always serious. That's the medical name. Angina pectoris, people mostly call it!'

She pressed her hands together. 'You mean – you mean, he's going to die?'

The American gazed at her compassionately – he had frank and honest eyes.

'I mustn't give you any false hopes. A sudden shock might carry him off. After an attack like tonight's, his only chance lies in absolute rest and quiet. He'll have to stay in bed for at least three weeks!'

She did not speak, staring at him in consternation.

'Obviously,' the doctor went on, looking about him, 'he can't stay here. He should be moved to a hospital. Not at once, but in a day or two!'

She shook her head blankly. 'It's impossible!' she murmured.

'Why?' And when she remained silent, 'If you're living in this big house, at least you can shift him to more comfortable quarters in it, can't you?' His voice had an irritable edge.

'You don't understand,' she said huskily. 'The rest of the house is dismantled. Only these two rooms and another off the lobby where I sleep are furnished.'

There was a heavy step outside, and a man's voice called softly, 'Mademoiselle!'

'It's my grandfather's servant,' she said. 'I must tell him what has happened!' She tiptoed out.

On the far side of the room a door broke the line of presses. It seemed to lead to the front of the house. Waiting until the girl was out of earshot, the doctor picked up the candle and tried this door. It was not locked and beyond the threshold he saw another small vestibule with a door in the corner and beside it what looked like a back staircase mounting to the upper floor. Two white doors, massive and tall, with elaborate bronze handles and finger-plates, faced him across the uncarpeted space. They yielded to his touch and he found himself peering into a wide dark chamber, empty and desolate.

Feebly the beams of his candle illuminated the dim void. To judge by the wallpaper – golden fleur-de-lys on a white ground – and a rag of yellow silk drooping sadly at one of the darkened windows, this had been the Manor drawing room. It had been stripped of its last stick of furniture. A few pictures were stacked together in a corner and one or two photographs in dusty frames remained on the walls – except for these, a painted shield representing a coat of arms and a panoply of ancient weapons hanging there, the place was bare. There was another pair of doors, similar to those by which he had entered, in the left-hand wall and he would have liked to have explored further. But fearful lest the girl should return and surprise him there, he reluctantly went back to the sitting room.

A moment later she rejoined him. 'You were very kind to help me,' she said rather formally,' and my grandfather and I are most grateful. I mustn't detain you any longer.'

'But I can't leave you like this,' he objected. 'Your grandfather...'

'Jacques and I will look after him – we shall follow out your instructions to the letter!'

'He should be moved to a hospital; but that's for you to decide. Anyway, I'm stopping at the fishing camp – I'll look in tomorrow and see how he is.'

She shook her head. 'Please, I'd rather you didn't! And I want you to promise me, on your word of honour, that you won't mention to anybody that you've seen us here.'

'But why?'

Her eyes grew angry. 'Isn't it sufficient that I ask it as a favour?'

He laughed shortly. 'No. I'm a doctor and you've called me in to attend your grandfather. In these circumstances, I'm responsible for seeing that he receives proper attention.' He broke off. 'Oh, for the Lord's sake,' he said impatiently, 'can't you see I'm only trying to help you?' He bent his gaze at her. 'I won't give you away, if that's what you're afraid of.' His voice grew gentler. 'Won't you tell me who you are and what you're doing here?'

She shook her head. 'You mustn't ask me that!' She broke off abruptly, raising her head to listen. 'Hush! Did you hear anything?'

'No!'

'I'll just see if grandfather's all right!' She crept away. In a moment she was back. 'He hasn't stirred!' She gazed at Wood in her direct, unsmiling fashion. 'You know,' she said hesitantly, 'sitting in this room at night one hears strange noises...'

'What kind of noises?'

'Footsteps. They seem to be in the house!'

He shook his head at her. 'This place is getting on your nerves, and no wonder! When I come round tomorrow I'm going to bring you along a good, stiff shot of bromide!'

'My nerves are all right,' she told him simply. 'I didn't just imagine it. I heard them the first night we were here. Jacques heard them, too. Footsteps. And a sort of scraping, bumping noise.' She shivered slightly. 'It's rather frightening. You know, they say the Manor's haunted?'

'Bunk. If you heard anything, it was this one-eyed poacher snooping around!'

'Old Mathias, do you mean?'

'I thought his name was...'

'"Le Borgne," they call him in the village. He'd never set foot in the house, not beyond the kitchen, at any rate – he's much too scared of the ghost!'

'You know him then?'

She nodded guardedly, but did not speak.

'How long have you been here, for goodness' sake?'

She counted on her fingers. 'This is the third night!' She went to the door and opened it. 'You must really go now!'

'And your grandfather?'

'He'll have to stay here for the present. I'll try and keep him quiet, as you say. But it won't be easy. He's been so excitable ever since he arrived here.'

'He can have his metaphylin in the morning as usual,' said Wood, lingering. 'And I'll drop around later in the day!'

She shook her head resolutely. 'No, no, I tell you! You might be followed. If he seems any worse, I'll send Jacques for you. You're at the fishing camp, you said? What is your name?'

'Dr. Wood, George Wood. My cabin's Number 3.'

With a brief nod she led the way out. He followed her through the kitchen where a middle-aged, dark man, who was reading a newspaper, stood up on her entry. She unfastened the outer door and held it for Wood.

He stopped on the threshold for one last appeal. 'I can't bear to think of you all alone in this place with a sick man on your hands,' he said huskily. 'Let me come back tomorrow!'

But she only shook her head and motioned him to pass out. He obeyed, thinking she was following; but no sooner was he outside than the door was slammed and bolted behind him.

There was that in her face which warned him that it would be useless to plead with her – besides, the door was shut. With a grateful glance at the full moon, glinting in the murmuring stream, that should light his way through the woods, he laughed rather ruefully and started to walk back to camp.

Chapter 8

GEORGE WOOD WAS BEGINNING to have quite an affection for his roommate. He found him the gentlest and most companionable of men. He was diverted by the latter's whimsical habit of sprinkling his conversation with quotations, always apt, from his beloved Tristram Shandy, a masterpiece which the doctor, to Mr. Treadgold's pious horror, had never read, but which the Englishman appeared to know by heart. The doctor found something transparently honest about Mr. Treadgold. Impossible to believe there was any guile in him when he looked at you out of those blue eyes of his. But what completed Mr. Treadgold's conquest of the young American was his candour in the matter of his fishing prowess.

That morning after breakfast, as agreed, they started out together on an all-day fishing excursion. They shared a guide and a canoe and had already entered the river when Mr. Treadgold, who had grown strangely taciturn, suddenly addressed his companion.

'Look here,' he said, 'I may as well own up now. I'm a sham – a hollow fraud!'

Their conversation on his arrival came to the doctor's mind. 'You mean, you're not a tailor?' he enquired in some bewilderment.

His companion laughed. 'No, that part's true enough. I mean, I'm not a fisherman!'

Wood grinned. 'If it comes to a show-down, old top, I'm no great shakes myself!'

'Shall I tell you the last time I fished?' said the other solemnly. 'It was more than forty years ago, in England, when another small boy and I broke bounds at school and went fishing for roach with a bent pin and a worm!'

Wood chuckled. 'Do you know anything about casting?'

'No more than the Mahatma Gandhi,' was the earnest rejoinder.

Wood's guffaw was so unrestrained that the guide, who was poling in the stern, glanced up in alarm.

'Don't worry,' said the doctor, patting Mr. Treadgold's shoulder. 'I'll show you. You'll pick up the knack in no time. And by the way, since it looks as if I were going to have you on my hands, how about calling me George, as the rest of my pals do?'

His companion perked up perceptibly. 'Right you are, George! But I'm not going to inflict Horace on you. I'm usually known as H. B.'

'Okay!' the young man cried. 'H. B., it is! But tell me, H. B., what made you come all this way to learn to fish?'

The other shrugged. 'I heard of this camp and it sounded pretty remote. I've had a hard summer and I wanted a complete rest and change of scene!' His gaze rested innocently on the doctor's face.

Wood did not answer. When Mr. Treadgold had asked him that morning what had become of him on the previous evening, he had prevaricated, saying that he had strolled along to take a look at the Manor and, finding all quiet, had started to walk back through the woods and had lost his way in the dark. Mr. Treadgold's frankness had impressed him. He was more than ever inclined to trust his roommate; but the girl had bound him to secrecy and he decided to hold his peace.

They had a long day's fishing, eating their lunch on a rock beside the limpid, shallow river, and bringing home twenty-two smallish trout, no less than five of which had fallen to Mr. Treadgold's new rod. It was past eight when they got back to camp, hungry and chilled, for the air was damp with the promise of rain. The lighted windows of the mess hut, from which the strains of the radio came jangling, seemed to beckon cheerfully as they disembarked at the landing-stage. The evening meal had long since been cleared away. But their supper had been kept hot and Madeleine served them at the end of the long table. While they ate, the tranquil evening activities of the living room went on about them. The bridge four was under way; the Tisserand family had sat down to pinochle; only Montgomery circulated, dividing his attention between plying Wood with questions about the day's fishing and trying to tune the static out of the early-Sarnoff set, under the direction of the youngest Miss Tisserand.

They were broadcasting in French from one of the Canadian stations. A syrupy French tenor – an especial favourite, it transpired, of the Tisserand tribe – was flatting his way lugubriously through Gounod's Berceuse. 'Ah, comme il changte bieng!' sighed Madame Tisserand in her nasal Canadian French.

'And to think, George,' Mr. Treadgold remarked sotto voce to the doctor, pushing back his plate and offering his cigar-case, 'to think I once believed that an American crooner was the worst thing on the air!'

'Except two crooners,' retorted the young man blithely, helping himself from the case.

Mr. Treadgold carefully chose a cigar. 'One lives and learns!' he proffered mildly.

The tenor had launched forth upon his second number. 'Parlez-moi d'amour!' the sugary falsetto trilled. 'Redites-moi des choses tendres!'

Resolutely Mr. Treadgold stood up. 'George,' he said, 'do you recollect what Uncle Toby said when he opened the window and let the fly go?'

By this time Tristram Shandy's Uncle Toby was, vicariously, quite a familiar of Mr. Treadgold's roommate. So, assuming a knowing air, the doctor asked, 'What?'

'He said,' replied the other with portentous solemnity, '"This world surely is wide enough to hold both thee and me!"' His head made a very slight movement towards the door. 'I believe there's some whisky left!' he added significantly.

Wood nodded and silently the two men slipped out.

They had been installed on their verandah for about an hour, slapping at the mosquitoes and watching the darkness deepen over the lake, when they observed the General approaching.

'Has either of you seen anything of Shiner?' he asked. 'He went out after dinner and hasn't come back. It's getting on for ten o'clock and he ought to be in bed.'

On their both disclaiming all knowledge of the youngster, the General stumped away with a light in his eye that boded no good for the truant.

'I hope nothing's happened to the kid,' said Mr. Treadgold when Rees had gone.

His companion yawned. 'He's probably taken a boat out and lost an oar or something!'

'Suppose we go as far as the landing-stage and see if there's any sign of him?'

The General and Adams were already on the little pier. As Mr. Treadgold and the doctor strolled up, Adams pointed silently to a canoe which was just emerging into the light of the lantern which burned all night at the end of the quay. In the bow, paddling vigorously, knelt the missing Shiner.

'What the devil's the meaning of this performance, sir?' his father rasped as the canoe came alongside.

The boy hopped out. He was breathless with excitement. 'I've been to the haunted house! I believe I saw the ghost, too!'

The General appeared about to choke. 'I thought I expressly forbade you...'

'You mean to say you really saw someone at the Manor, old man?' Adams asked.

'Well, I didn't exactly see anybody,' the lad admitted. 'But there was a sort of dim light at the side – it seemed to be shining through a shutter – and I heard footsteps, too! I didn't wait to see any more – I just ran!'

His father grabbed him by the arm. 'You go straight to bed, my friend! I'll deal with you in the morning!'

'But, hang it, General,' Adams expostulated, 'let the boy tell us about the ghost! It sounds interesting!'

'Obviously, that one-eyed poacher's camping in the house,' Mr. Treadgold remarked aside to the doctor.

But Wood, staring absently into the darkness, did not answer.

'Off with you!' the General barked at his son, disregarding Adams's intervention. 'At the double! Quick march! And let me hear no more of this childish nonsense!'

Thus admonished, the youngster departed precipitately in the direction of the Rees camp, followed at a distance by his still fuming parent, and Mr. Treadgold and the doctor returned to their verandah.

Wood lit his pipe and lay back in his chair, gazing aloft, his hands clasped behind his head. He seemed disinclined for speech. Mr. Treadgold was content. He had no particular wish to talk, either. After his long day in the air he felt healthily tired, but he was not ready for bed. His second cigar was going well, his deck chair was adjusted at the right angle, and he was enjoying the sombre stillness of the night, the fragrance of the woods. A little while and his cigar, which had gone out, fell from his lips to the floor, his head drooped...

A shout awakened him. It had begun to rain. Along the duckboards Montgomery, a raincoat draped over his head, was hailing them.

'Hey, Doc, what's the time? My watch has stopped!'

'A quarter to eleven,' Wood shouted back.

'Gracious,' exclaimed Mr. Treadgold, sitting up, 'I must have dozed off. Well, here's the rain all right!'

'It's only a shower,' his companion replied, and relapsed into silence.

He was haunted by the vision of the girl and her grandfather cowering in that ghostly house. The light young Rees had seen must have come from their improvised sitting room. Tonight the story was all over the camp – tomorrow the village would have it. What was he to do? Go off and warn the girl to find a fresh hiding-place? Pitilessly the rain descended, like a sheet of water. On a night like this, with the old man at death's door, where could these two go? If only his car were not out of action!

The snap of Mr. Treadgold's watch broke a long silence. The rain had stopped as abruptly as it had started. 'Eleven o'clock,' said Mr. Treadgold. 'Bedtime, I think!'

'Wait a bit!' Wood answered.

He had just remembered that large and expensive coupé in the garage. Well, it would mean entrusting his roommate with the girl's secret. After all, why not? The open countenance at his side, so sage and so serene, gave him confidence. On the instant, his mind was made up. He would tell H. B. The whole story and see what he suggested...

The mess hut was long since dark: one by one the lights in the cabins had disappeared: the night wind rustled in the birches, bringing down a spatter of raindrops. Still from the verandah of Camp Number 3 came the murmur of the doctor's voice. At length it ceased.

'So that's the light young Rees saw,' said Mr. Treadgold musingly. 'Well, I believe I can tell you who your patient is.'

Wood looked at him sharply. 'What do you mean?'

'It's the Seigneur.'

'The which?'

'A sort of local Lord of the Manor.' Treadgold waxed a little learned on the seigneurial system as the curé had explained it to him. 'It seems he got into a mess of some kind and had to skip.

Adams was telling me about it at dinner.' He craned his head in the direction of the adjoining cabin. 'Is Adams still up?'

'His light's out,' said the doctor, and asked. 'What kind of a mess?'

'Adams didn't say!'

'So the old boy's on the lam and hiding in the family mansion, eh?'

'That's about the size of it. The young woman hasn't sent for you, has she?'

A brief head-shake. 'Not yet!'

'My advice to you is simple. If she does, go to your patient. Otherwise, stay away. You don't want to get yourself mixed up more than you need with a fugitive from justice.'

Wood sighed. 'I can't help being sorry for the girl. She's so plucky, so – kind of proud. I'd like to help her if I could. Why don't we take your car and run over there now?' He regarded his companion hopefully.

Mr. Treadgold started. 'At this time of night? No, no, my boy, I'm much too old for such knight-errantry. Besides, I'm going to bed. Hello, what's that?'

They both heard the muffled thump of oars on the dark lake at their feet. 'It's a boat,' said Wood. 'Who can be out at this hour?'

'I expect it's Adams. He told me he likes rowing the last thing at night – it makes him sleep.'

The doctor pointed. 'It isn't Adams!'

A figure was visible under the pier light, a man in a shining rubber coat who stood peering about him, as though uncertain of his bearings. 'It's Jacques!' cried Wood suddenly.

Springing from his chair, he went plunging along the duckboards, Mr. Treadgold at his heels. As they emerged from the darkness upon the lighted landing-stage, the man sprang forward. Under his straw hat his face glistened with perspiration.

'Ah, Docteur, I am happy I find you,' he faltered in broken English. 'Mademoiselle say for you to come quickly. My master is unconscious and we cannot revive him!'

Chapter 9

'I'll get the car!'

Mr. Treadgold spoke and was gone. His words galvanised the doctor into action. 'Go with him!' he bade the servant and rushed back to the cabin. There he gathered up his stethoscope, the black satchel containing his emergency kit, without which he never travelled, his torchlight and his raincoat, and was out in the dripping darkness again. As he raced for the garage the roar of a motor warming up came back to him. On the roadway behind the main hut the car was already throbbing, with Mr. Treadgold, swathed in his cape, at the wheel and Jacques in the rumble. Wood sprang in. The clock on the dash marked midnight.

Mr. Treadgold nudged his companion. 'I asked him,' he said in an undertone, jerking his head backward towards the rumble, 'who these people at the Manor are. But he says his orders are to give no name. I guess it's the Seigneur all right, though. He's a Catholic, anyway – we have to stop by for the curé. And anyone can see that this fellow's a gentleman's servant.' In a spatter of mud the car shot away.

As the rain had stopped, they had not waited to put up the hood. Leaning back, Wood began to question the servant behind. As Mademoiselle had sat up with Monsieur all the previous night, Jacques said, after supper that evening Monsieur sent her to lie down. When, around nine o'clock, Jacques looked in to give Monsieur his tablets, Monsieur told him he could go to bed. Monsieur had seemed so much better, he had complied – he slept in a small room off the kitchen. The next thing he knew he found Mademoiselle at his bedside – the old gentleman had had another attack, she said. He accompanied her to the room they used for meals – la lingerie, Jacques called it – and saw Monsieur, fully dressed, on the floor: he did not speak or move. Between them they got the old man to his room, but he did not come round. Then Mademoiselle had sent him to the camp for the doctor. He had run all the way through the woods, and if he had not happened to find a boat on the other side, he would have had to make the whole tour of the lake. He was to fetch the curé, too – Mademoiselle was very insistent about this. The other gentleman had agreed to stop at the presbytery – it was only a little bit out of the way. 'A matter of two or three minutes,' Mr. Treadgold put in. 'I guess it won't make any difference,' the doctor agreed gravely.

The curé had not yet returned from Trois-Ponts, Mademoiselle Agathe called to the waiting car from an open window of the presbytery. He should have the message the moment he got back. But who should be ill, in danger of death, at the Manor? 'Drive on!' Wood ground out between his teeth to Mr. Treadgold and, with a roar that awoke all the echoes of the silent square, they were on their way again.

It was twenty-five minutes past twelve when the coupé drew up at the Manor. The doctor, clutching his satchel, was out and over the gate before the car had ceased to move. Leaving his companions to follow as best they might, he sprinted up the avenue and round to the back porch.

The house was plunged in darkness – not even the linen room showed a light. But the back door was unfastened and, with the aid of his torch, he groped his way through the black kitchen to the lobby beyond. A narrow band of radiance, falling athwart the gloom, denoted the old man's room. All was still as death within.

Fully dressed in a dark suit, the old man lay stretched on his truckle-bed. His eyes were closed and in the uncertain ray of the single candle that flared on a chair, his finely moulded face was ashen. Putting his satchel down on the table, Wood went forward. For the moment he thought he was alone with the patient. But then something stirred in the shadows and the girl was before him.

'Why was he allowed to get up?' He spoke sternly, his eyes on the figure on the bed.

Her fingers tore at the little handkerchief she carried. 'He insisted that I should go and rest. I must have fallen asleep. I awoke, thinking I heard a cry. I ran in here, but he was gone – his clothes, too. He must have dressed himself – I found him on the floor of the linen room, unconscious as you see him now. I tried to give him brandy, coffee, but his teeth were clenched so firmly...' She spoke in breathless, broken sentences, hands fluttering, eyes imploring.

Stepping past her, Wood went to the bed. She followed slowly after, watching his every movement with a sort of dreadful fascination.

Mr. Treadgold entering just then – Jacques had remained at the gate to await the priest – saw the doctor, his stethoscope in his ears, bending over the seemingly lifeless form stretched on the pallet. Laying the stethoscope aside, Wood took the candle and, opening one of the patient's eyes with finger and thumb, passed the light before it. Then with an absorbed, purposeful air he went to the table and, unstrapping his satchel, found a hypodermic needle and a small bottle. He filled the needle, tried it, and returned to the bed.

Soft-voiced, soft-footed, the servant was at the door. He signalled to the girl. 'Psst, Mademoiselle! Monsieur le Curé is there!'

In dismay she glanced about the impoverished room. 'But we must prepare an altar,' she said in lowered tones. Removing a cup and a glass from the crate that stood beside the bed, she flew to a suitcase against the wall, and returning with a large, white handkerchief, spread it over the box. 'Quickly, Jacques,' she ordered, 'bring another candle! You'll find one in the linen room!'

As the servant turned to obey her, he receded a pace, then reverentially dropped on one knee. A cloaked figure stood in the doorway. It was the Abbé Bazin. His rapt air, and the way he carried his hands beneath his cloak, told Mr. Treadgold that he bore the viaticum.

The girl had placed the solitary candle on the improvised altar. She was on her knees. Jacques had tiptoed away. Looking neither to right nor left, the priest advanced to the bed.

Just then the doctor, with a faint shrug, turned away. He met the curé face to face. 'I'm sorry,' he said gently, 'this man is dead!'

The priest did not speak – he was staring fixedly at the dead man's face. But it was evident that he understood, for he took one hand from under his cloak and, raising it, made the sign of the cross over the bed, then fell to his knees. Through the hushed room rolled, above the sound of the girl's stifled sobbing, the prayer for the Dead: 'De profundis clamavi ad Te, Dominum; Domine, exaudi orationem meam!' Mr. Treadgold and the doctor knelt.

The door was flung back violently, making the candle-flame leap. Jacques stood there, mouth sagging, eyes staring. Mr. Treadgold rose hastily and went to enjoin him to silence.

'Ah, mon Dieu,' the man gasped. 'Quel malheur! Back there in the salon...'

'Quiet!' the other whispered peremptorily. 'Your master's dead!'

'Dead?' Aghast the servant echoed him. He was a pigeon-breasted, sallow man with a curiously guarded air. His glance flashed to the bed and the priest beside it praying on his knees, but instantly came back to the Englishman's face. 'But, Monsieur,' he cried distractedly under his breath, 'it is as I say. Back there in the salon – I saw it myself...'

Firmly Mr. Treadgold pushed him into the lobby and closed the door behind them.

'What are you talking about?' he demanded sternly.

The man's hands fluttered wildly. 'I go to the linen room for the candle, as Mademoiselle ordered. But the room is dark – someone has taken the lamp that stands on the table. Now I see a faint light under the door at the end. I open the door, and what do I perceive across the vestibule, through the doors of the salon beyond? Standing on the floor is the lamp – it is burning, you understand – and beside it the body of a man!'

'What man?' Mr. Treadgold's tone was irritable, incredulous.

The yellowish eyeballs rolled in terror. 'I was drawing nearer to look when I see that he is lying in a pool of blood. I call to him, but he does not budge, and I know he is dead. So I come back here. If Monsieur would go with me...'

The door behind them opened and the doctor appeared. 'What's going on here?' he asked.

'He insists there's a dead man in the drawing room,' Mr. Treadgold explained.

Wood stared at him. 'What do you mean, in the drawing room?'

The other shrugged. 'It's what he keeps on telling me. We'd better investigate!' He signalled to the servant to lead on.

The doctor's torch lighted them through the darkened linen room to the vestibule beyond. Across the vestibule the lofty doors of the dismantled drawing room gaped wide, and beyond them, sprawling on the uncarpeted boards like a sack dropped from a truck, a formless mass was visible. It lay on the brink of the pool of light cast by the lamp which stood on the floor close by. As they approached, they could see it was a man, prone on his back, with one knee drawn up and limp hands flung wide.

Mr. Treadgold was the first to catch sight of the face. He stopped dead and turned, with a shocked expression, to Wood.

'My God,' he whispered, 'it's Adams!'

Chapter 10

ADAMS IN HIS NEAT flannel suit and gay yellow pullover, silken ankles showing above trim brown shoes; Adams on his back with knee crooked and limbs flaccid like a man who has flung himself down on the grass, face to the sun; Adams with eyes closed, his small, rather delicate features puckered in a puzzled frown.

'Adams!' echoed the doctor blankly: then he was down on his knees beside the body.

Swiftly, gingerly, his hands moved about it. 'He's dead all right!' He spoke unemotionally over his shoulder. Softly he replaced the limp arm he had raised from the floor. 'But he's not dead long: the matter of an hour or two, at most! What the devil does it mean?' He began to fumble with the body, unbuttoning the jacket, rolling up the jersey, opening the blood-stained shirt. Then he switched on his torch. The dead man's skin shone whitely in the bright beam. 'Look here!' said Wood, sitting back on his heels.

His two companions leaned forward. Wood's finger indicated a discoloured hole high up in the left breast – he held a swab of cotton wool in his hand with which he had wiped the wound clean. 'He's been stabbed!' he announced laconically.

Turning the torchlight this way and that, the American was searching the floor about and beneath the dead man. 'I can't find any weapon,' he announced, glancing up at the others. 'I never saw a wound quite like that before. It wasn't made with a knife, I swear – the opening's too large. It seems to be triangular, as if he'd been stabbed with some sharp tool, like a file, or a chisel, with a triangular base!' Shaking his head he stood up. 'Well,' he remarked, brushing his hands together, 'we'd better not touch anything until the police arrive. But what beats me is what the blazes he was doing here!'

By way of reply his companion snapped his fingers. 'Show me that light a minute!' He was gazing intently upon the floor. Taking Wood's torch, Mr. Treadgold switched the beam upon the ground and began to make the circle of the body.

The dead man lay at an angle, towards the right-hand near corner of the drawing room as you looked in from the vestibule, his feet pointing towards the double doors and at a distance of not more than a dozen paces from them. Perhaps a yard from his head, between him and the right-hand wall, the lamp shed its rays upon the edges of the viscous stain which had welled out on either side of the body. Beyond that little oasis of light the rest of the dismantled chamber was dimly seen – its two windows, close-shuttered, breaking the line of the wall opposite the vestibule entrance, its other set of doors in the centre of the left-hand wall.

On the near side of these doors a faint glitter, high up on the wall, caught the doctor's eye. It was the rack of arms he had remarked on his previous visit. With a muttered ejaculation he was about to cross the room to it when Mr. Treadgold called him. 'George,' he cried softly, 'look here!'

He stood at the foot of the body, close to the left leg – the one that was partly drawn up – the torch deflected upon the pool, already congealing, in which it reclined. In the glare of the torchlight Wood saw that the edge of the spreading stain was cut by the upper part of a broad, squat footprint. 'And now here!' Mr. Treadgold went on and, swinging round, turned the light towards the vestibule, and upon the floor between the double doors. A reddish smear was visible upon the age-worn beams.

'Gosh!' said the doctor under his breath.

'He left his tracks all right,' was his companion's dry comment. He paused. 'Unless...' he murmured as though to himself and glanced involuntarily towards Jacques, who, with wooden features but eyes unceasingly watchful, waited in the shadow within the doorway.

'My friend,' said Mr. Treadgold gently, 'just let me see your shoe!' With an unwilling air the servant caught his right foot in his hand and displayed the sole. It was damp from the evening's rain but clean. 'Now the other!' the Englishman encouraged him. The left sole, too, showed no trace of blood. 'Good!' Mr. Treadgold exclaimed briskly. 'And now to see where this trail will lead us!'

Torch in hand, his two companions following, he plunged into the vestibule – there was an eager, exploring air about him that put the doctor in mind of a large dog hunting rabbits. In the vestibule they immediately picked up another smear and there was a third just inside the linen room.

'The window!' cried Mr. Treadgold, brandishing his torch.

The window was of the casement type, opening inward. One side was set back against the wall. The shutter was closed, but not fastened – it yielded to a slight push. There were what looked like fresh scratches on the wooden sill and, as the torch was focussed upon the marks, they all saw the faint smear of scarlet upon the faded and blistered paintwork. Outside, below the window, a line of bushes swayed gently in the night breeze. Leaning over the sill, Mr. Treadgold shone the light upon the path they lined.

'Where does it lead to?' he asked of Jacques, who was behind him.

'But, Monsieur,' the man replied, 'it is the path by which you 'ave come. It go from the front to the kitchen door.'

The path gleamed wetly in the torch's beam: its surface, softened by the shower earlier in the evening, was crossed and re-crossed by footprints.

Mr. Treadgold grunted and drew in his head. 'Four of us, besides the murderer, have left their marks there,' he remarked soberly. 'We'll have to wait for daylight to investigate out-of-doors, anyway. Fortunately, it's a fine night!'

'Let's go back to the drawing room, shall we, H. B.?' said Wood suddenly. 'There's something I want to look at!'

So saying he led his companion back to the sombre chamber and before the panoply of ancient weapons that hung on the wall. They saw, exhibited upon a board, gilt-nailed and covered with threadbare, red velvet, two curved swords, with brass hilts and leather sheaths, a brace of antique horse-pistols, such as highwaymen are depicted with, and an ancient musket, no bigger than a carbine, corroded with rust.

'Tracking down your weapon, eh?' Mr. Treadgold remarked, absently rubbing his finger along the barrel of the musket. 'Well, it didn't come from here!' In effect there was no empty hook and no sign of any of the arms the board displayed having been disarranged.

Mr. Treadgold had drifted off. He was gazing moodily at the painted shield which flanked the other side of the door. It showed the familiar device of the pelican feeding its young from its lacerated breast, with a scroll below bearing the motto, 'Je tiendrai foy' – obviously the St. Rémy crest.

The doctor touched the other's sleeve. 'Look here, H. B., hadn't we better do something about notifying the police? Also, we have to find out what Adams was doing here.'

His companion turned away from the shield. 'I believe I can tell you that,' he answered quietly, while his eye sought out Jacques. 'Do you know a man they call Le Borgne?' he asked the servant.

The American's eyes snapped. 'The one-eyed poacher, eh?' Excitedly he pounded his palm with his fist. 'Then those blood marks we found...'

A plump hand stayed him – Mr. Treadgold was awaiting the servant's reply. 'Yes, Monsieur,' said Jacques with his habitually guarded air.

'Have you seen him this evening?'

The man hesitated. 'He was in the kitchen before supper. I did not see him since!'

'Does he sleep here?'

'Oh, no, Monsieur! He have his own hut on the riverbank above the old mill.'

'But he's in the habit of coming into the house, eh?'

'Only as far as the kitchen. He fetch us our supplies.'

Mr. Treadgold nodded austerely. He pointed with his foot towards the body. 'How did *he get here*?'

Jacques shook his head. 'I do not know.'

'You didn't let him in?'

'No, Monsieur. I do not know anything about him until I walk in and he is lying there.'

'Yet he was a friend of the family, I think?'

A shadow seemed momentarily to darken the yellowish face.

'For that, I cannot say. Me, I never see him before.'

Mr. Treadgold turned to the doctor again. 'I meant to tell you, but it slipped my memory. Last night, while you were out, Adams caught this tramp, Le Borgne, skulking in his cabin. If it hadn't been for me...' He briefly described the scene. 'Do you remember,' he asked, 'the last time we saw Adams tonight?'

'It was on the landing-stage, wasn't it? When young Shiner came in.'

'Exactly. The boy spoke of seeing a light in a window of the Manor and I observed – I don't know whether you recall it – that probably Le Borgne was camping in the house. Whether Adams overheard my remark or not, I believe he decided on the spur of the moment to go and investigate and, taking a boat across the lake...'

The American was swift to catch his drift. 'I'm on. You mean that that boat which Jacques found on the other side was left there by Adams, is that it?'

'Precisely. I've been turning this over in my mind. Adams, an old friend of the family, is led to believe that Le Borgne is making free of the Manor house. Just what he knew to this man's detriment, beyond the fact that he's a drunkard and a general bad lot, I'm unable to say; but I surmise he jumped to the conclusion that Le Borgne was there to no good purpose – you know, there's a lot of easy loot in an old house like this in the way of brasswork and lead sheeting...'

'And old One-Eye caught him prying and killed him, eh?'

'That's the way it looks to me.' He paused. 'With the data we already possess, it shouldn't be hard to arrive at the approximate time at which Adams met his death. Young Rees came in about ten, didn't he? To row across the lake and to walk through the woods to the Manor took me, as far as I can remember, about thirty-five minutes, easy going, by daylight: let's say forty minutes at night – Adams probably hurried. If he started at once, therefore, he must have reached the Manor round-about... Wait!' He stooped suddenly and felt the dead man's coat, then glanced at the soles of the shoes. 'The rain,' he cried, straightening up to look at the doctor. 'Do you remember the rain tonight?'

'Sure.' Wood looked down at the figure on the floor and nodded admiringly. 'Smart!' he murmured. 'I get you! You mean, that Adams had no raincoat and that his clothes and feet are dry; in other words, that he arrived here before the rain?'

'Exactly. The rain stopped at eleven o'clock – I remember looking at my watch. The point is, when did it begin?'

'I can tell you that,' was the other's triumphant answer. 'The shower had just started when Montgomery called out to ask me the time. It was a quarter to eleven – don't you remember?'

'Gad, you're right!' said his companion softly. 'It means, then, that Adams cannot have got here after the period between ten-forty-five,' – he dragged out his watch – 'and, say twelve-forty-five when Jacques found him. Isn't it possible to say how long he's been dead?'

Wood shook his head dubiously. 'Not with any great degree of accuracy.' But he bent down and felt the dead man's hand again. 'He's certainly been dead for more than an hour!'

'You'd depose to that on the witness stand?'

'Absolutely!'

'That narrows the critical period down to the hour between ten-forty-five and eleven-forty-five, then.' He rounded swiftly on the servant. 'At what time did Mademoiselle awaken you?'

But Jacques could not help him. He had not looked at the time. And he had heard no untoward sound from the direction of the salon, or, indeed, anywhere in the house, which was still as death when Mademoiselle had fetched him to the linen room.

Mr. Treadgold shrugged. 'It's not important for the moment,' he told the doctor. 'The essential point to discover is what Le Borgne was doing between ten-forty-five and eleven-forty-five!'

'That's up to the police,' said the American. Then his face grew rather blank. 'Do you suppose there are any police in the village?'

'I doubt it,' replied Mr. Treadgold. 'I've been thinking the matter out while we've been talking and I believe the best thing we can do is to have the curé in and tell him what's happened.'

In the lobby a little light fell through the door of the death-chamber. A blurred shape darkened it – it was the priest who was just emerging. Behind him, within the room, on the humble altar the silver box in which he had brought the Last Sacrament gleamed in the rays of the solitary candle. The girl was a motionless figure kneeling beside the bed.

'Ah, Monsieur Treadgold,' the curé said softly, closing the door and coming forward, 'I was looking for you. For the moment I am loath to intrude upon this young girl's grief. But since I find you two gentlemen here' – he looked from Mr.

Treadgold to the doctor – 'perhaps you are able to tell me in what circumstances...'

Mr. Treadgold broke in. 'It is the Seigneur, isn't it?'

The curé inclined his head and sighed. 'Yes, Monsieur. I wasn't well acquainted with him, for I've been curé here only for the past three years and he went abroad to live soon after my arrival. But I recognised him at once, changed though he is from my memory of him. It is indeed Hector de St. Rémy, the last Seigneur de Mort Homme. That he should have come home to die in an obscure corner of this ancient house is the climax of the tragic events which overshadowed his closing years.'

'Monsieur le Curé...' Mr. Treadgold began.

The priest misunderstood the purpose of the interruption. 'Let us speak no ill of him, Monsieur,' he reproved gravely, 'for he is now with God.' He glanced interrogatively from Mr. Treadgold to the doctor. 'But who is this young girl?' he asked.

'His granddaughter, Monsieur le Curé,' Mr. Treadgold put in.

'So!' The other was fidgeting, but the Abbé Bazin was not accustomed to being hurried. 'She would be the daughter, then, of Charles de St. Rémy – Seigneur Hector had but the one child – who married an Irish lady and was in business in London. They were both drowned in a yachting accident, I remember hearing, the year before I came here. So, she's the granddaughter...'

Mr. Treadgold could contain himself no longer. 'Excuse me,' he interposed firmly, 'but all this has no importance for the moment. Monsieur le Curé, a terrible thing has happened. A man was murdered here tonight!'

At last the abbé was shaken out of his inexorable composure. 'A man murdered – here?' he exclaimed incredulously.

'A gentleman named Adams, a guest with us at the fishing camp. For reasons which I shall explain to you suspicion attaches to this half-witted tramp who prowls about the Manor, the man they call Le Borgne.'

The priest frowned quickly. 'First the miller and now a second victim,' he murmured, as though to himself. 'One would say that Ruffier was right.' He looked coldly at the speaker. 'How was the name of this man?' he asked.

'Adams. Gideon Adams.'

The curé seemed to start. 'It's not possible!' he murmured.

'You know him?'

But the other disregarded the question. 'How did it happen?' he demanded sternly.

Mr. Treadgold shrugged. 'For the present we are reduced to conjecture. The servant found him, not ten minutes ago, when he went to fetch another candle. He's been stabbed!'

The abbé's face was like a mask of stone. 'Where is he?'

'In the drawing room. We haven't moved him.'

'Let me see!' The words had a peremptory ring – it was the curé, unchallenged leader of the community, speaking.

Once more the lamp cast long shadows across the lawyer's lifeless form. Wood displayed the gaping wound, and in his lucid, rather ponderous French Mr. Treadgold described the finding of the body. He showed the footprint, told of the blood marks they had traced, and outlined, step by step, the case he had built up against Le Borgne. The priest, his features stern and inflexible in the lamplight, listened in a deeply attentive silence.

Jacques had lit candles in the linen room and presently they adjourned there.

'There are no police nearer than Trois-Ponts, seventeen miles away,' said the curé. 'In any event, such cases are handled by the Provincial Police at Quebec, under instructions from the Attorney-General's office. I shall make it my business to immediately telegraph the Attorney-General to have someone sent to investigate, and in the meantime, on my return to the village, I will notify the coroner and the mayor of the parish who will, no doubt, if they see fit, have a warrant sworn out for the arrest of this unhappy creature. As your testimony will be of value, I must request you two gentlemen to have the goodness to remain here until the coroner and mayor arrive.'

Mr. Treadgold bowed majestically. 'We are, of course, entirely at the disposal of the authorities.'

The priest paused. 'I may not stay longer now, for I must return the Blessed Sacrament to the church. Also, it is advisable that the coroner should be informed of what has occurred without delay. In the circumstances I've refrained from putting any questions to the young lady. But in the light of this fresh tragedy, I feel that she should be acquainted with what has taken place – indeed, she may be able to throw some light upon it. Perhaps you'd see her, Monsieur Treadgol', and tell the coroner what she has to say?'

With that he inclined his head briefly to each and was gone. They saw him disappear into the room where the dead seigneur lay, and a moment later Jacques was lighting the bowed figure to the exit.

Chapter 11

AGAINST FAINT EXPLOSIVE NOISES of a car starting, a voice made itself heard behind them: 'The curé said you wished to speak to me...' The girl contemplated them from the threshold of the linen room. She had bathed her eyes and spoke with composure.

Wood introduced his companion. 'You're Mademoiselle de St. Rémy, aren't you?' he asked.

Brushing her lips with her handkerchief, she inclined her head silently.

'Excuse me a moment,' she said, and going to one of the cupboards, fetched candles which she gave to Jacques who waited at the door. 'You will arrange the room,' she bade him in a low voice. 'After, when it grows light, we will gather flowers.'

The door closed upon the servant. Mr. Treadgold cleared his throat.

'I beg you to believe how very deeply we sympathise with you in your great bereavement, Mademoiselle,' he said. 'I shouldn't venture to intrude upon your grief at this moment but for certain circumstances.'

'Won't you and your friend sit down?' Her manner was self-possessed. 'No, thanks' – she shook her head at the doctor who brought forward a chair for her – 'I prefer to stand.'

'There were certain questions...' began Mr. Treadgold, seating himself.

'I'll tell you anything I can,' she assured him graciously.

He paused. With a faintly embarrassed air he was examining his nails.

'Do you know a man named Adams, Gideon Adams, a lawyer in Toronto?'

She bowed her head. 'Yes.'

'What brought him here tonight?'

She did not reply at once: indeed, her silence lasted so long that Mr. Treadgold looked up.

'You didn't know he was here?' he questioned gently.

She shook her head.

'Didn't you know he was staying at the fishing camp?'

Once more she shook her head, gazing at him steadily, her manner faintly expectant.

'I'm afraid you must prepare yourself for a shock,' said Mr. Treadgold, his blue eyes regarding her sympathetically. 'Mr. Adams is dead!'

A little V of perplexity creased the smoothness of her forehead between the slender eyebrows. 'Dead?' she echoed tonelessly. Her voice was husky and she cleared her throat.

'It's not pleasant, but you'll have to know the truth. Adams was murdered, stabbed.'

He was struck by the deathly pallor of her face in the candlelight. She made no sign. She seemed numb: no instinctive recoil: no movement of horror.

'Your servant found him lying dead in the dismantled salon back there, a few minutes after the curé arrived.'

The graceful head slowly drooped to the handkerchief which she pressed to her lips.

'But who... who should have killed him?' she asked tremulously. She raised her eyes to the pink, good-natured face that contemplated her so compassionately.

Mr. Treadgold shrugged. 'That is what we're trying to find out,' he answered soothingly. 'Meanwhile, there are one or two points which I'd like, with your assistance, to establish...'

The listless movement of her hands told him to proceed.

'What time was it when you woke and went to your grandfather's room?' he asked.

She looked at him so blankly that he repeated the question, thinking she had not understood him.

She started and her eyes stirred to life. 'I looked at my watch. It was a little after eleven.'

Mr. Treadgold's face registered satisfaction. It was as though he said, 'Here's a witness after my own heart.' He paused – he seemed to be assembling his thoughts.

Wood struck in. 'Mademoiselle told me she thought she heard a cry when she awoke.' He turned to her. 'Was it your grandfather, do you think?'

She was looking down at the floor. 'I can't tell you,' she answered, with a brief head-shake. 'You know how it is when a sudden noise awakens one. It's a sort of echo ringing in one's ears – you can't analyse it.'

'On your way here,' said Mr. Treadgold, 'did you hear any sound from the front of the house – voices or footsteps?'

She shook her head quickly. 'I wasn't listening for any sound,' she retorted rather wearily. 'I was wholly occupied with my grandfather.'

Mr. Treadgold pointed across the room. 'That window – was it open when you came in?'

She nodded. 'Yes. Or rather it was ajar. Thinking that Grandpapa had only fainted, I opened it wide to give him more air.'

'Was the room dark?'

'Yes. I brought a candle with me. I remember asking Jacques, when we came back here, what he'd done with the lamp. He said he'd left it burning when he went to bed.'

Mr. Treadgold glanced significantly at the doctor. 'A brass lamp with a white glass shade, is it?' he asked the girl.

She nodded.

'The big drawing room on the other side of this door – have you been using it?' was the next question.

She shook her head. 'No. We walked through the rooms the morning after we arrived, that's all.'

'When did you arrive?'

'Four nights ago.'

He paused. 'I don't wish to say anything to give you pain, but – well, your grandfather had his reasons for not wanting his presence at the Manor known, hadn't he?'

She flushed. 'He had his reasons, yes,' she answered rather proudly. 'But they were nothing to be ashamed of.'

'I wasn't suggesting it. I was just wondering why he came back.'

Her lips trembled. 'He was ill – he must have known he was going to die, though he never told me. He wanted to see the old house again.'

Mr. Treadgold's nod was compassionate. 'I understand. But tell me, how did you manage to arrive here without being observed?'

She hesitated. 'We took the steamer from Quebec to Trois-Ponts,' she returned unwillingly. 'Jacques, who had gone on ahead, met us there with Mathias. Mathias had his boat and brought us up the river.'

'Mathias?' Mr. Treadgold seemed to prick up his ears. 'That's the man they call Le Borgne, isn't it? When did you see him last?'

She stopped to consider. 'Not since yesterday afternoon, I believe. Jacques says he was here before supper this evening, but I didn't see him.'

'What was the trouble between Le Borgne and Adams?'

'None so far as I know.' Then she seemed to catch the implication in his voice. 'Surely you're not suggesting...?' She laughed nervously. 'Simply because unkind people say that he killed the miller? You mustn't believe it – it's a lie. The old man looks and behaves wildly, but he wouldn't harm a soul.'

'I can only tell you that last night he broke into Adams's cabin at the camp. Adams caught him and handled him pretty roughly. Adams seemed to think he was looking for something – what, I don't know.'

'Mathias never killed this man, if that's what you're hinting!' she cried, with feeling.

With a faint shrug Mr. Treadgold left the subject.

'You say you didn't know that Adams was at the camp? Did your grandfather know?'

She shook her head quickly.

'He mightn't have mentioned it to you?' Mr. Treadgold persisted.

She shook her head again. 'He would certainly have told me!'

'Adams was an old friend of your family, I believe?'

'As a matter of fact,' she answered slowly, 'he was a connection of ours by marriage, a stepson of my Aunt Anita's, Grandpapa's youngest sister. She married a widower called Adams who had this son by his first marriage.'

Mr. Treadgold seemed surprised. He gazed at her tentatively, dangling his glasses.

'Listen,' the doctor now broke in, 'this explains a lot. I warned this young lady yesterday that her grandfather wouldn't survive a sudden shock. It occurs to me that the old gentleman may actually have witnessed the murder or, at any rate, unexpectedly have come upon the body; in the state of his heart, either experience would have been enough to carry him off. Seeing that this man was a relation of his, his sister's stepson.'

His lips pursed up under the grey moustache, Mr. Treadgold was contemplating him thoughtfully.

'One moment!' he now broke in, and went swiftly out.

The girl's eyes followed him. As the door closed, she swung to Wood.

'Why does he have to interfere in matters that don't concern him?' she asked hysterically.

'Between you and me,' said the doctor soothingly, 'it was the curé who asked him to make these enquiries. But the coroner will be here any minute now and he'll take over the investigation.'

She drew back, her eyes startled. 'The coroner? Does that mean there'll be an inquest?'

He nodded. 'I suppose so.'

'Shall I have to give evidence?'

He shrugged. 'They'll call us all, I imagine.'

'You mean, they'll put me in the witness-box, cross-question me?' Her voice was agitated.

He looked rather embarrassed. 'I expect so – I don't know a thing about the procedure here. But don't worry – it's not like a trial, you know. And, anyway, my friend and I will be there to take care of you.'

She shivered, making the gesture of drawing the little cape of her frock closer about her shoulders.

Then Mr. Treadgold reappeared. He drew Wood aside.

'I had a look at the old man's shoes,' he whispered confidentially. 'I thought perhaps it was he who left that footprint. But it wasn't – his shoes are clean. By the way, we heard a car coming up the drive. Jacques has gone to see if it's the coroner.'

At the same moment there were footsteps and voices in the lobby. The door swung inward, disclosing the servant, ushering in three men. At the sight of the first to enter, Mr. Treadgold repressed a movement of surprise.

It was the storekeeper, Joseph Ruffier.

He came in briskly and, at the sight of the girl, pulled off his black béret. He had evidently dressed in haste – his open raincoat showed an old grey sweater tucked into dark trousers, and there were slippers on his feet. Behind him appeared a lanky old man, grasping a bag, and a dapper individual in whom Mr. Treadgold recognised Maître Boucheron, the notary he had met at the curé's.

'Ah, Monsieur Treadgol',' said the storekeeper composedly, 'Monsieur le Curé said we should find you here. Mademoiselle!' He made a dignified bow to the girl. 'And this, I take it,' he continued, looking hard at Wood, 'is the doctor?' His gesture embraced his two companions. 'Mademoiselle, Messieurs, permit me to present these gentlemen. Dr. Côté, the coroner' – the old gentleman, who was mopping the inside of his hat with his handkerchief, inclined himself civilly – 'and Maître Boucheron, the St. Rémy family lawyer.'

The notary's black eyes flashed Mr. Treadgold a glance of recognition, then, with a stiff bow, he addressed the girl.

'Mademoiselle,' he said gravely, 'as one who was honoured with the confidence of your grandfather, the Seigneur, whose soul rest in peace, I beg to offer my most respectful condolences.'

The girl did not receive the little speech very graciously, Mr. Treadgold thought. Her eyes narrowed and she only murmured distantly, 'Monsieur!'

But Boucheron was not rebuffed. 'The mayor,' he went on, 'has lost no time in taking the preliminary steps to avenge the dreadful deed which has cast its shadow across the Seigneur's death-bed. On receiving Monsieur le Curé's communication, he immediately despatched my neighbour, Fortin, and Narcisse Laframboise, the baker, to apprehend this miscreant who has already once escaped the penalty of his crimes.' He rolled this off with a flamboyant air, his birdlike eyes darting rapid glances at the girl's rather disdainful countenance.

'With my full approval,' said the coroner. He was white-haired and stooping, with a lean, sunburned face.

'Seeing that his shack is off the road,' Ruffier supplemented in a rapid aside to Mr. Treadgold, 'and I wished us to lose no time in arriving on the scene, I took it upon myself to order two of our neighbours to bring him here to answer the charges which, as the curé tells me, you, Monsieur, have so intelligently formulated.'

It suddenly dawned upon Mr. Treadgold that the mayor was none other than Joseph Ruffier himself. It struck him that the latter was taking a good deal for granted.

'You understand, of course,' he said, with some alarm, 'that there's nothing more than a presumption of guilt against this man at present?'

'I understand it very well,' was the good-humoured reply. 'But I shall be very surprised if he can tell us anything to disprove Monsieur's most astute reasoning. Step by step – very good.' The dark eyes twinkled. 'I fancy that these gentlemen from Quebec, who think they know everything, will get a bit of a shock when they arrive here and find their man already behind the bars. This is no time for recriminations,' he added somewhat self-complacently, 'but you, at least, Monsieur Treadgol', are my witness that I, the mayor of the parish, foresaw the danger of leaving this savage at large. If the coroner's jury had evinced any intelligence in the case of the miller, Le Borgne would now be where he could do no further harm.' He turned to the coroner. 'N'est-ce pas, Docteur?'

'Quite right, Joseph, quite right!' the other agreed.

With a glance at the girl Ruffier beckoned Mr. Treadgold aside. 'Did you have a word with the young lady, as the curé suggested?'

Mademoiselle de St. Rémy could throw no light on Adams's presence in the house, Mr. Treadgold assured him. Apparently, neither she nor the manservant had seen or heard him arrive.

'She's quite definite in saying, too,' he added, 'that neither she nor her grandfather had any idea that Adams was at the camp.'

'How long has he been there?'

'Since Sunday, he told me.'

Ruffier nodded. 'None of us in the village had heard of his being here and, of course, Ange Tremblay wouldn't know him – he comes from Montreal. It's pretty clear that Monsieur Adams had no suspicion that the old gentleman was back at the Manor or he'd have been round before this.'

'He was a connection of the family, the girl told me.'

'Oh, yes. But there was no love lost between him and the Seigneur, allez!' He lowered his voice. 'The story is that if Monsieur de St. Rémy had not fled to France three years ago, Monsieur Adams would have put him in jail.'

Mr. Treadgold nodded. 'Adams hinted as much to me. What was the trouble?'

The mayor shrugged. 'I never heard the rights of it and Maître Boucheron was never the one to gossip about his clients' affairs. But it seems that Monsieur was trustee under his sister's marriage settlement – the stepmother of Monsieur Adams, you understand. When their father, Seigneur Pierre, died and the capital should have been paid over, it was decided to leave it invested in the estate, Mademoiselle Anita, as we always called her, receiving the interest as before. Then, three years ago, her husband died, and the stepson, who was settling up his father's affairs, called upon the Seigneur to pay out Mademoiselle Anita's dowry. But what with the depression, mortgages, and so forth, the coffers, it would appear, were empty. The Manor was sold up and the Seigneur disappeared to France – the rumour was that Adams had sworn to send him to prison if ever he set foot in Canada again.'

Mr. Treadgold pursed up his lips. 'So that's why they were in hiding...'

The coroner, who was standing by with Wood, now spoke up. 'Eh, bien, Joseph, do we go to view the body?'

'Go with the doctor. I'll join you in a moment.' The two men departed. Ruffier glanced unostentatiously to where the girl was standing with the notary. 'I ask myself,' he said, in an undertone to Mr. Treadgold, 'what can have brought him back. What does the young lady say?'

'She told me he wanted to see the old house again before he died.'

The other sighed, his dark eyes suddenly tender. 'Poor old man! He had no enemies here. To think that none of us knew he was back, not even his own lawyer. Well, shall we follow the others?'

Boucheron stepped forward. 'I hope the coroner does not expect Mademoiselle to be present at the examination.'

'There'll be no need of that, I think,' Ruffier answered kindly.

He had stopped before the girl, his rugged countenance respectful, his eyes compassionate.

'Mademoiselle,' he said, 'we are strangers to you, but you should be no stranger to us. All our lives we have known your family. As a young man, many is the night your late father and I camped together in the woods, hunting the moose and the caribou and, had God blessed me with children, my eldest son would have borne the name of Charles. I would that your homecoming had been happier, but all the same I bid you welcome home. And if there's anything in which the mayor of the parish can serve you, I beg of you to call on me.'

Mr. Treadgold felt quite moved. In his rough clothes the man looked the peasant he was. But he spoke his little piece with a sincerity of accent, a chivalry of address, that would not have done discredit to a courtier of Versailles. The girl's expression revealed that she, too, was touched. The candle-rays glinted on damp lashes as she bowed her head, murmuring in a small, husky voice, 'Merci, Monsieur le Maire.' She might have swept to the floor in a curtsy and one would scarcely have been surprised, Mr. Treadgold mused; like the soft light, the unaffected rhetoric of the little speech, the courtesy of the gesture, seemed to summon back the atmosphere of a simpler, more gracious age. 'Gracious,' that was the word – it was graciously done. He felt his respect growing for his friend the mayor.

In the salon the shutters had been folded back and by the first light of dawn straggling in upon the dusty boards the room appeared more gaunt and desolate than ever. The coroner was on his knees beside the body, probe in hand, spectacles on nose, engaged in what appeared to be an extremely leisurely and protracted examination of the wound. Wood, erect, was watching him with every symptom of extreme impatience.

The coroner might be officially in charge of the investigation: nevertheless, it was the mayor who directed it, Mr. Treadgold observed. Ruffier was down beside the corpse in a second and, beckoning to Wood to join him, proceeded to put to the latter a series of highly pertinent questions – the cause and approximate hour of death, the course taken by the weapon, the nature of the weapon, where the deceased had stood when struck. The mayor might know no English, but by dumb-show and with the aid of an English word here and there, which he repeated after Wood, he contrived to make himself understood.

The American had to demonstrate for Ruffier's benefit how, in his opinion, the victim had received the fatal blow. Nothing loath, the young man obliged. According to his theory, Adams, guided from outside by the light shining through the shutter, had made his way to the linen room and, finding no one there, had picked up the lamp to explore further. Once in the salon, he had heard a suspicious sound in the room he had quitted and, to rid himself of the lamp, had set it down and was in the act of turning to face the door when his assailant, who had followed him from the linen room, sprang at him and struck him down.

Ruffier was evidently impressed. 'That would be the way of it, I make no doubt,' he opined gravely. 'And you didn't find the knife?'

The weapon was missing, Mr. Treadgold intervened to remark, and explained that, in the doctor's opinion, not a knife but a sharpened chisel or file had been used. The mayor nodded – such an instrument might well have been in Le Borgne's possession, he conceded.

It was he who reminded the coroner that the lamp must be impounded for the police who would surely wish to examine it for fingerprints: it was he who turned out the dead man's pockets. The search disclosed nothing of interest – cigarette case and lighter, bunch of keys, some change, a wallet with driving and fishing licences, visiting-cards, and a small wad of bills. Ruffier counted the bills – two hundred and fifty dollars in fifty-

and ten-dollar bills. 'At least robbery wasn't the motive.' he remarked, adding the wallet to the pile. In an inside breast-pocket were one or two papers – a letter from the Forgeron office, addressed to the deceased at Toronto, confirming his reservation at the camp; a receipted bill from the Château Frontenac Hotel with some figures pencilled on the back; an hotel folder; a garage account.

The coroner, having concluded his examination, drew the mayor aside and conversed with him in whispers. Then Mr. Treadgold showed them the footprint on the floor. With an important air Dr. Côté produced a footrule and notebook and proceeded with all leisureliness to take measurements. By this time Ruffier was on the other side of the room, following up the blood track under Mr. Treadgold's guidance. In a party they returned to the linen room to inspect the marks on the window-sill. Voices were audible in the lobby and Jacques, appearing just then, explained that two nuns, sent by the curé to keep the death-watch, had arrived. Mademoiselle had taken them into the bedroom.

Ruffier nodded approvingly. 'Now that the young lady's out of the way,' he told the coroner, 'it's a good chance to remove the body. As coroner it's your duty to take charge of it, pending the inquest.'

The old gentleman nodded solemnly. 'Bien sûr, it's the law.'

'We can put him in your barn for the time being, as we did with the miller, hein?'

'C'est bien, Joseph.'

The mayor turned to Jacques. 'Find a hurdle or a couple of planks, will you, my friend, and bring them to the salon. Young Israel Fortin, who's outside with my car, will lend you a hand.'

After a brief interval they appeared in the salon, Jacques and a thickset youth incongruously sporting a baseball cap quartered in white and red. Between them they bore one of those wooden trays with shafts which gardeners use for the conveyance of plants. The dead man was lifted upon it. 'Té!' exclaimed young Fortin suddenly. 'The gentleman dropped his pencil.' He stooped to the floor.

A small gold pencil lay in his grimy palm, a dainty trinket, flat in shape with a ring at the end.

'It was under him as he lay,' the youth explained sheepishly.

Ruffier took the pencil, glanced at it, and handed it to the coroner. Then, 'To the car!' he ordered the bearers.

They raised the litter. It was too short and its burden sagged upon it. The first rays of morning touched with pink the dead man's face. The story Adams had told at dinner suddenly crept into Mr. Treadgold's mind. He seemed to see Adams again, triumphant, unconquerable, and found the contrast too much for him. The poor devil has found his match at last, was his thought, as he turned away. Sombrely, he watched the others file out behind the stretcher.

He was still standing there when Dr. Côté came back.

'A bad business, Monsieur,' the old man remarked, contemplating the other out of narrow, hazel eyes.

A bad business, Mr. Treadgold agreed absently.

'It must be twenty years since I last set foot in the Manor,' observed the doctor reminiscently, filling his pipe. 'The last Seigneur was not here much. He was a great musician, was Seigneur Hector, and he preferred to live in Quebec, Montreal, where he could attend the concerts. But in his father's day, Monsieur – you should have known the old house then!' Wagging his head mournfully, he scratched a match on his sole and applied it to his pipe. 'It was in this very room, for instance, that on the first of the year the whole family – Madame, the sons and daughters and their children – would kneel to receive the Seigneur's blessing, according to the custom of our people. And when the Seigneur had given his benediction, he'd kneel in his turn and the youngest child present, often the tiniest tot, would be led forward to make the sign of the cross with its little hands over the Seigneur's head!' He sighed. 'Ah, Monsieur, those were the good old days!' Pipe in mouth, his hands behind his back, he began to trail round the room.

'So,' he murmured, stopping before the coat of arms, 'the family crest? I thought everything had gone at the auction. Three years ago, it was, soon after we heard that Seigneur Hector had gone away to France. Many dealers came from Quebec – the house was richly furnished then, *pardi!* I remember my wife wanted me to attend the sale – there was a sofa in yellow damask she coveted – but I didn't have the heart!' Moving on, he came to a halt before the panoply of arms. 'Té,' he ejaculated softly, 'the pistols of Seigneur Ignace! Yes, yes, I remember now, they were withdrawn from the sale, they and the swords – it was said they were heirlooms. And, see, the little musket! A souvenir, Monsieur, of an adventure Seigneur Ignace had in Corsica where, I have heard, the family had its roots. He was travelling there – it's more than a hundred years ago – when his carriage was attacked by bandits and he is said to have taken that old gun from the hands of one of the brigands who was slain. Seigneur Pierre, father of Seigneur Hector who lies dead within, used to like to tell the story. He said the musket was very curious on account of its being so small, and its little bayonet...'

He broke off and with extreme deliberation took his spectacles from their case and putting them on peered at the rusty weapon.

'So,' he murmured, 'I don't see the bayonet any more. But there, it must be thirty years since Seigneur Pierre showed it to me and in that time the old house has known many changes. The swords, I perceive, are still there. One belonged to an ancestor who was a privateer against the English: the story is that the King of France sent it to him along with his letters of marque. Let me see now, which one was it? Isidore de St. Rémy? No, he was the intendant. Ferdinand? Seigneur Pierre told me – he had all the family history by heart...'

He was rambling on garrulously when the door beside him opened brusquely. Ruffier poked his big head in. 'Le Borgne!' he announced to the coroner and was gone.

Chapter 12

THE DOOR GAVE UPON the entrance hall, wide and deep and high. There was a stairway mounting on one side, a door beyond it, and the broad arch of the front door at the end. The front door was open and through it, over the rail of the platform that ran before the house, Mr. Treadgold had a glimpse of a buggy driving away. Ruffier was giving a parting injunction to the muffled figure that held the reins. 'Be as quick as you can!' he shouted. Returning to the hall, he drew the coroner aside for a whispered confabulation. 'I sent Narcisse back to look for them,' Mr. Treadgold heard him say. Then, the door beside the staircase opening, he saw Wood beckoning to him.

The room beyond was as naked as the other, with plastered walls and beamed ceiling painted white. Maître Boucheron, as jumpy as ever, was talking in undertones to a burly man with a scarf about his neck who was in charge of the suspect. Bareheaded and barefoot and wearing the same shapeless garments in which Mr. Treadgold had seen him before, Le Borgne presented a lamentable appearance. Tanned and shaggy and grimy, he seemed to reek of the earth – one thought of a ground hog or a badger dug from its hole and dragged to the light. Mr. Treadgold studied him with interest. No doubt, the single eye threw the whole face out of balance and the fellow was of low mentality. Yet he could discern no trace of madness there, only the sort of suspicious, man-shy look of any wild thing cornered.

A table had been improvised out of planks laid across two barrels and here, the notary having been sent for a chair, the coroner seated himself, the others remaining standing. The burly man opened the proceedings.

'Eh, bien,' he said, addressing the coroner in stentorian tones, 'Neighbour Laframboise and I went to the shack, as Monsieur le Maire directed. This man was there asleep. He'd been drinking and we had a job to rouse him – *pfui*, one could smell the bagosse on his breath three ells away!'

'What you call in the United States "le bootleg,"' Ruffier whispered behind his hand to Mr. Treadgold.

'We told him,' the witness went on, 'that a gentleman from the camp was killed up at the Manor and that he must answer for it, but he made no reply.' He laid a hunting-knife in a sheath on the table. 'He had this knife on his belt, but it is clean. And he has no blood on his clothing. We brought him along as ordered.'

Dr. Côté unsheathed the knife, examined it, and passed it to Wood. Mr. Treadgold glanced at the young man's face and found it non-committal.

'Mathias,' said the coroner, surveying the suspect over the top of his glasses, 'a gentleman named Adams, who's been stopping at the fishing camp, was murdered here tonight. Do you understand what I say? He was killed, stabbed. What can you tell us about it?'

Le Borgne stared at him without speaking.

'Come, we know that he beat you yesterday. You wanted to revenge yourself, didn't you?'

There was still no answer.

'One would say he'd lost his tongue as well as his senses, maudit!' the burly man grumbled.

'Softly, Neighbour Fortin!' Dr. Côté addressed Le Borgne again. 'Why did you break into this gentleman's cabin? To rob him, was it?'

The scarecrow figure shook its head.

'He wasn't after money, he means,' Ruffier broke in. 'It was booze he was looking for, eh, Le Borgne?'

The same slow head-shake.

'Why did you go to the camp?' the coroner persisted patiently.

Unexpectedly a grimy finger was pointed at Mr. Treadgold. 'I saw him here,' a cracked voice mumbled. 'It was to find out what he wanted.'

'Correct!' said Ruffier. 'Monsieur Treadgol' told me he took a stroll by way of the Manor yesterday afternoon and that Le Borgne saw him. But that doesn't explain why you broke into the other gentleman's cabin,' he reminded the prisoner.

'It was to see...'

'To see what?'

Bare feet shuffled. 'To see if it was really he...'

The coroner struck in. 'You mean, you caught sight of somebody you took to be Monsieur Adams?'

A surly nod. 'C'est bien ça! He was coming out of one of the cabins.'

'And you wanted to make sure?' The same gesture. 'You knew him, then?'

'It was from the old days,' the harsh voice mumbled, 'when Mademoiselle Anita was first married. She and her husband brought him once or twice to the Manor to visit.'

'That may be,' the coroner remarked testily. 'But what had Adams to do with you?'

'He was the enemy of Monsieur,' said the accused gruffly.

Maître Boucheron cleared his throat. 'It's a fact,' he proffered stiffly, 'that of recent years the Seigneur and Mr. Adams were not on good terms.' He shrugged. 'But you're familiar with this poor creature's obsession, Monsieur le Coroner – for him every stranger has designs on the Manor.'

They were now aware that the door had opened and that the girl was among them. She paid no heed to any of them, but posted herself on the edge of the circle, her eyes on the shaggy figure facing it.

'Did you tell the Seigneur that Monsieur Adams was at the camp?' Ruffier asked the accused.

Le Borgne nodded, his solitary orb furtively seeking out the girl. It seemed to Mr. Treadgold that she started.

'When was this?' the mayor's voice chimed in, incisive.

'Tonight.' Le Borgne was still stealing glances at the girl – anxiously, Mr. Treadgold thought.

'Tonight?' Coroner and mayor spoke simultaneously.

The tatterdemalion figure suddenly became expansive. In a confused way the prisoner seemed to be on the defensive, as though he sensed a reproach – Mr. Treadgold had the impression that he was addressing himself to the girl. It was not his fault, the scarecrow blurted out: Monsieur was sick all day – he hadn't been able to speak to him before.

'Why didn't you tell Mademoiselle?' Ruffier demanded.

He hadn't seen Mademoiselle, either; Jacques had said she was with Monsieur and must not be disturbed.

'Jacques, then?'

A shrug which plainly said that this was a private, a family matter. 'But tonight' – the grotesque mask lit up and the puny form seemed to strut – 'when I brought the bread and eggs for Jacques, Monsieur met me at the kitchen door and I told him.'

The girl spoke, gravely, tensely. 'At what time was this, Mathias?'

The single eye dropped to the floor. He wouldn't know that. Wait! The church clock had struck the quarter after ten as he came into the village.

'You mean you left the Seigneur and went down to the village?' the coroner enquired sharply.

A vigorous nod. 'By Monsieur's order.' proudly.

'For what?'

'To fetch Maître Boucheron.'

The notary rolled his eyes. 'To fetch me?' he cried, tapping his chest dramatically. He turned to the coroner. 'This is the first I've heard of it. In any case, I've been away at Trois-Ponts on a case all day and I didn't get home until late.' He spoke very fast. His speech, like all his movements, was jerky. He spun round to the prisoner. 'Did you come to my house?' he snapped at the prisoner. 'Because,' he added, addressing the coroner, 'as you know, my servant sleeps out and if he came before eleven there was no one to let him in.'

'Not so fast, Maître,' said the coroner. 'You only bewilder him.' He surveyed the accused over his glasses. 'You say that the Seigneur despatched you to fetch Maître Boucheron, is that it?'

Le Borgne, sniffing, drew his sleeve across his nose and nodded. He was to tell Maître Boucheron it was most urgent – Monsieur expected him that very night. He had called at the notary's, but nobody answered the bell. So he had gone off home.

'Ah,' said Boucheron, with an air of relief.

'What time was it when you went home?' the coroner asked.

The man flicked an anxious glance across the table; he was suddenly on his guard, it seemed to Mr. Treadgold.

'I don't know,' he answered sullenly.

'You were drunk, eh?' put in the mayor crisply.

The other shivered and shuffled with his feet. 'It was raining. A man wants something to keep out the cold.'

The coroner leaned back to speak to Ruffier. 'It's as I told you, Joseph. They're selling liquor in the village again.' He gazed sternly at the prisoner. 'Where did you get it?'

Mathias was silent, his reddish eye shifting apprehensively from Dr. Côté to the mayor.

'What does it matter where he got it!' Ruffier exclaimed. 'It's perfectly clear what happened. When he says he went home, he's lying. What he did was to return to the Manor to tell the Seigneur that our friend Boucheron was out. At the Manor, with the drink in him, he comes across Adams and kills him.' His glance swung to the suspect. 'That was the way of it, wasn't it? Come, Le Borgne, denials won't help you. You killed him, didn't you?'

The druggist's large hand gripped the puny figure by the neck of the tattered sweater. 'Answer when Monsieur le Maire speaks to you, maudit!' he rasped, shaking him.

The girl sprang forward. 'Leave him alone!' she cried. 'Can't you see you frighten him? You know he's weak-minded – it's cowardly and... and abominable to bully him like this.'

Ruffier signalled to Fortin, who, with a sheepish air, stood back.

'Mademoiselle,' said the mayor suavely, 'we know you are acting with the best intentions, but you would do better to leave this matter to the coroner.'

'Not if you're going to take advantage of this poor fellow's weak wits to force him into confessing a crime he never committed.'

The coroner drummed with his fingers. 'But the evidence, Mademoiselle...'

'I know you have a case of sorts against him. This gentleman, if I'm to believe my servant' – she directed a scathing glance at Mr. Treadgold – 'is already convinced of his guilt...'

'Really, my dear young lady...', Mr. Treadgold expostulated.

'I tell you as I told him,' she cried to the coroner, ignoring the interruption, 'this inoffensive old man is incapable of such a crime. He's scared now – he doesn't know what he's saying. Let me speak to him alone: I'll make him tell me anything you want to know.'

Ruffier had suddenly raised his head – there was the sound of wheels outside. A moment later the door was flung open and a clumsy, gangling man in a lumberman's striped blouse strode in. He carried a pair of shoes in his hand. Walking up to the table, he dumped them down in front of the coroner.

'Hidden in the roof,' he announced briefly and stretched his long arms.

Dr. Côté turned the shoes over in his hands. They were ragged and down-trodden and the mud with which the leather was caked was smeared with reddish stains. In a deathlike hush he held the shoes aloft.

'Are these your shoes, Mathias?' he asked.

All eyes were turned to the scarecrow. The head was drooping, drooping, and the solitary eye kept turning to right and left, furtively, despairingly. With his customary deliberation the coroner pulled out his notebook and, after a leisurely search, found his footrule. He measured the shoes, referring to the book. Then he glanced at the mayor over his spectacles.

'The measurements tally,' he pronounced.

Ruffier nodded briefly. 'You'll order his detention, I suppose,' he remarked to the coroner. 'You have the right, you know. "With or without a warrant," the law says. Just give me the order and I'll lock him up in my shed.'

He stooped to the coroner's ear and the two men conferred in whispers.

The girl had not moved – she was staring with frightened eyes at the woebegone figure before the table. Wood looked round for Mr. Treadgold and found that he had disappeared; he also perceived, with a sense of surprise, that the windows were crimson with the sunrise.

He touched the girl on the arm. 'You'd better come away now,' he said.

A nun was seated in the lobby reading her office. In his halting French Wood explained that the girl should get some rest. He understood the nun to say that, for the time being, Mademoiselle Adrienne was to stay at the Manor in the charge of the two sisters.

So her name was Adrienne! He repeated it under his breath and liked the sound. The girl did not speak or even look at him; she seemed listless and on the brink of collapse, but let the sister shepherd her to her room.

'I'll leave her something to make her sleep, ici, sur la table!' Wood told the nun, as they disappeared, and then remembered he had left his satchel in the Seigneur's room. Unwilling to disturb the peace of the death-chamber, he went in search of Jacques.

The kitchen was empty. He opened the outer door and saw Mr. Treadgold standing on the walk outside. His hands were behind his back, his eyes were lost in thought; it was evident that he was miles away.

'Hello, H. B.,' said the doctor, 'what became of you?'

His roommate started. 'Ah, George!'

The young man sniffed. 'Gosh, the air feels good. Been having a look round? Any more trails?'

The other shook his head.

'Did you take a peek at the path under the linen room window for footprints?'

Mr. Treadgold nodded rather sombrely. 'Just a mess!' he sighed. 'Did the curé come in a car?' he asked suddenly.

'I think so – at least, I heard an engine starting up when he went away.'

'Did you happen to notice whether he was wearing goloshes?'

The doctor shook his head. 'I'm afraid I didn't. Why?'

Mr. Treadgold shrugged faintly. 'Nothing. I was just wondering.'

'Well, they nailed old One-Eye, didn't they?' said Wood.

'It would seem so.'

His companion laughed. 'You don't seem very sure about it.'

Mr. Treadgold sighed. 'Perhaps I feel rather like Uncle Toby on a celebrated occasion.'

Wood chuckled. 'Well, what did he say?'

'He said, "I wish I had not known so much of this affair, or that I had known more of it!"'

His companion grinned. 'That guy pulled as many wisecracks as Jimmie Walker. Come on, let's go home to bed!'

Jacques was in the kitchen and the doctor sent him for the satchel.

'While he's fetching it,' said Wood, 'we'd better find out if it's all right for us to leave, hadn't we? Besides, I want to ask my aged colleague about the inquest.'

They were passing through the salon and had reached the door leading into the hall when Wood suddenly stopped. 'Hello,' he said, 'that's odd!'

'What's odd?' demanded Mr. Treadgold, coming up behind him.

His roommate was pointing at the panoply of arms. 'Why, that contraption – a bayonet or whatever it is – on the end of the musket. I don't remember it.'

Mr. Treadgold uttered a stifled cry. He was staring at the musket.

'God,' he murmured, 'I must have been blind!'

His companion shot him an incredulous glance, then bent forward to examine the bayonet. It was no more than a foot or fifteen inches long, scarcely larger than the bayonet of a toy gun, with a ring that fitted over the muzzle of the little musket.

'Look,' came Wood's awe-struck whisper, 'the blade's triangular!'

Chapter 13

'Old Côté told me there used to be a bayonet on that musket,' declared Mr. Treadgold in a hollow voice, 'not half an hour since, when he and I were together in this very room, waiting for Le Borgne to arrive. It wasn't there then. To think that he actually drew my attention to the fact that it was missing and I never guessed!' He smote his brow dramatically.

Wood put out his hand gingerly towards the bayonet and withdrew it again.

'We'd best not touch it, perhaps. fingerprints, you know.'

His companion laughed harshly. 'No fear. Whoever put it back there wiped it clean, you bet.' His finger pointed at the blade. 'Look at that rust – it's smooth and dark! The rust on the barrel is all powdery.' He sighed and extracted from his pocket a large red-and-yellow bandanna handkerchief. 'No harm in being cautious, though. That velvet' – he indicated the material covering the board – 'would take a print well – that rusty barrel, too. Whoever put the bayonet back took good care not to leave a mark on it, but he may not have thought of leaving marks elsewhere. Criminals are like that, you know, George. Dr. Hans Gross, in his Handbuch für Untersuchungsrichter, which is by way of being one of the textbooks on criminology, says, "Never overlook the possibility of the one glaring blunder which is customarily made in every serious crime!" – and he goes on to observe that many a criminologist has been switched from the right track by the feeling, "He couldn't have been such a fool!"'

While speaking, with the aid of the handkerchief wrapped about his fingers, he was gently and painstakingly easing the bayonet loose.

'But, see here, H. B.,' the doctor exclaimed excitedly, 'this discovery puts an entirely different complexion on things. I mean, old One-Eye can't have put the bayonet back, for the simple reason that he didn't arrive here until after you and the coroner had seen the musket without it.'

'Quite.' The bayonet was free now. Mr. Treadgold was gazing at it sombrely as it lay on the handkerchief in his hands. 'I suppose you're sure that Adams could have been stabbed with this?' he asked.

'Absolutely.' Wood took bayonet and handkerchief from him. 'See how it springs from a triangular base and tapers to a point,' he remarked, his finger following the blade along. 'It's impossible to establish positively that this is the weapon with which the crime was committed, of course, until it's been microscopically examined – I don't mind betting they'll find traces of human blood soaked into the rust. The wound should tell us something, too – I mean, it's quite likely there are particles of rust in it.' Then, perceiving that the other had fallen silent, he glanced at him questioningly and said, 'Whom have you in mind?'

Mr. Treadgold shrugged faintly. 'Jacques found the body,' he observed impersonally. Then, as voices resounded from the passage, 'We'll have to turn this in,' he declared. He took the bayonet from Wood and, going to the door, looked out.

They were leading Le Borgne through the hall – his bare feet pattered on the flags. Ruffier and the coroner stood by, looking on. Seeing Mr. Treadgold there, the bayonet in his hands, the mayor came across. It was evident from his face that he grasped the situation on the instant – the man had a rapier mind, Mr. Treadgold decided.

'This bayonet...' began Mr. Treadgold.

The storekeeper's eyes snapped. 'You mean...?' He whisked round, fingers snapping, to where the coroner was industriously polishing his spectacles. 'Docteur, viens icitte!'

The old man lumbered across. 'Té, the brigand's bayonet!' mumbled Dr. Côté, showing his gums in an affable smile. 'And I was just telling our friend that I thought it was lost!'

Ruffier interrupted him peremptorily. 'Monsieur Treadgol' thinks it's the weapon Le Borgne used...'

The coroner seemed utterly nonplussed. 'It was, in truth, with some such instrument that he was killed,' he agreed, dandling his snowy head. 'But how should the bayonet have found its way back to the little musket, Joseph? How do you account for that?'

At that moment Jacques appeared from the vestibule with Wood's satchel.

With a swift glance enjoining his three companions to silence, Ruffier went forward to meet him.

'It was you who found Monsieur Adams's body, my friend?'

The sallow face was impassive. 'Yes.'

'You saw no weapon?'

'No.'

Ruffier held up the bayonet. 'Ever seen this before?'

Jacques shook his head, his gaze steady, deferential. 'No.'

The man's calm was unshatterable. He wore the mien of the trained servant like a mask.

'It's believed that Monsieur Adams was stabbed with this bayonet,' said Ruffier pointedly. 'The murderer took it from that trophy on the wall. Half an hour ago the bayonet was missing from the rack: just now it was discovered there. How do you explain that?'

Jacques shrugged faintly – his every action was restrained. 'I can't. I know nothing about it.'

'What about Mademoiselle? Did she find it?'

'It's possible. In any case, Mademoiselle said nothing to me.' Perceiving that the mayor had no further questions, he timed a judicious pause and turned to Wood. 'Your satchel, Monsieur.' He set the satchel down against the wall and went quietly out.

Ruffier signalled to Mr. Treadgold and Wood to follow him into the hall. There he closed the salon door.

'Gentlemen,' he said, 'this discovery places us in something of a dilemma. This surly fellow is lying for a certainty; but whether he or the girl abstracted that bayonet from the scene of the crime is immaterial.'

'You think that one of them took it?' Mr. Treadgold suggested.

'Who else should it have been?' With his hands on their arms he drew them closer. 'Adams and the Seigneur were at daggers drawn, it's agreed? The old gentleman was up and dressed. Mightn't one assume that Adams walked in upon him and that an altercation ensued in the course of which Adams was stabbed?'

Mr. Treadgold gave the sense of the above to the doctor. 'Bunk!' said Wood forcibly. 'Tell him, H. B., that whoever killed Adams did it in one bound and finish. It's not so much a question of physical strength as of speed and agility. If His Honour believes that frail old man was the murderer, he's crazy.'

'But of course! I agree with every word you say,' cried Ruffier to the doctor when Mr. Treadgold had conveyed the gist of Wood's remarks. 'It's the girl I'm thinking of. I'm very sure she was under this impression until the sight of those shoes told her differently. And it would explain the way she came to this wretched man's defence.' His eyes softened. 'One can't blame her, I suppose, for wanting to get rid of that bayonet.'

'I don't see how she can have possibly believed that her grandfather did it,' Mr. Treadgold declared bluntly. 'We don't know where the bayonet was picked up, but it was presumably lying in the salon, beside the body, if it wasn't sticking in the dead man's breast. But the Seigneur, let me remind you, was found unconscious, if not dead, in the linen room.'

The mayor's smile was tolerant. 'And do you really imagine that a young girl reasons as closely as that at such a moment? Consider the circumstances.' His hands fluttered: he became dramatic. 'She's aroused from sleep to find the old man, whom she had left ill in bed, fully dressed and seemingly lifeless on the floor. He has obviously sustained some terrible shock. When she hears that his bitterest enemy has been discovered mysteriously murdered in the next room, isn't it natural she should assume that her grandfather killed him and died himself of the exertion?'

Mr. Treadgold nodded. 'Dr. Wood warned her that a sudden shock might prove fatal. She'd remember that when she heard about Adams. I dare say you're right.'

'You see? Now, then, the inquest is set for ten o'clock this morning at Dr. Côté's house. Presumably Mademoiselle will give evidence. In the interests of the family and of the young lady herself, the coroner is prepared to pass over the circumstances of the Seigneur's presence here – he'll confine the evidence to the actual facts of the murder. If we bring up the question of the bayonet, its disappearance and recovery, inevitably the whole sordid story of this family quarrel must come out. As we know, it has no bearing on the murder, and I see no reason why it should be raised at the inquest – if the police want to go into it later, that's their affair. Mademoiselle de St. Rémy is an innocent victim in all this terrible affair and I've the greatest sympathy for her. Her father was a fine man, and I'm unwilling to expose her to unfavourable comment by reason of this impulsive action of hers. You understand my point of view?'

'Absolutely,' said Mr. Treadgold. 'But what about the jury? Aren't they likely to inquire about the weapon?'

'The coroner will know how to deal with them – I'll have a word with him. In the meantime, would you and your friend have the goodness to say nothing about the matter?'

Mr. Treadgold thought he had better explain the situation to the doctor.

'Sure,' said Wood promptly. 'I'm all for keeping the girl out of it.'

His companion relayed this assurance to Ruffier.

'I felt sure I could depend on you,' said the mayor composedly. 'Meanwhile, the coroner or I will have a word with the young lady and get at the truth about the bayonet.'

Wood caught the sense of this last remark. 'Pas maintenant,' he said to the mayor in the loud and distinct tones he reserved for his efforts in French. 'Mam'zell beaucoup fatiguay. Couchay.' And closing his eyes and laying one hand against his cheek, he gave a realistic impression of his idea of a young woman in an attitude of slumber.

Only Anglo-Saxons are diverted by the efforts of foreigners to make themselves understood.

The storekeeper did not smile. 'Okay,' he cried idiomatically. 'Later. Before the inquest.' He shook hands ceremoniously with each. 'Until tomorrow, gentlemen.' The salon door swung to behind him.

'I call that darned decent of His Honour,' declared Wood, gazing after him. 'He's dead right, you know. Inquests are the devil. No rules of evidence or anything. A fool coroner can simply raise Old Harry with a witness, if he wants to. I'd hate to see that nice girl manhandled on the stand. Her name's Adrienne. It sort of fits her, don't you think? Did you notice how beautifully she moves?'

Mr. Treadgold was silent, fingering his moustache.

'I liked the way she stood up for that poor devil tonight, didn't you?' his roommate continued. 'She certainly put the fear of God into that fat druggist. You know, H. B., I don't notice women much as a rule, but there's something genuine about this girl, even if she did try and put one over about that bayonet. His Honour's perfectly right – it has nothing to do with the material facts of the case.'

His companion shook his head dubiously. 'The whole proceedings strike me as being devilish irregular. However, I suppose they know what they're doing.'

'They've got their man, haven't they? So what are you beefing about?'

Mr. Treadgold did not speak for a moment.

'Was Maître Boucheron wearing rubbers, do you know?' he asked absently.

'No,' the other gave him a withering look; 'he had on patent-leather jackboots with gold tassels. What's all this about rubbers, anyway?'

'Nothing,' said Mr. Treadgold, as before; 'I was just wondering!'

The doctor took his arm. 'You've got rubbers on the brain. Come on! I just have to fix the young woman a sedative and then we'll hit the hay.'

'Give me five minutes,' said Mr. Treadgold. 'Now that it's light I'd like to have a look round outside. I'll meet you at the car.'

With that he strode quickly down the hall and disappeared through the open front door.

Chapter 14

THE INQUEST WAS HELD in what was obviously the parlour of the coroner's house, in the village, across the square from the church. It was a sombre apartment, low-ceilinged and airless and darkened by the window hangings. Side by side with the doctor's diplomas, half a century old and yellowing in their frames, the walls displayed a tarnished coffin plate under glass and an enlarged photograph of an old lady ornamented with two initials worked in human hair. Le Borgne was not present nor did anyone appear for him – Maître Boucheron seemed to be the only lawyer there. The parlour was jammed to the doors, the atmosphere almost unbreathable. Stolid peasant faces, bony and weather-beaten, made a frieze at the back.

All the men guests from the camp attended, with them the Angel, very fluttery, and Batisse, who had been the dead man's guide. General Rees was in a querulous mood. He was evidently under the impression that it devolved upon him to see that the instinctive inclination of the Gallic temperament to tamper with the ideals of British justice was firmly resisted. He received his first shock on discovering that there were only six jurors, although Maître Boucheron, whom Mr. Treadgold introduced to him, declared that this was the number prescribed by the law of the Province of Quebec. 'Never heard of it,' Rees muttered gloomily. 'Every part of the British Empire I've ever been in, it was always "twelve good men and true," as in King Alfred's day.'

He was even more exercised on learning that the jury had been picked at random from among the more responsible householders by the worthy Dr. Côté in the course of an after-breakfast saunter. 'It may be their way of doing things,' he breathed in Mr. Treadgold's ear. 'But it's slapdash, Treadgold, that's what it is, slapdash. Just like the French in the War!'

Actually only five jurors presented themselves, the absence of the sixth leading to a wordy altercation between the court and the greater part of the audience packed in and about the doorway. There were loud cries for someone called 'Alcide,' and an urchin arriving breathlessly to announce that 'Père' was getting in the hay. There was a wait until the missing juryman hurried in with his hair full of burrs, explaining that his watch had stopped.

The jury took the oath in French which again filled Mr. Treadgold's neighbour with the deepest misgiving. 'They're British subjects, ain't they?' he growled. 'Why can't they be sworn in English like the rest of us?' Mr. Treadgold did not agree, though he was careful not to say so – he was inclined to think that 'Que Dieu vous soit en aide!' sounded even more impressive than 'So help you God!' The jury having clumped out through the kitchen to the barn to view the body and clumped in again, the coroner adjusted his glasses and, gazing down at his gnarled hands clasped before him, proceeded to outline the circumstances of the murder.

Mr. Treadgold's attention soon wandered off to the girl. She had come in with the curé and one of the nuns from the Manor and had let the mayor guide her to where chairs were set apart for her and her companions in a window facing the jury. She looked very distinguished in black – there was a certain Parisian chic about the simple little hat, the plain crêpe frock, that was curiously incongruous in that rustic setting. Her face was in shadow; but it was easy to discern from the very rigidity of her pose that she was desperately nervous. She gazed straight in front of her as though unconscious of the fact that, heedless of the coroner's placid droning, every eye in the room was on her, from the six jurymen sitting bolt upright in Madame Côté's dining room chairs to the throng of villagers blocking the door.

The name 'Mathias Hurtibise' sounded upon Mr. Treadgold's ear. He was conscious of a little stir of excitement rippling through the crowded parlour. The coroner was holding up the bayonet, still enveloped in Mr. Treadgold's gaudy bandanna.

'Some of you who have been at the Manor in the old days,' he said, 'may remember the blunderbuss of Seigneur Ignace and this bayonet which formed part of it hanging on the wall in the salon. The dead man's wound suggests that he was stabbed with some such instrument as this: moreover, I have examined the bayonet through a magnifying-glass and traces of what appears to be human blood are visible round the hilt. Laboratory examination by the police will very easily establish the point. I do not propose to hand this weapon to the jury because we must take care not to efface any fingerprints.'

Mr. Treadgold was all attention now. Nothing about the circumstances in which the bayonet was found, he noticed – Ruffier had been as good as his word. Dr. Wood, who was standing up against the wall, caught his eye and they exchanged a meaning glance.

The coroner had lifted a newspaper and was displaying the shoes. 'As you will hear from Narcisse Laframboise,' he told the jury, 'these shoes, which you may examine for yourselves, were found concealed in the roof of Mathias's hut...' On a sign from him one of the jurors came forward and took the shoes which passed from hand to hand among the jury. 'In these circumstances,' Dr. Côté went on, 'by virtue of my powers as justice of the peace, I issued a warrant in the name of Our Lord the King for the arrest of the said Mathias Hurtibise, which warrant has been duly executed by the mayor of the parish.'

There was a sort of low murmur. Everybody looked to where, under an ancient eight-day clock solemnly ticking, the mayor sat against the wall behind the coroner. He had donned what was evidently his best suit for the occasion and a stiff white collar. It was characteristic of the man's delicacy, Mr. Treadgold reflected, that he had not seated himself at the coroner's table – the empty chair placed there was obviously intended for him. With one leg crossed over the other, his arms folded, he leaned back in his seat, staring up at the heavy beams of the ceiling, his air aloof as though to stress the fact that the coroner alone was in charge of the enquiry.

The clerk – a humpback – who sat beside the coroner, had called: 'Ange Tremblay!' The Angel, blinking owlishly, was at the table, holding the Bible as though it were a hot brick, while the clerk gabbled the oath. The gardien formally identified the body. Adams had arrived at the camp on the previous Sunday – as far as the witness knew, it was the first time he had stayed there. The last time he – Tremblay – saw the deceased alive was in the dining-hut at the camp after supper on the night of the murder when the witness was arranging the guests' fishing excursions for the following day. Adams had made no complaint about anyone having broken into his cabin.

The gardien was excused. 'Jacques Legaré,' the coroner called, glancing up from a paper before him. 'The late Seigneur's servant,' he explained to the jury. Heavy-footed and slow, the valet came forward. 'By your name you should be Canadien,' Dr. Côté suggested paternally.

'I was born in Quebec,' was the sullen answer.

'Where did your father come from?'

The man hesitated. 'St. Florentin,' he replied sulkily.

A voice piped up from the back of the court, an old, cracked voice: 'It'll be one of the Legarés who hauled lumber for Seigneur Pierre. One of them went to Quebec to work on the railroads. Ask him, Monsieur le Coroner, if he's not the son of Onésime Legaré's Joachim.'

'Joachim Legaré was my father,' said the valet, without looking round.

'How long have you been with Monsieur de St. Rémy?'

'Three years.'

'You weren't with him when he lived at the Manor, I think?'

The man shook his head. He had worked as a valet in the Quebec hotel where the Seigneur used to stay: Monsieur had engaged him to go to Europe with him.

One of the jurors was on his feet, a weedy individual with sandy hair combed into a topknot, pince-nez looped over one ear with a chain, and a sharp, inquisitive nose. Nervousness made him slightly truculent.

'With respect, Monsieur le Coroner,' he said importantly, 'strange rumours are current in the village regarding the late Seigneur. It is said that he and the young lady have been at the Manor, unbeknownst to everybody, for several days. I'd like to ask the witness what he can tell us about it.'

'We're not investigating the Seigneur's death, friend Pelletier,' Dr. Côté observed mildly. 'No inquest is necessary in his case – the American doctor has given a certificate of death from natural causes in which I fully concur. I've already explained that the old gentleman and his granddaughter have been at the Manor since Monday, and that last night, as the result of a heart attack, he passed away in circumstances that have nothing to do with the present enquiry, except in so far as the tragedy may have hastened his death through shock.' He turned to the witness. 'Please tell the jury how you found the body of Monsieur Adams.'

Jacques complied as the juryman reluctantly sat down.

'Mathias was in the habit of bringing you supplies, I believe?' the coroner enquired when the servant had finished.

'Yes, Monsieur.'

'He had free access to the house, eh?'

'To the kitchen, yes.'

'When did you see him last before the discovery of the body?'

'About seven p.m. when he came with some milk.'

'Did he then, or at any other time, say anything to you about Adams being at the camp?'

'No, Monsieur.'

The witness withdrew, and Wood took his place. He was sworn and spoke in English, Maître Boucheron acting as interpreter. He told of examining the body and described the cause of death. He agreed that, from the nature of the wound, it might have been inflicted by the bayonet. Prompted by the coroner, he narrated the circumstances in which he had found himself at the Manor and told of his having attended the Seigneur on the previous day.

'Did you then warn Mademoiselle de St. Rémy of the possible consequences to her grandfather of any sudden strain or shock?' the coroner demanded.

That was correct, Wood agreed. 'And am I right in saying,' the other went on, 'that if a man in the late Seigneur's physical condition had witnessed the murder or even unexpectedly come upon the body of the victim, the resultant excitement might have proved fatal?'

'Absolutely.'

'Thank you, Doctor. Mr. Treadgold!'

The coroner helped Mr. Treadgold through his evidence. The latter was first asked to describe the scene he had witnessed between Adams and Mathias and thereafter young Rees's appearance at the camp on the night of the murder with the news that he had seen a light shining in a window of the Manor. Mr. Treadgold spoke in French and the packed room listened in tense silence as, coming to the events that followed the discovery of the body, he told of the footprint he had found beside the dead man and the trail that led to the window. There were no questions from the jury and the witness gave way to Laframboise, the baker, who identified the shoes and deposed to unearthing them from the rafters of Le Borgne's shack. Gawky and self-conscious, the lanky baker strode back to his chair.

With a faintly hesitant manner Dr. Côté was polishing his glasses on his sleeve. 'I feel sure I speak for you all, my friends,' he observed, looking round the room, 'when I express to Mademoiselle de St. Rémy our sincere condolences on the great loss she has sustained in the person of the late Seigneur, her grandfather, last male representative of a family which has been connected with the parish since its first beginnings. She is a newcomer in our midst, but her late father, Monsieur Charles de St. Rémy, is affectionately remembered by many of us. At my request she is present here today' – he glanced towards the figure in black in the window – 'ready to answer any questions' – here he paused and let his eye rest upon the inquisitive juryman – 'that fall within the scope of this enquiry. I would draw your attention, however, to the fact that her evidence is necessarily of a negative order, since she was asleep in her bedroom at the Manor at the time when, as far as we have been able to establish, the murder took place.'

The General's raucous whisper rustled in Mr. Treadgold's ear: 'Gad, he don't mean to call her!' The atmosphere in the room was taut with suspense.

'In these circumstances,' the tranquil voice at the table proceeded, 'I should like to respect the young lady's grief...'

The juryman Pelletier had stood up. The serried ranks of spectators at the back seemed to sway as every neck was craned in his direction.

'Well, Aristide...' With an audible sigh the coroner popped on his glasses and surveyed the speaker.

The juror, a thumb thrust in the armhole of his waistcoat, glanced about him for support. 'I disagree,' he said in a loud voice. 'From what we have heard from you and the witnesses it would seem that Mademoiselle was the first person stirring in the house after the murder. I say we should hear the young lady!'

There was a murmur of assent from his fellow-jurymen, which, as the audience took it up, swelled in volume and broke into some hand-clapping.

'Silence!' cried the coroner angrily, banging the table. Rather apprehensively he glanced behind him to where the mayor sat. But Ruffier merely shrugged, his face contemptuous.

Settling his spectacles on his nose with a resigned air, the coroner looked towards the girl.

'Will you come forward and be sworn, please?' he said.

She stood up at once and advanced slowly to the table in a hush so intense that the tranquil ticking of the clock was plainly audible. A watchdog with jangling chain barked furiously in the yard outside.

It was the coroner himself who administered the oath, handing her the Bible, directing her to take off her glove. His rather flat voice broke in upon the stillness: 'Le témoignage que vous rendrez en cette cause sera la vérité, toute la vérité et rien autre chose que la vérité. Que Dieu vous soit en aide!' A pause.

'Face the jury, please, Mademoiselle! Your name?'

'Adrienne Stephanie de St. Rémy.'

'Your age?'

'Twenty-one.'

'You have been living at the Manor with your grandfather and his servant for several days?'

'Since Monday night.'

'The day before yesterday your grandfather had a serious heart attack, as the result of which he was confined to his room. When you left him yesterday evening to go and lie down, he was still in bed. What time was that?'

'Soon after eight o'clock.'

'Will you tell us what happened after that?'

'I lay down in my clothes. I didn't mean to go to sleep, but I had been up all the previous night with Grandfather and I must have dropped off. I awoke thinking I heard a cry. I naturally believed that Grandfather was calling me and ran to his room.'

'What time was this?' a juror asked.

She had been gaining confidence as she spoke, but the brusque interruption appeared to fluster her. In some confusion she glanced about her to locate the speaker and said, 'A few minutes past eleven.'

She was pitiably nervous, rolling and unrolling her handkerchief.

Seeing that she had lost the thread of her evidence Dr. Côté came to her aid. 'The Seigneur was not in his bedroom, so you went to the *lingerie*, where you took your meals. You found your grandfather fully dressed and unconscious, didn't you?'

She nodded, moistening her lips.

'Tell the jury what happened then.'

'Seeing that he didn't revive, I went and aroused Jacques. Between us we got him to his room. Then I sent Jacques to the camp for Dr. Wood.' She appeared to be more composed now.

'There's just one more point, Mademoiselle,' said the coroner. 'You know the accused Mathias?'

'Oh, yes.'

'Was he in the habit of roaming about the Manor grounds at night?'

She made the slightest pause before replying. 'Yes.'

'At all hours?'

She nodded.

'When you discovered your grandfather, did you hear any sound in the house or grounds?'

'No.'

'Or see anyone about?'

She shook her head.

'From eight o'clock until eleven or a few minutes past, you were asleep?'

'That is so.'

'So that you wouldn't have heard either Adams or the murderer arrive?'

'No.'

'And in fact you heard nothing?'

'No.'

Adjusting his spectacles, the coroner began to fumble among his papers. 'That seems to be all. I don't think we need detain...'

'One moment!' Pelletier was on his feet again. 'I'd like to ask Mademoiselle a question.'

The coroner shrugged. 'As you will, my friend.'

The juror cleared his throat and turned to the witness.

'When you first went into the linen room, where exactly was the Seigneur lying?'

She hesitated. 'As a matter of fact, when I first came upon him, he was in the vestibule,' she said in a low voice.

'In the vestibule?' repeated the coroner sharply. 'I understood from the doctor...' His eyes travelled towards Wood.

The girl moistened her lips. 'I'm afraid I unintentionally misled the doctor,' she answered nervously. 'But I was so alarmed about my grandfather, I scarcely knew what I was saying. It was only later, when I had time to think back...'

'I'd be glad if the young lady would answer my question,' Pelletier put in rather truculently. 'Just where was the old gentleman lying when she found him?'

She looked about her rather desperately. 'He wasn't lying. He was standing...'

'*Standing?*' exclaimed the coroner. 'Standing where?' His voice had a querulous edge.

A hand was laid on his arm. The mayor had come forward: he now dropped into the vacant chair at the table.

'He was outside the doors of the salon,' came the answer in a low and hurried tone,' tearing at his chest and moaning. As I reached him, he' – she paused to steady her voice – 'he collapsed in my arms. I managed to get him as far as the linen room where I'd left the candle.'

'Did he say anything?' the coroner asked.

She shook her head. 'He was already unconscious. I put him down and went to fetch Jacques...' She broke off and pressed her handkerchief against her lips.

'The Seigneur was outside the salon, you say.' Pelletier returned to the charge. 'Were the salon doors open or shut?'

She hesitated. 'I didn't notice – then.'

The coroner leaned forward. 'What do you mean "then"?'

She pressed her hands together. 'After Jacques went for the doctor, I discovered that my grandfather's heart tablets had been left in the linen room. I went to fetch them and then saw that there was a light in the salon. It must have been there all along, but before I was too concerned about Grandfather to notice it...' She broke off.

'Well?' said the coroner.

'I went out into the vestibule and saw that the salon doors were ajar. I pushed one side back. There was someone lying there on the floor beside the lamp. It was Gideon Adams.'

'You recognised him?'

She bowed her head. 'I could see that he was dead. There was nothing I could do for him, and Grandfather was unconscious in his room – all I thought of was of bringing him round. Then the doctor came and... and the curé, and the doctor said that Grandfather was dead, and by the time I thought of Adams again, Jacques had already discovered him...' Her voice trailed off.

'It's all very fine for her to make these admissions now,' Mr. Treadgold reflected as he sat on his very hard kitchen chair between the General and Maître Boucheron, 'but she certainly didn't let on to me when I questioned her that she knew about that dead body in the salon, and, judging by the way George Wood's staring at her, she didn't tell him, either – and anyway, if she had, he'd have mentioned it to me. Of course,' he mused, rubbing his chin, 'it's quite evident why she said nothing about it: she believed it was the old man who had killed Adams, as Ruffier was sharp enough to recognise. Hello, Ruffier's on his feet – he's coming out of his shell at last.'

'If Monsieur le Coroner would allow me a word?'

The mayor had risen at the table. People were whispering and nudging and peering at the girl, but absolute quiet fell as, pausing deliberately for silence, Ruffier faced the room.

With a friendly wave of the hand towards the persistent juryman, he remarked in a colloquial tone: 'I only wanted to point out that our friend Aristide, with the aid of Mademoiselle's very frank statement, has established a point of considerable importance for the enquiry. Thanks to neighbour Pelletier, we know now that Adams was already dead by eleven o'clock, or a few minutes later, the hour at which Mademoiselle came upon the Seigneur.'

He smiled knowingly at Pelletier. 'That was what you were after, eh, my old Aristide?' he remarked in a confidential aside, loud enough, however, for the whole room to hear.

The juryman was delighted. He smiled craftily at the mayor and with a self-righteous air, resumed his seat.

Mr. Treadgold's opinion of the mayor shot up a hundredfold. The note struck was perfect. The casual, almost chatty tone immediately took the sting out of the situation: in one breath Ruffier had contrived to stress the witness's candour, short-circuit the cross-examination by switching it over to a side-issue, and soft-soap into inaction the only troublesome member of the jury. Already the girl was returning to her place. Well, Ruffier had undertaken to shield her. He was evidently a man of his word. A pretty good strategist, too, and how he knew his villagers!

A word from the mayor in Dr. Côté's ear and, rapping for silence, the coroner began to resume the evidence for the jury. Mr. Treadgold's attention wandered again. He glanced round the court. There was a khaki-clad constable at the back and Mr. Treadgold remembered the car inscribed 'Police Provinciale' he had noticed outside the house – he had a sudden conviction that Le Borgne was destined to be whisked off to jail at Trois-Ponts in that car. George Wood was gazing solicitously at the girl; Maître Boucheron was mopping inside his collar with his handkerchief, as though he felt the heat; old Tisserand was looking drowsy.

A note was passed up from the door and the coroner broke off to glance at it. 'I now leave you, my friends, to return your verdict,' he concluded a very brief speech; '... the sooner the better,' he added benevolently, 'for neighbour Mathieu's Angélique is in labour and, if I don't hurry, the baby will arrive before me.'

There was a laugh at this and the laugh released a buzz of conversation. The jury did not leave the room: they were putting their heads together where they sat, leaning forward and conversing in whispers...

The murmur of voices died away, but people behind were still talking. Pelletier was on his feet. In the hubbub Mr. Treadgold could not catch the words, but he divined their purport. It was a verdict of wilful murder against Mathias Hurtibise.

Chapter 15

THE ROOM EMPTIED RELUCTANTLY. Mr. Treadgold looked for Wood, and found him gone. The doctor had got his car back and had driven himself over in it; but there was no sign of the somewhat battered roadster when Mr. Treadgold ultimately reached the street. Ruffier and the girl had vanished, too.

At the camp, going from the garage to his cabin, Mr. Treadgold came face to face with Tisserand, rod in hand, waddling down to the landing-stage. The beady, black eyes greeted him with a penetrating look.

'They talk and talk and talk,' the clerk wheezed confidentially, jerking his head towards the main hut, 'as if by talking they could bring the unfortunate gentleman back to life. Evidently, it is all very shocking, but what should one do? For me, I go to take a trout, and I think, if you're wise, Monsieur, you'll follow my example. You have your rod, yes?'

'I shall be delighted to watch you,' Mr. Treadgold told him, 'but I don't believe I want to fish.'

They took a flat-bottomed boat, and in silence Tisserand pulled to the farther shore. Twenty yards from the bank he dropped the killick and from a battered tin case selected a fly which he proceeded, with pudgy fingers extraordinarily deft, to tie to his line. Then he glanced at the sky, emitted a brief grunt, and with a dexterous twist of the wrist began to cast.

For a long time he fished in stolid silence, his companion, pipe in mouth, idly watching from the stern. The lake was drowsy with the noontide. A majestic array of clouds, fleecy white, piled billowing one upon the other, tempered the heat of the sun to an agreeable warmth. The air throbbed softly to the propeller beat of a plane somewhere out of sight; the reel made a little whirring noise from time to time. Suddenly a triumphant 'Ah!' burst from the fisherman's lips, the rod was arched bowlike, there was a flick of the wrist and a shining trout with belly pinkly flushed was threshing the boards at Mr. Treadgold's feet. The clerk's moonlike countenance beamed: thereafter, the spell was broken and, as he cast again, he began to talk.

'Eh bien,' he observed, as once more his fly delicately skimmed the water, 'they lose no time, these gentlemen of St. Florentin! He seemed to know what he wanted, this coroner of theirs, diable! At this rate, they'll have their man safely hanged before the police arrive! This poor young lady! What a terrible experience!'

His companion nodded soberly. 'What are your detectives like?' he asked, trailing his hand in the water. 'Pretty efficient?'

The other shrugged, his eye on the line. 'Evidently, they haven't the same opportunities as your New York police,' he replied, not without a certain malice. 'I know one or two of them at Quebec. One went to school with me – Napoléon Bigoury, a highly intelligent type. Educated, too – he speaks both languages – and a great traveller. He has been to Chicago – he was hotel detective there for three years. I shouldn't wonder if they didn't send him down here again. It was he who investigated the miller's death, you know...'

Mr. Treadgold nodded. 'I heard a detective was down from Quebec. When was this?'

'About a month ago. It was before I came, but Bigoury told me about it.'

'He found no evidence against Le Borgne, I think?'

'Not enough to hang a cat. They were all for arresting the poor wretch then, but Bigoury told me no jury would convict.'

'In the circumstances I think they might have waited with the inquest.'

The fat man cast. 'Voyez-vous, Monsieur, these little parishes of ours are jealous of their independence. They like to do things in their own way, without interference from outside. This time they have the evidence and they're taking no risks.'

His companion looked thoughtful. 'Such evidence as it is; but then any stick's good enough to beat a dog with, I suppose.' He paused. 'That would explain why they made no attempt to look into the possibility of an alibi...'

'An alibi? In the face of those marks on his shoes? Did he put forward an alibi?'

'Not in so many words. But he'd been drinking and, although he claimed to have had a bottle with him, the coroner evidently disbelieved it. He seemed to think he'd been boozing somewhere in the village.'

Tisserand nodded. 'At Lhermite's, no doubt!' He glanced suddenly aloft. 'Tiens, an aeroplane!'

The deep hum of propellers came echoing back from the woods. A plane, wings glistening in the sun, was visible high above the trees.

Mr. Treadgold scarcely looked up. 'There is such a place in the village, then?' he enquired with marked interest.

The fat man nodded guardedly, his head in the air. 'The guides go there. The Restaurant de la Gaieté. There's said to be a back room...' He was still staring aloft. 'Hello, he's cut off his engine! One would say he were coming down...'

The drone of the propellers had abruptly ceased. The plane was circling above the lake.

Mr. Treadgold disregarded it. 'But, look here,' he broke in earnestly, 'suppose Le Borgne actually was drinking at Lhermite's place, but is afraid to admit it for fear of getting the fellow into trouble, don't you realise that the hour at which Le Borgne left is absolutely vital?'

But Tisserand's attention was now wholly centred on the plane. 'Bon Dieu!' he wheezed irately, 'is there no place sacred to these damnable machines? He means to land on the lake – look, one can see the floats!'

The plane was now below the level of the trees, its white floats clearly distinguishable. Now with a sudden, shattering roar the engine picked up.

'Seigneur de Miséricorde!' trumpeted the fat man – he had flung his rod into the bottom of the boat and was hauling frantically at the stone anchor – 'he'll hit us!'

But at that instant the plane, its motor silent again, swooped down to the water, and, after bouncing along on the surface in a flurry of spray, came to a halt not a hundred yards from the boat.

Tisserand had flopped into the rowing-seat and grasped the oars, preparatory to making for the shore. A shout came rolling across the water, 'Ho-là!' With a sudden ejaculation the clerk put the punt about and began to row furiously towards the plane. 'It's Bigoury!' he exclaimed.

A stocky man, wearing a fleecy greatcoat and tweed cap, leaned down to draw the punt alongside.

'Napoléon!' cried Tisserand joyously. 'So it's you, you rascal, who tumble from the skies and frighten the trout, not to mention my friend and myself! This is Monsieur Treadgold, of New York,' he introduced, 'my friend, Sergeant Bigoury, of the Sûreté Provinciale!'

Gimlet eyes glittered a greeting through horn-rimmed glasses. 'Pleased to meetcha,' said the sergeant in English, jaws moving rhythmically, and, calling to another man who was watching a policeman unload some luggage from the cabin, presented him as Dr. Perronneau, 'médecin-légiste – what you call the Medical Examiner in New York,' he explained to Mr. Treadgold. 'And Constable Bissonnette,' he went on, jerking his head at the police officer, 'our fingerprint expert.' Dropping into French, he said to Tisserand: 'Yes, it's I, old friend. They told me at your office you were here. The trains didn't suit, so, seeing that the Assistant Attorney-General was in a hurry, we came by air. You take us ashore, hein?'

The three men piled into the punt and Tisserand stood off while the plane, having taxied to the end of the lake and turned, came roaring by to take the air and disappear over the trees.

'So your chief's in a hurry?' said Tisserand to the sergeant as they made for the landing-stage.

Bigoury laughed. 'Two deaths in a month at the Manor — three, if you count the Seigneur! What do you think?' He had an explosive manner of speech. 'Can you give us some food?'

'Surely...'

'How do I reach the Manor from here?'

'You'll want a car,' Tisserand replied, and looked at Mr. Treadgold, who promptly placed himself at the detective's disposition.

'You'd like to call on the coroner first, I dare say,' he remarked to Bigoury.

The sergeant made a sound with his lips suggesting that he had extended his travels beyond Chicago to the Bronx.

'We'll let the doctor handle that old windbag,' he observed succinctly. 'I'm going to the Manor.'

Shiner sat on the rail of the dock, his elbows on his knees, his feet tucked under him, the picture of desolation. Mr. Treadgold had not seen the boy since the tragedy and stopped to speak to him, while the others went on to the main hut. The youngster brightened up sufficiently to ask about the plane. He was greatly impressed to hear that it had brought the detective.

'I say, which is he?' he demanded, staring after Tisserand and his companions. It was the one in the cap with glasses, Mr. Treadgold explained. Shiner seemed disappointed. 'Not much to look at, is he?' he declared. He made a pause, his small face secretive. 'I suppose they're sure they've got the right man, sir?'

'Le Borgne, do you mean?'

The lad nodded.

'The coroner's jury returned a verdict against him, Shiner.'

'Yes, but...' He broke off. 'Look here,' he burst out, 'I promised not to tell anybody, but I think the detective ought to know – I'd have spoken to Daddy, but he's been in such an absolute fury with me ever since last night...' He stopped again.

'What is it, old man?'

'Batisse thinks that Le Borgne didn't do it...'

'Oh?'

'I had a talk with him when he came back from the inquest. He was frightfully mysterious. "So long I was leev'," he said – you know the rum way these guides have of talking – "I never see nodding lak' dat. If everyt'ing was tell, Le Borgne no go to prison," he said. "But somebody no lak' for to spik, I guess." What do you make of that, sir?'

'Did he mention any name?'

'No. I tried to pump him, but he dried up.' His glance consulted Mr. Treadgold. 'Do you s'pose we ought to tell the detective?'

The other reflected. 'I'd better have a word with Batisse first.'

With a pensive air he went to his lunch.

Chapter 16

GEORGE WOOD DROVE HIS car onto the grass beside the trail and jerked it to a halt in a tangle of blueberry bushes. With a purposeful look in his eye he switched off the engine and turned to the girl beside him.

'First stage of the cure,' he announced. 'Forest air for the lungs, tobacco for the nerves. Halt for a cigarette and a little polite conversation, then we push on!' He extended a frayed packet.

She was saying good-bye to the curé when Wood stepped up to her after the inquest. He gathered from their conversation that the Seigneur's body had been taken down to the church against the funeral next day and that she was going to stay at the convent in the village for the moment – the curé said he would send to the Manor for her baggage later. It was then that Wood struck in with his suggestion. He had his car there – if it would be any convenience for Mademoiselle, he would be very happy to drive her to the Manor and wait while she packed. The girl seemed to welcome the proposal and, as though the young man's strictly professional air gave him confidence, the priest raised no objection.

It was not until they were rattling up the hill towards the Manor, however, that Wood disclosed his plan. 'You look wretchedly ill. What you want is fresh air,' he told her. 'I'm going to take you for a drive before we fetch your things.'

She gave him a rather wan smile. 'I think I should like it,' she answered simply.

No nonsense about her, he told himself: no gush, no pose, no primness. She was not on the defensive as other girls in her situation might have been – she seemed to be glad of his company and not to care if he knew it. Yet she wasn't one of those hearty females – on the contrary, there was something adorably feminine about her. He liked the demureness of the white collar and cuffs that relieved the severity of her simple black frock: he found her small black hat set at just the right angle to suit the shape of her face and show the graceful line of the head with its crisp, dark hair looped back over the prettiest ears. He felt it vaguely as a compliment to his intelligence, too, that she did not think it necessary to parade her grief.

She took a cigarette and let him give her a light. Sinking back in her seat she said: 'It's just what I wanted. A cigarette and this perfect peace. I think you must be a very good doctor.'

He nodded solemnly. 'None better. Me and the Mayos. Look at the income I make. Take this car, for instance...' With a humorous glance at her he poked a finger into a rent in the shabby leatherwork.

She smiled indulgently, half-closing her eyes against the smoke curling up from the corner of her mouth – in the sunlight her eyes were exactly the colour of wood violets, he decided. She leaned her head back against the folded hood, her serene face tilted to the sky. 'It's heavenly here. I'm so glad you brought me.'

They had passed the Manor and the mill and, where the woods came down to the road, had taken at random a road which, driving deep into the thick of them, soon became no more than a grassy trail. They had stopped in a little clearing dotted with stacks of corded lumber and hemmed in closely by trees. Before them the trail, slashed by long pencils of sunlight, melted into a bluish vista. The air was warm and loud with bees droning among the blueberries and wild raspberries: crows cawed hoarsely in the top branches of the firs; and somewhere out of sight a brook gurgled softly.

The girl sighed happily and blew a cloud of smoke. 'You live in New York, don't you?' she said, watching a white butterfly that went dancing between the bushes.

The young man nodded. 'Know it?'

She shook her head

'A healthy city,' he said. 'Too darn healthy!'

She smiled at him. She had a slow, caressing smile, as though it were something she were loath to part with, a smile that turned the corners of her mouth right up like a small child's, and displayed even, milk-white teeth.

'I'd like to see New York,' she confessed. 'I love cities. Although I'm a Canadienne – my father would never let me speak of being French Canadian – I've never been to Canada before, or indeed anywhere, except England and France – I was born in London. But I've heard about Canada all my life – the rivers, the woods, the mountains, the moose and the salmon – and just to sit here and listen to that stream and breathe in the divine scent of the pines is to realise some of the beauty Daddy used to tell me about as a child. He was going to show it all to me some day. But the War came and he joined up, then he had to start in business all over again and afterwards he and my mother were drowned.'

'Yachting, wasn't it? The curé told us.'

She nodded.

'And now I suppose you'll settle down here.'

She shook her head dubiously. 'I don't believe I could ever become acclimatised after Paris. There's a narrowness about the life of these people that... that stifles me. At the inquest this morning all those peasant faces staring – they were so strange, so unfamiliar. And Sister Marie Célestine, that dear old nun who brought me to the inquest, imagine, she's been a nun for forty-seven years! And never travelled farther than Quebec. I always have a feeling that I'm scandalising her.'

Wood chuckled. 'Paris is about two centuries away from St. Florentin, remember!'

Her nod was rather forlorn. 'The sisters are very sweet. But how I'm going to stand a convent for even twenty-four hours...'

'How long have you been living in Paris?'

'For the past four years – since I was seventeen. I was at a finishing school when Father and Mother died. Grandpapa was anxious for me to come out to Canada then. But I wanted to study art – I was entered for the Beaux-Arts. So he made me an allowance until, about three years ago, he came over to Paris himself and took me to live with him.'

'That was after the trouble with Adams, was it?'

She nodded. 'His income was very much reduced. No more allowance. But I was able to go on with my studies until he fell ill and had to give up his work.'

'He had a job, eh?'

'He was in the orchestra at the Opéra Comique. He played the flute and gave lessons in his spare time. We had a little money coming in from the estate and we managed all right until his heart became bad and he had to stay away from rehearsals. Then he lost his position and he couldn't go on with his teaching, either. If it hadn't been for the few hundred francs a month I was able to earn...'

'Painting?'

'Commercial work – dress designing for the big shops, posters – when I could get it. What with the slump and the Americans staying at home, things haven't been too easy. And since our rents stopped coming in, what I was able to make wasn't really enough.'

'Yet you managed to find the fares to come all this way?'

'That was a nest-egg of Grandpapa's – five hundred dollars. He always wanted to be buried here – it was meant to defray the cost of bringing him back to St. Florentin, if he should die abroad...' Her eyes clouded over. 'I realise now he must have known he hadn't long to live. I'm glad I didn't oppose him – he wanted so much to see the old house again. Besides, something had to be done about our rents. Grandpapa kept writing to Boucheron, but he didn't answer...'

'He collects the rents for you, is that it?'

She flushed. 'He's supposed to. But six months ago Aunt Anita died and since then we've received nothing because, of course, Gideon Adams ordered him to keep them back. At least, that's what I say, but Grandfather wouldn't believe it of Boucheron.'

'Your grandfather wasn't afraid that Boucheron would give him away to Adams?'

The idea seemed new to her and she turned her head to regard him sharply. 'He wouldn't have dared. The tenants idolised Grandpapa. If they'd found out that Boucheron had done anything to harm the Seigneur, his practice would have been ruined.'

She spoke assuredly, but he was aware of a certain misgiving behind her words.

'What about Adams finding out, anyway? Was your grandfather prepared to risk it?'

'There seemed to be no risk – Adams hasn't been near the Manor for years and years. I can't imagine what brought him – no one, not even Boucheron, knew we were coming.' She paused. 'You heard about the trouble between them, I suppose?'

He nodded. 'Oh, if you'd known Grandfather as I did,' she cried, pressing her hands together, 'you'd realise that he wasn't a thief. He never had a head for business, that's all. He was an artist, a musician, not a businessman. Besides, he always left everything to Boucheron. The truth is that Adams hated Grandpapa, because Adams was a Westerner and looked down on the French Canadians, Grandpapa used to say. Besides, he had his knife into Grandfather, anyway, because, years ago, when he was staying at the Manor, they got into an argument about politics which ended in Adams leaving the house. But for Aunt Anita he'd have seized the few miserable rents which were all we had to live on. As it was, he sold everything in the Manor, as you've seen – he'd have sold the Manor, too, if he could have found a purchaser. Aunt Anita died six months ago and from that moment our money stopped. That was Adams's doing, of course.'

'And your grandfather didn't see Boucheron to ask him?'

She shook her head. 'No. He was going to, but he had to rest after the journey and then he had that attack.'

'As far as I gather, the real object of your grandfather's return was to enquire about the rents.'

She was staring in front of her. 'I don't know the real reason.'

He looked at her intently. 'You said it was because he wanted to see the old house again,' he reminded her.

'That was true. But it wasn't the only reason. The rents, either. As a rule, he had no secrets from me. But from the time we arrived at the Manor I could see he had something on his mind.'

Wood nodded. 'You told me he was restless and excitable, I remember. Didn't he give you any inkling?'

She did not reply. For a moment her eyes rested tentatively on his face.

'Your friend who was with you at the Manor last night...' she began.

'Treadgold?'

'He's very intelligent, isn't he?'

'Rather. And simply bursting with culture. Ever read Tristram Shandy?'

She shook her head.

'Never heard of Uncle Toby and Corporal Trim?'

'Never!'

The young man chortled. 'Well, you will if you meet old man Treadgold more than once. He's by way of being a bit of a criminologist, too!'

Blankly she stared at him. 'You mean he's a detective?'

Wood laughed. 'Don't look so rattled. Only in an amateur way!'

She gazed down at her neat black shoes. 'He doesn't believe that Mathias killed this man, does he?' she said abruptly.

Her companion slapped at a mosquito. 'I don't know why he shouldn't. The evidence is clear enough...'

'I was sitting across the room from him at the inquest. I never saw a man look so unhappy about anything. When the jury announced the verdict, he frowned, and I'm almost sure I saw him shake his head.'

'He didn't say anything to me. Wait a moment, though – this morning, after you went to bed, he seemed very anxious to know whether anyone at the Manor had been wearing rubbers...'

'Rubbers?'

'That's what he said.'

'Who's anyone?'

'The curé, Boucheron.'

She frowned quickly. 'Boucheron?'

He clapped his hand over hers as it rested on the seat beside him. 'Drop this idea that Le Borgne isn't the man, will you! You can't get over the evidence of those shoes. He left a footprint beside the body, you know. You thought your grandfather killed Adams, didn't you?'

She nodded.

'Well, take it from me, the thing's a physical impossibility.'

Her face was suddenly eager. 'You're sure of that?'

'Positively. I can't imagine what ever put such an idea into your head.'

She made a long pause. 'The last time they met, Grandfather threatened to kill him...'

'How do you know this?'

'I was there. Gideon Adams came to see us in Paris with a certain proposal.'

'What proposal?'

'He wanted me to marry him.'

'No!'

'Yes.' She smiled at the horror in his voice. 'He had it all worked out. I was to marry him and we were to live at the Manor – he wanted to retire and live the life of a country gentleman. Grandpapa was to return to Canada if he liked and have an apartment in Montreal or Quebec – Gideon would make him an allowance.'

'What did you tell him?'

'I told him to ask Grandpapa.'

'And what did your grandfather say?'

She was looking down on the brown hand that imprisoned hers. 'He was like a madman. He frightened me. Before I could stop him he had opened a drawer and pulled out a pistol he kept there. He told Gideon that if he didn't get out he'd shoot him.'

'And Gideon took the hint?'

She nodded, her face contemptuous. 'He was a bully – he had no real courage.' She drew her hand away.

'When you looked into the salon last night and saw Adams, was that bayonet on the floor?' he asked after a pause.

She shook her head. 'I meant to ask you about that. I didn't see it.'

'Then Jacques must have picked it up and put it back.'

'Put it back where?'

'On that stand on the wall. It was found there, wiped clean.'

'Didn't Mathias put it back?'

'No. At the time he was under guard in that room across the hall. Did Jacques know Adams?'

'Oh, yes.'

'He claimed he didn't.'

'He saw him only once as far as I know, the day Gideon came to see us in Paris and there was the row.'

'Was Jacques present?'

'He heard Grandfather shouting, and came in. It was he who took the gun away from him.'

Wood nodded. 'I expect he had the same idea as you and wanted to get rid of the evidence. It makes no difference, really. Le Borgne's the man...' He gave her his quick smile. 'You've had a bad time, haven't you? Gosh, I hate to think of you being buried alive in that convent. Why don't you come over and stop at the camp?'

For the first time she laughed. 'And the curé? And all the village gossips? How could I stay there with a lot of men?'

'Mercy, girl, the place is overrun with women. You'll be chaperoned to death. Just leave this to me, will you? As soon as you've packed your traps we'll drive over – the gardien can telephone the convent that you've changed your mind.'

She looked at him out of her tranquil eyes. 'Why are you doing all this for me?'

He laughed. 'It's my daily good deed – Boy Scout stuff, you know.'

She smiled back at him. 'Couldn't you be serious for once?'

This time he glanced away – the tips of his ears were red.

'I don't know,' he answered hesitantly. 'I like you and I have a sort of feeling, somehow, that you ought to be happy, at least happier than you are...' He stopped. 'When you've seen the other women at the camp,' he said, with a flash of his old jesting tone, 'I dare say you'll understand why I wanted you to come and stay...'

She looked at him for a long moment, then rather shyly laid her arm on his sleeve.

'Let's go to the Manor now,' she suggested. 'I want to ask your advice about something.'

'Can't you tell me here?'

She shook her head. 'Let's go; do you mind?'

Obediently his foot pressed the starter. The car was moving forward when she caught his arm.

'Listen,' she cried excitedly, 'there's something moving in the bushes. Oh, do you think it could be a moose?'

With the unlooked-for onslaught his foot slipped off the clutch, the engine stalled and the car lurched into a hole.

'You won't believe me,' he remarked resignedly, 'but I'd scarcely know a moose if I saw one. We've all manner of wild animals in New York, but...'

'There was a sort of crashing. Look at that branch – it's still swaying!'

He gazed where she was pointing. 'It might have been a moose,' he agreed gravely. 'On the other hand, it might have been Madame Tisserand, one of your prospective chaperones, gathering blueberries. She's about the same weight and, judging by the head on the dining room wall at the camp, there's a distinct facial resemblance.'

The girl laughed and, all remaining still, they regained the trail and presently were bumping along in the direction of the main road.

Round a curve, a hundred yards or so from the clearing, the doctor lifted a hand from the wheel to point. 'There's your moose!' he chaffed. 'It's only a lumberjack on the job!'

The hood of a battered flivver projected from behind a bush. The car had been backed almost out of sight up a side path. It was unattended.

'A lumberjack? What's that?' she queried.

'A lumberman. A woodcutter.'

She smiled her delicate smile. 'The only woodcutters I know are in the fairy stories I used to read as a little girl. It's queer to think of them riding about the forest in cars. At that rate, I suppose Red Riding Hood would drive up to her grandmother's cottage in a limousine!'

With a whimsical air he considered the point. 'More likely a sports roadster,' he finally pronounced. 'Something rather natty, probably, with a scarlet body to match her frock, and lots of chromium plating. The wolf would have the limousine – you know, one of those overpowering affairs, about twenty feet long, all shiny and black and slinky, with three different kinds of klaxon and a Filipino chauffeur. And there'd be a large "No Parking" sign hung up outside the cottage, and, of course, dear little Red Riding Hood would park right under it, the way everyone does on this continent.'

The girl simmered with amusement. 'You're too absurd!'

'And Red Riding Hood would take one peek at the wolf's limousine standing there,' he proceeded imperturbably, 'and she'd bounce right into the cottage and "Gran," she'd holler, "who's the new boyfriend?" And Gran would open her mouth and flash her long, white fangs and tell her, very blasé-like, "The Prince is simply c-crazy about me!" And Red Riding Hood would notice the teeth and come right back with "Why, Gran, that new dentist of yours is certainly the cat's whiskers. If those aren't the swellest teeth!"'

She crooned a little laugh. 'And what'd happen then?'

'Gran would lick her chops and smile ever so craftily and she'd say, "Red, sweetheart, just give me time to have my massage and get into my clothes and you and I'll take a little ride!"'

At that the girl laughed outright. 'You have the craziest imagination!' She shook her head at him. 'Do you always go on like this?'

'It's a poor heart that never rejoices, Adrienne!'

She nodded demurely. 'All the same, I know why you're doing it. You wanted to cheer me up, didn't you?'

He turned and grinned at her. 'You read me like a book!'

Her cool fingers touched his brown hand as it grasped the wheel. 'I shall never forget how kind you've been to me,' she said in a low voice.

'Nonsense,' he told her, flushing. And added, 'the front name is George.'

'Thank you, Georges,' she said, softening the name in the French way.

They spoke no more after that and so in silence came to the Manor.

Chapter 17

Leaving the roadster parked on the drive, they made their way round to the kitchen door – she wanted to see if Jacques was back from the inquest, the girl explained. But there was no sign of the servant. Within the house was the expectant hush of empty places – their feet rang on the uncarpeted boards, as, with her graceful gait, the girl led the way to the linen room. There she drew up a chair to the table and sat down. Opening her handbag she produced a slim leather wallet.

'It was in Grandpapa's pocket,' she explained, unfolding it. 'I found it last night, but I didn't examine it until this morning: the curé was waiting for me then and I didn't have time to do anything about it...' She paused. 'There's a letter in it addressed to me – "For Adrienne, in the event of my death," it says on the envelope.'

She had drawn from the wallet a letter which had been sealed with three seals in green wax, now broken. 'It's in French – I'll translate for you. Grandpapa wrote it in Paris last year. It's dated October 17, the day he went to see the heart specialist.' In a husky voice she began to read:

My dear Adrienne, Professor Gauthier gives me no hope. He warns me that, with my heart in its present condition, I must be prepared to die at any moment without warning. I have decided to keep the doctor's verdict to myself. Death is the natural portion of old age and I have not the right to let this dark shadow fall upon your youth already clouded by the troubles my folly has brought down on us...

Her voice quivered and she halted to steady it.

You know [she read on, after an instant's pause] *that, driven from home by the unrelenting animosity of a single individual, I had no opportunity before my departure to dispose of the Manor or its contents. As you are aware, Gideon Adams obtained possession of the Manor in part settlement of your aunt's claim against the estate and, after my departure, had its contents sold by auction. Hitherto, I have allowed you to believe that nothing was saved from the sale; but this is to let you know that, before leaving, I took steps to place certain of the most valuable of the family possessions beyond his reach. They include the gold snuffbox given to Seigneur Ignace by General Brock, Seigneur Ignace's silver candlesticks and silver inkstand, the set of Sèvres vases presented to him by King Louis XVIII of France, your great-grandmother's Stafford tea service inscribed with the family crest, some Waterford glass and other articles. These I placed for safekeeping in a hiding place I contrived in the attic...*

Wood put out his cigarette. 'Hidden here?' He gave the girl a sharp glance. 'Doesn't this perhaps explain Adams's presence at St. Florentin?'

She nodded shrewdly. 'I thought of that. But let me finish the letter.' She resumed, going back to the last phrase she had read:

These I placed for safekeeping in a hiding-place I contrived in the attic. I still hope to return to the Manor before I die, but if I am not destined to see the old house again, it is my wish that you should go there in my place and take possession of these heirlooms, which are your sole inheritance. You have never been to the Manor, so let me tell you how to proceed...

The doctor was listening intently. She read on:

In the right-hand corner of the wall facing the stair that mounts to the attic from the bedroom floor – it is the little stair in the wall I mean and not the back stairs descending to the vestibule – a panel conceals a cupboard. Look three feet from the right-hand wall, at a height of four feet from the ground, and you will find a hole plugged with paper the same colour as the pitch pine. Remove the paper, and a nail or a pencil inserted will release a hidden spring and the panel will open. The things are on the two shelves behind it...

George Wood whistled. 'Gosh!' he exclaimed softly.

The girl stayed him with her hand – she had not finished the letter.

You, dearest child [she pursued rather tremulously], *are the only one to share this secret. You will remember that carpentry has always been a hobby of mine...*

She looked up. 'It's true,' she said. 'Grandpapa was quite a carpenter. In Paris, before he fell ill, he made all kinds of things for our apartment...' She turned back to the letter and read on:

It was a simple matter for me to replace the cupboard door by a panel which I stained the same colour as the matchboarding and I did the work single-handed. By the time you receive this letter, therefore, you will be the only one in possession of my secret, for I shall have gone to my last account. Rest assured, though, dearest child, that, wherever I am, I shall be with you in thought, praying that you may live long to cherish these precious heirlooms which are all your loving and broken-hearted...

She choked and laid the letter down, unfinished. 'That's all that matters,' she said brokenly. 'We were such good friends – he was always so brave and gay...' She turned her head away. Wood clamped his hand over hers. She gave him her wistful smile. 'It's all right,' she assured him and sniffed forlornly, 'I'm not going to cry. Give me a cigarette!' and when her cigarette was alight, 'I must go to the attic,' she went on. 'I thought perhaps you'd go with me...'

'Sure!' Wood stood up briskly. His head was slanted at a listening angle. 'There's no one about. Why don't we go now?'

She nodded, her eyes very bright. 'All right!'

'How do we get to the attic? Do you know the way?'

'There's a flight going up from the first floor. I realise now that Grandpapa was trying to visit the attic the day after we arrived. I was with Jacques in the kitchen after lunch when we heard Grandpapa calling out. His voice seemed to come from upstairs. We found him on the first landing – the bedroom floor. He was breathless, clutching at his heart and terribly, terribly agitated. He kept on saying to himself, "Je ne peux plus! Je ne peux plus! Il faut attendre!" – that means, "I can't manage it! I shall have to wait!" you know. Jacques and I brought him down to his room and put him to bed. He stayed there until the evening he had his first attack!'

Her companion nodded. 'Poor old boy! Stair-climbing was about the worst thing he could have done in the circumstances. I dare say it brought on that seizure of his in the garden. Well, shall we go? Wait, we want a nail or a pencil – something to work that panel!'

'I have a pencil,' she replied, and drew up from the front of her black frock the other end of a thin gold chain she wore round her neck. There was a round clasp at the end of the chain, but no pencil. In dismay she stared at the clasp. 'Oh, dear!' she cried, 'I believe I've lost it!' She was glancing down inside her dress.

'Never mind, I have one,' Wood told her and showed a pencil. 'Let's go!'

He went across to her and slipped his arm in hers. She seemed to draw nearer to him so that he felt the warmth of her body through the thinness of her frock.

'I shall be glad to get out of this house,' she said in a suppressed voice, clutching his arm rather tightly, as they went out into the vestibule; 'even in broad daylight, with the sunshine pouring in at the windows, it fills me with terror. It's so still and… and uncanny: I feel myself listening to the silence, waiting for some sound to break it. I'd never have dared to go up to the attic alone…'

They were in the front hall now, at the foot of the main staircase.

'We might as well make sure we have the place to ourselves,' the doctor suggested. Relinquishing his companion's arm, he ran to the vestibule door and called sharply, 'Jacques!'

But there was no reply. His voice reverberated sadly in the surrounding emptiness, and in the hush that re-descended as they waited for an answering hail, they could hear the murmur of the cascade in the grounds outside.

'Lead on!' cried Wood. Arm-in-arm they marched up the flight.

The staircase with slender balustrade in one piece mounted curving to a cramped, irregularly shaped landing, low of roof and dusky by contrast with the light and airy entrance hall below. It was a mass of corners with its ceiling sloping down at all manner of unexpected angles, its pair of windows close-shuttered and sunk in immensely deep embrasures, and a whole series of cupboards with doors, skilfully fitted into the panelling. Three doors, obviously bedrooms, broke the line of the left-hand wall: opposite, flattened in a corner, was a tiny, built-in stair.

The stair was dark. 'We'll want a candle!' said Wood.

'Wait there! I'll fetch one.' The girl tripped away. When an instant later she came up again, a lighted candle in her hand, he was at the foot of the attic flight, leaning forward listening.

'It's odd,' he said, turning to take the candle from her, 'but I could have sworn there was a footstep overhead!'

She gazed at him intently. 'I told you already, Jacques and I heard strange sounds from this part of the house the first night we were here. Jacques said it was rats, but the noise seemed to me to be too heavy – it was a kind of distant, heavy scraping, a sort of fumbling tapping. Until I found this letter of Grandpapa's, I couldn't help thinking – I know it was childish of me – of these stories about the Manor being haunted. But now I'm wondering...'

The young man was staring fixedly at her. 'I'm wondering myself,' he broke in abruptly. 'Come on, Adrienne, let's get to the bottom of this, shall we?' As she made no answer, he turned with an encouraging grin and reached for her hand. 'Not scared, are you?' She shook her head and tried, but not very successfully, to smile back at him. Then he took her hand in his and, drawing her along behind him, went up the narrow stair.

Straight and steep it mounted, in a darkness that was stifling hot and so intense that it seemed opaque, to what appeared at first glimpse to be an elaborate scaffolding, a regular cat's-cradle of tremendous timbers. Hand-in-hand they came out into the middle of the attic, upon an open space hemmed in by the framework of enormous beams, upright and diagonal, supporting the roof. Here odd pieces of derelict furniture, propped, lopsided and lamentable, against the scaffolding, impeded the immediate view, and in the centre of the space a number of dilapidated trunks with lids flung wide gushed a mass of papers, books, and old clothes in wild confusion upon the floor. It was as warm as a furnace room under the eaves and the blended reeks of dust, moth-balls, and dry-rot was sour in their nostrils.

Wood's candle flung giant shadows as he moved it up and down. So large and high was the attic that the feeble ray scarce penetrated to its uttermost corners or to the recesses of that cavernous roof. They stood for a moment to listen while the light slowly travelled from wall to wall. But the place was as still as the grave: the thick walls, the spreading roof-tree, seemed to shut out all sound.

'Well,' said Wood briskly, 'there's no one here.' He let go the girl's hand to point in front of him. 'The wall opposite the stair, didn't he say?' he questioned. 'Well, there we are, behind that old sideboard or whatever it is!' They darted forward and, round a decrepit buffet, came upon a transverse beam between them and the wall.

As Wood ducked under it, there was a sharp ejaculation from the girl who had remained on the other side. 'Oh, look!' she cried.

There was the wall and there was the panel. But the panel stood open, and by the flickering candlelight they could see that the shelves behind it were bare. With a muttered exclamation Wood sprang forward...

It seemed to him, when he looked back on the incident afterwards, that his mind registered simultaneously the girl's scream and the sudden appearance on the wall before him of a tall shadow with arm swiftly uplifted. Instinctively he must have whipped round, for the blow that immediately descended, heavy and numbing, glanced off his shoulder, knocked him off his balance, and struck the candle from his hand. As the metal candlestick clattered on the bare boards and he reeled backwards to land full length upon the floor, he heard, out of the clammy darkness that instantly descended, the girl scream out in terror for the second time.

'Adrienne,' he called out, 'Adrienne! Are you all right?' As he spoke, his ear caught, somewhere in the darkness surrounding them, the sound of a door softly closing.

'Yes, yes,' the girl's voice came back to him, very near at hand.

'My dear, where are you?'

Then their hands met in the dark and she helped him to his feet.

'Wait!' he told her, breathing rather hard. 'Let me get a light!' His lighter snapped and the tiny flame revealed her, tense and pallid, standing there.

'I thought you were killed,' she exclaimed huskily. 'Are you sure you aren't hurt?'

He was rubbing his arm. 'The old arm's a bit sore. But what the heck! If you hadn't cried out, I'd have had a fractured skull, I wouldn't mind betting – it was a pretty solid belt, I tell you, from a blackjack or a piece of lead piping, I'd say!'

She caught his hand. 'It's bleeding. And look, it's all swollen!'

He pulled his hand away. 'It's just the skin broken.' He wrapped his handkerchief about it. 'Don't fuss over me! Tell me what happened!' Lighter in hand he began to search the floor for the candle.

'There was a dark figure – it seemed to step out from behind that open panel. I screamed, and at the same moment its arm came down on your head.'

He had found the candle and rekindled it. Holding it aloft, he scrutinised the empty cupboard and the panel before it. 'It's the Seigneur's cache all right,' he pronounced. 'Look, there's the hole he spoke of!' He showed her a hole drilled in the thin, varnished panel. 'We're too late, my dear. That letter hasn't been out of your possession, I suppose?'

She shook her head. 'Not for a single instant. Ever since I first found it in the wallet this morning, sealed up with the seal unbroken, it has been in my bag.'

He stooped to gather something from the floor. 'This figure you saw, what did it look like?'

'I couldn't see the face. It didn't seem to have any – it was all shrouded, like one of those mutes of the Inquisition.'

He laughed. 'Here's the explanation!' He held up a small sack and, thrusting his uninjured hand inside, poked finger and thumb through two wide slits in the fabric. 'It was on the ground where our unknown friend dropped it. He'd no further use for it, I guess. Whoever he was, he didn't intend to be recognised. You didn't see which way he went before the light went out, did you?' He folded the bag and thrust it down his waistcoat.

She shook her head.

'It seems to me,' he said musingly, 'that just before I went down, I heard a door shut.' He snapped his fingers. 'Of course, the back stairs!' He was moving the candle about, glancing round the room. Now he steadied the light and pointed to a corner of the attic where, through a gap in the timbers, the upper part of a door was visible. They crossed to the door, opened it, and perceived a flight of steps leading down.

'It's the staircase that goes up from the vestibule outside the linen room,' the girl reminded him.

She saw him with his finger on his lips. A heavy footstep was audible below. Wood sprang down the stairs two at a time to where a door opened off the staircase. Jacques stood just inside it, peering out – behind him the low-pitched ceiling of the bedroom landing was discernible.

The sallow face registered no surprise at the sudden irruption. 'I think I 'ear someone cry out,' he said in his ungracious way.

'Was it you who was in the attic just now?' the doctor demanded.

An impassive head-shake. 'No, Monsieur. I return from the village only at this instant.'

'Did anyone come down these stairs?'

'No, Monsieur.'

'Is there anybody in the house except ourselves?'

'No, Monsieur.' The valet paused, then stepped back, holding the door. 'Are Mademoiselle and Monsieur coming down?'

'In a moment, Jacques!' the girl struck in.

The servant bowed without speaking and, letting the door swing to behind him, disappeared.

She drew a deep breath – she was staring blankly at Wood.

'He's lying,' said the American crisply. 'He was here all the time and followed us to the attic. Why? Because it was he who robbed that cache. He was in your grandfather's confidence, wasn't he?'

She nodded. 'Yes. But he may only have removed the things to a safer hiding-place. He's a rough, queer creature, but he's thoroughly devoted.'

The doctor rubbed his arm. 'Then why did he slug me? I don't want to scare you, but, if you ask me, neither of us was intended to leave the attic alive.'

'You may be right,' she answered, her eyes dreamy. She paused, leaning back against the bannisters, her face perplexed, her forehead puckered in a little frown. 'Suppose Gideon Adams suspected that these heirlooms were hidden in the house and came here to tax Grandpapa with it?'

Wood's eyes snapped. 'And Jacques, who'd looted the cache, killed Adams to save himself from exposure!'

She shook her head. 'Jacques was devoted to Grandpapa, I tell you. If he did kill Adams, it was to prevent him from getting his hands on those heirlooms.'

'Then why not tell you the truth? Instead, he makes a murderous attack on me in the hope of shutting my mouth. Why? Because he killed Adams and he's obviously afraid that the discovery of the robbery will incriminate him.'

She shrank back aghast. 'But it's horrible!'

'The first thing we have to do,' Wood told her briskly, 'is to get hold of old Treadgold and see what he has to say about it. He's bound to be over at the camp, so chuck your things together and we'll be off at once. In the meantime, not a word about this business to anyone, you understand?'

She nodded. 'Very well.'

They descended to the vestibule. A heavy footstep resounded from the lobby and, glancing through the open doors of the linen room, they had a glimpse of Jacques in his shirt-sleeves with a mop and bucket, moving about. Otherwise, the house was sunk in silence. In the salon the sunshine poured through the windows upon the parquet where a row of planks now hid the traces of the crime: the front hall was empty, likewise the big room across it, where Le Borgne had been examined.

There was the sound of a car approaching up the drive. They opened the front door and looked out. At the same moment they heard a light step behind them and, turning, saw Maître Boucheron coming from the end of the hall. Wood gave the girl a warning glance.

At the sight of the lawyer, the girl frowned. 'Have you been here long, Maître?' she asked quickly.

'I was walking down by the stream,' Boucheron replied stolidly. He had doffed his hat and with a jerky, nervous movement was brushing the nap with his sleeve – his thick black hair was dank at the temples with perspiration. 'The gardien at the fishing camp rang me up to say that the detective from Quebec had arrived. His plane landed on the lake and he's coming here as soon as he's had his lunch. I thought I'd better be on hand in case he wants to question me.' He turned his hat over. There was a little smear of dust on the crown and he went on with his brushing operation, grave and absorbed.

A car had drawn up at the front door, a trim, blue sedan. A square-set figure jumped out and came swiftly into the hall. It was Ruffier.

'Well,' he said briskly to the notary, 'is he here?'

Boucheron looked up from his hat. 'Not yet.' He paused. 'How did you know that he'd arrived?'

Ruffier chuckled. 'There's not much going on round here that I don't hear about.' Then, perceiving that the lawyer was staring at Wood's bandaged hand, he addressed himself to the girl. 'The doctor has hurt himself?'

'He had a fall,' she answered briefly.

They spoke in French. The American who had followed the sense of the conversation struck in quickly. 'Pas beaucoup blessé,' he remarked, with his brightest grin, wiggling his hand. 'Bientôt okay!'

The mayor snatched at the familiar word. 'Okay, hein?' he echoed, all smiles. 'Bien, bien!'

Boucheron said nothing, staring down at his hat.

Wood turned to the girl. 'Better get packed up,' he said. 'I'll bring the car up to the front.'

'I won't take long,' she answered and, smiling at Ruffier, moved towards the end of the hall.

But Boucheron stepped in front of her. 'One moment, Mademoiselle,' he said in a dead voice. 'Where are you going with the doctor?'

The girl coloured angrily: she did not attempt to conceal the frank contempt of her regard and tone.

'Dr. Wood has been kind enough to ask me to stay at the camp,' she rejoined icily.

'The doctor is most thoughtful,' the notary replied. 'But I'd suggest you postpone your departure until the detective arrives. He'll certainly want to question you.'

'Then he can come to the camp.'

Boucheron's jet eyes seemed to glow, but his manner was as carefully aloof as ever.

'It would be unfortunate if you gave him the impression that you're evading him, Mademoiselle. I know this Sergeant Bigoury and I warn you you'll find him less – less accommodating than the coroner showed himself this morning...'

'Just what do you mean by that, Maître?' she demanded, dangerously calm.

The notary was fidgeting with his hat, spinning the brim round and round in his fingers.

'The sergeant will doubtless want to know,' he rapped out in his staccato way, 'why under oath you found it necessary to change your evidence. There's also the matter of the bayonet to be cleared up. These are points which I'm sure you can satisfactorily explain, but if you'll take my advice...'

Her eyes flamed suddenly. 'I don't want your advice, Maître Boucheron,' she told him hotly. 'And you can take it from me, when the time comes for explanations, I shan't be the only one who'll be required to explain.'

On the instant the lawyer stopped rotating his hat. His livid face seemed to become paler and the black eyes were suddenly wary.

Before he could reply, the doctor sprang between them. He thrust his face into Boucheron's.

'Listen to me!' he said. 'This house has terrible associations for Mademoiselle, she's sustained a severe nervous shock, and she's not stopping in the place another minute, for this detective or anybody else. I'm her medical adviser and what I say goes!' He turned to the girl. 'Cut along and get your things!'

But Boucheron still barred the way. He swung to Ruffier.

'She must stay,' he said rapidly in French. 'Tell her so, Monsieur le Maire! Assert yourself!'

The storekeeper's shrug was expansive and bland. 'If she wishes to go to the camp, why not? Our friend Bigoury can see her there just as well. The American doctor is right – the sooner Mademoiselle turns her back on the Manor and its painful souvenirs the better.' He turned to the girl. 'Go, Mademoiselle! We won't detain you!'

Sulkily Boucheron stepped aside. But the doctor had not done with him.

'There's one thing more,' he declared loudly. 'My French isn't so hot, but I understand enough to realise that you made certain insinuations against this young lady. If you'll repeat them in English...'

The girl laid her hand on his arm. 'Please! It's not worth bothering about...'

Wood shook her off. 'He can't get away with that stuff!' he exclaimed furiously.

She lowered her voice. 'Georges, please!'

'Oh, all right!' Shaking himself like a wet puppy, he strode to the door and disappeared.

With a grateful glance at Ruffier the girl went off to pack.

The detective had still not arrived when, some ten minutes later, Jacques brought her two suitcases and hatbox to the car. Ruffier and Boucheron had retired to the salon – their voices raised in argument drifted through the open window as Wood and the girl drove away.

Chapter 18

FOR THE DRIVE FROM the fishing camp to the Manor, Sergeant Bigoury, slightly flushed with his meal and dispersing a strong odour of mint from jaws in steady motion, sat beside Mr. Treadgold at the wheel, while Dr. Perronneau and the constable bestowed themselves and their attaché cases in the rumble.

'I'd no idea the Canadian police were so up to date,' Mr. Treadgold observed urbanely, as they bumped over the rutted track that led to the main road. 'Do you always travel by air, Sergeant?'

'There ain't any ways from dog-sleigh to plane we don't travel,' was the placid rejoinder. 'The Province of Quebec's a big field to cover, yes, sirree. Our bailiwick stretches all the way up to the concessions beyond Lake St. John on the north and eastward to the shores of the Gulf of St. Lawrence. If there's a train, we train it: if not, it's a plane; and if we can't make it by air, then it's a sleigh or the old raquettes – snowshoes!'

Mr. Treadgold stole a sidelong glance at his companion. Types always fascinated him and he found his curiosity engaged by this individual who spoke English like a travelling salesman and at the same time the purest idiomatic French as French Canada knows it. It was not easy to picture the little sergeant, with his trim moustache and natty clothes, fighting his way on snowshoes, into the open spaces beyond the reach of civilisation.

'You certainly seem to get around,' he hazarded.

The detective laughed drily. 'I'll tell the world! Why, once I travelled all the way from Quebec to the Magdalen Islands to pull in a guy and, boy, was I seasick? Another time it's a call from the coroner of a village in the Gaspé, out Fox Cape way. A poisoning case – a dame was feeding her old man weed-killer, or so the story ran – her mother was said to be in on it as well. They turned the investigation over to me. Mid-winter it was, with the thermometer down to forty below on the north shore of the Gaspé and six-foot drifts on the roads. I took the Canadian National as far as Matane, where the railroad ends, then a sleigh on to Fox Cape, and fin'ly snowshoes to reach the farm where these folks lived.'

'And you arrested the women?'

'Sure, I arrested 'em and landed 'em all snug in jail at Rivière-du-Loup. Constable Bissonnette in the rumble back there was with me and we had two sleighs. I took the wife and put the old woman in with him. The trip back to Matane wasn't so bad. We borrowed a brace of dogs from the village, I remember.'

'Dogs? What for?'

'To put in the bottom of the sleighs to keep our feet warm. Afterwards, the wife wrote me a letter from jail to say how nice they had been treated on the way down, her and her Ma.'

Mr. Treadgold laughed. 'It sounds like an active life to me. You were down here before to investigate the miller's death, weren't you?'

Bigoury shifted his gum. 'That's right!'

'They suspected Le Borgne of that murder, too, didn't they?'

The detective sniffed. 'It was like this, see? There wasn't no motive that I or anybody else could spot. 'Course, this guy was cuckoo and used to hang around the Manor, so some of these smart Alecks, like this mayor of theirs, wished it on him. As a matter of fact, from what the widow told me, Le Borgne was pretty friendly with them all at the mill – he'd drop in from time to time with a string of trout or a trapped rabbit and they'd give him a bag of flour. Mind you, Gagnon, or whatever his name was, may have slipped off a rock and broke his neck: then again, someone might have pushed him. Out getting trout, they said he was, but I knew better.'

Mr. Treadgold cocked up his ears. 'You're not going to tell me that the miller was responsible for the mysterious noises at the Manor, that he was the ghost?'

The sergeant laughed drily. 'Ghost, my eye! There wasn't any ghost nor any noises, neither. If you knew these villages as I do, you'd realise that every one of 'em is full of stories of spooks and corpse-lights and feux follets – whatever that is in English...'

'Will-o'-the-wisps?'

'That's the word. Our habitant's the most superstitious son-of-a-gun alive. Gagnon was just as bad as the rest of 'em, or so I gathered from his widow – none of 'em at the mill would go near the Manor after nightfall. But on the night of the tragedy it seems like he had a drink or two of whisky blanc under his belt. He would have it he'd seen a light in one of the upper rooms and went off to investigate. The eldest kid found him dead in the stream next morning.'

'Mightn't Le Borgne have been camping in the house?'

'That was my original hunch. But it didn't stand up. With the mayor and the notary I went over the whole place from garret to cellar – there's an attic as big as a church. Barring a few sticks of furniture below-stairs and some trash in the attic, the place was as bare as your hand. The lawyer, who seems to have been the last man in there when the house was shut up three years ago, assured me that nothing had been touched so far as he could see, and certainly I saw no evidence of anyone having broken in, let alone lived there...' He paused to get rid of his gum over the side of the car. 'Our friend Tisserand says you were responsible for them pulling in Le Borgne again on this charge.'

Mr. Treadgold sighed. 'I'm afraid that's true.'

'Why "afraid"?'

Mr. Treadgold coloured. 'I'm by way of being interested in the elucidation of crime. Mainly out of vanity, I fear, I outlined a certain line of reasoning which tended to cast suspicion upon this man and without further enquiry, the mayor and coroner between them ordered his arrest.'

The sergeant's nod was contemptuous. 'Hicks!' he murmured disgustedly. 'I remember this mayor of theirs particularly, the sort of guy who knows it all.' He flashed a penetrating glance through his glasses at his companion. 'So now you're not so certain of Le Borgne's guilt, is that it?'

The other nodded.

'What's happened to make you change your mind?' Bigoury persisted.

'You know the case against Le Borgne, Sergeant?'

'As far as friend Tis was able to outline it, yes!'

'He told you of the footprint they found beside the body?'

'Yeah!'

Mr. Treadgold suddenly looked positively haggard. 'Did you ever hear of liquid blood retaining a footprint?' he demanded sharply.

Pushing his spectacles up on his forehead, Bigoury turned round to look at him. 'Ah!' he observed quietly.

'Adams couldn't have reached the Manor after ten-forty-five because the rain started at that hour and his clothing and shoes were dry. And by eleven o'clock or a few minutes after he was already dead, as the girl's evidence at the inquest showed. Which means that he had been dead for no more than twenty minutes at the best when she found him, possibly less. Can blood coagulate in a quarter of an hour or so sufficiently to retain the impression of a foot, I ask you?'

'No,' said the sergeant; and added, 'So what?'

'The blood on Le Borgne's shoes and the fact that they fit the footprint show that he actually visited the scene of the crime. But it was after the murder – after, as I believe, the girl had taken her grandfather away and the salon remained empty until, a good hour and a half later, Jacques, the Seigneur's servant, discovered the body. Le Borgne had been drinking and the sight of the murdered man on the floor probably frightened him out of his wits: he scrambled out of the linen room window, leaving his tracks on floor and window-sill, and fled to his shack, where the mayor's deputies found him in a drunken stupor. There's another thing — I've a notion that Le Borgne can produce an alibi...'

The detective sniffed. 'An alibi, eh? I'm not so hot about alibis. In Chi, where I used to live, they're manufactured by the gross...'

'If it's anything, this alibi is genuine!' Mr. Treadgold was excited. His state of mind was evinced by the fact that involuntarily his foot was pressing down upon the accelerator and the car was bouncing so violently over the washboard surface of the main road which they had now reached that from the rumble Dr. Perronneau cried plaintively, 'Doucement!' Mumbling, 'Sorry!' Mr. Treadgold slowed down and rather breathlessly went on: 'Le Borgne admits going off on a drinking bout after he'd called at the lawyer's, but he won't say where. It seems there's a place in the village kept by a man called Lhermite — the Restaurant de la Gaieté, where hard liquor can be had. The camp guides go there. One of them, a fellow named Batisse, is saying that if somebody had cared to speak up at the inquest, Le Borgne would have been cleared.'

'You mean he was boozing at this speak and that someone — the boss or one of the chaps in the place — can prove it?'

'That's my idea — yes!'

'Then why don't Le Borgne pipe up and tell about it?'

Mr. Treadgold shrugged. 'Too dumb, or too scared.'

'And if he didn't croak Adams, but only came upon the body after the job was done, why not say so, will you tell me that?'

'That's easier to answer. He's the son of one of the Seigneur's old tenants and obviously devoted to the family. If he's content to take the rap, it's because he believes that either the old man or, maybe, the girl killed Adams.'

The detective's attention was concentrated upon the piece of gum he was stripping. Now, with a stolid grunt, he inserted the wad in his mouth and drew a bulging notebook from an inner pocket.

'How was the name of this bird who runs the speak?' he demanded.

Mr. Treadgold repeated the name and Bigoury wrote it down.

'And if Le Borgne's cleared,' the detective asked quietly, 'what then?'

Mr. Treadgold gazed stonily at the ribbon of road unwinding before them between the weather-beaten rail fences. 'In that case, Sergeant,' he pronounced delicately, 'you'll be faced with a mystery which, in my humble opinion, is likely to test your ingenuity to the utmost.'

'You said it,' the other agreed heartily, jaws champing. 'There's several points about this case I don't get, anyway. This bayonet the murderer used, for instance, where was it found and who found it? Old Tis didn't seem to know...'

Mr. Treadgold explained about the bayonet and the mystery of its reappearance on the rack of arms in the salon.

'It was immediately apparent,' he said, 'that either the girl or Jacques, who were the first persons to find the body of the murdered man, must have picked up the bayonet, wiped it clean, and restored it to its place on the musket.'

'In the belief that the Seigneur was the murderer?'

'In the girl's case, yes, I should say. Jacques, on the other hand, who's nobody's fool, must have known that his master couldn't possibly have had the physical strength to stab Adams. I fancy he suspected the girl of having done the killing...' And he proceeded to describe how, on the mayor's prompting, the matter had been hushed up at the inquest, out of consideration for the girl.

'And suppose the dame had a better reason for getting rid of the sticker than the wish to shield the Seigneur?' Bigoury broke in roughly. 'Why shouldn't she have killed Adams herself?'

'Why not?' his companion conceded blandly.

'She was wrapped up in her grandfather, you say, and Adams had ruined him. The servant – Jacques, or whatever his name is – may have been in it, too. They could have done the job together.'

'Why not?' Mr. Treadgold said again.

Bigoury glanced at him sharply. 'Crime investigation interests you, you say?'

'Very much!'

'If you were handling this case, from which angle would you tackle it?'

Mr. Treadgold paused. 'Well,' he said, 'I believe I should concentrate on finding the answers to three questions.'

'What are they?'

'The first is, What was Adams doing at St. Florentin?'

'You don't think he simply came down here for a week's fishing?'

His companion arched his eyebrows. 'That would be an amazing coincidence, wouldn't it? We all know that coincidences occur in life; but I prefer to believe that they're the exception and not the rule. In other words, they're all right to fall back upon as a final explanation, when all else fails; but at this stage of the game, no, no, my dear Sergeant, it won't do!'

The detective gave an amused laugh.

'And your second question?'

'How did Adams come to be in the salon?'

'Any theory?'

'None as yet.'

'Your last question?'

'Who was wearing goloshes on the night of the murder?'

'Goloshes?'

'Rubbers.'

'I know, but just what's the idea?'
Mr. Treadgold laughed mysteriously.
'Wait until we reach the Manor and perhaps I can explain!'

Chapter 19

As they crossed the bridge over the mill stream in the Manor grounds, a glitter ahead caught their eye. The afternoon sun was striking highlights on the gleaming cellulose of a sky-blue sedan standing at the front door.

'If I'm not very much mistaken,' Mr. Treadgold remarked to the sergeant as he brought the coupé to a full stop in rear of it, 'that's the mayor's car.'

Bigoury frowned. 'What does he want here?' he growled.

'Why not let the doctor and the officer go in and get to work?' was the other's diplomatic suggestion. 'Ruffier will be delighted to lend them a hand. While the officer is examining that musket for fingerprints, the doctor could take the mayor to the back of the house for a talk, leaving the salon free for you to look it over at your leisure. In the meantime, you and I might take a stroll around outside – there are one or two things I'd like you to see!'

The sergeant was delighted to fall in with this proposal. He despatched the doctor and the constable inside and returned to where Mr. Treadgold was absently fingering his stiff grey moustache and staring on the ground.

'Eh bien?' said the detective.

The other looked up. 'Have you read Gross, Sergeant?' he asked.

'One of the sports writers, is he?'

Mr. Treadgold smiled. 'Dr. Hans Gross. He's perhaps the most practical of any Continental criminologist. He says somewhere in his Handbuch für Untersuchungsrichter – I quote from memory – "Once you are launched upon an investigation, the most important thing is to determine the right moment at which to form a fixed opinion about the case."'

The little man made an expansive gesture.

'Okay by me. And has the moment arrived?'

His companion shook his head – he smiled no longer.

'Not yet. But if we can eliminate this wretched tramp, it will be close at hand. For the time being Adams is the pivot. Why did he suddenly appear at St. Florentin? He obviously didn't know that the Seigneur was due to arrive at the Manor or he wouldn't have waited for three days – until, indeed, the boy's story told him that something untoward was afoot – before coming here. The examination of his luggage at the camp may throw light on this. In the meantime, let me show you something.' So saying, he strode off along the path.

They were at the side of the house. Mr. Treadgold stopped at the first window they came to, a casement window with a narrow sill about four feet from the ground. The window was shut, with curtains drawn on the inside. Motioning his companion to silence, Mr. Treadgold approached the window, bent his head to listen, then beckoned to the detective to draw near.

'There's no one there,' he said. 'This is the linen room. It was by this window that Le Borgne apparently made his escape. You can see the marks he left.'

He pointed to sundry scratches on the woodwork at the base of the window-frame.

'Early this morning,' he went on, 'as soon as it was light enough to see, I came out into the grounds here. It seemed to me important to look for such clues as might exist before they were effaced. I should tell you again that last night, from ten-forty-five to eleven o'clock, it rained in torrents so that this path was quite soft. Unfortunately, before I reached it, at least half a dozen people had trampled it so that it was impossible to pick up any definite footprints. Under this window, however, I was luckier.'

The path of fine grey sand reached right up to the side of the house. Low bushes, set in small, circular beds of black earth, were spaced out at regular intervals to form a hedge. Between two of these bushes, immediately below the window, a couple of short boards rested on the path.

'Your work?' Bigoury demanded, pointing at the boards.

With a slightly self-conscious air Mr. Treadgold nodded.

The sergeant wagged his head. 'Do you know your onions?' he muttered admiringly. 'If we always had gents like you to work with...'

Mr. Treadgold had removed the boards. The firm sand had taken the impressions like a mould. Two footprints were revealed, parallel and close together, one a few inches closer to the wall than the other. They were quite large and displayed a mass of dots, a sort of stippling effect, where the soles had rested.

Stooping, the detective examined them lengthily.

'Rubbers, eh?' he observed at length, straightening up.

'I think so,' Mr. Treadgold replied.

Bigoury was peering down behind the bushes.

'And there were no other footprints under the window?'

'None.' He hesitated. 'It suggests to me that Le Borgne must have entered the house elsewhere – probably by the back. When he left by the window, he jumped and landed clear in the middle of the path where his footprints were lost in a mass of others.'

'And these prints here?' the sergeant questioned, pointing.

'They're obviously not Le Borgne's – unless you wish me to believe that a tramp like that, a poacher and trapper, would wear rubbers.'

Bigoury nodded, fiddling with his small black moustache.

'You're right, I guess. Then who?'

'Let's go back a piece, do you mind?' said Mr. Treadgold.

Under his guidance they headed off along the drive and passed out at the front gate.

'We're going to the side entrance,' Mr. Treadgold explained. 'We could reach it through the house, I imagine, only I don't know the way.'

They turned right and entered the side road that followed the outer wall of the property round. As the road curved, it brought in sight a pair of tall masonry pillars supporting a wooden gate with red-tiled roofs rising beyond – clearly, the Manor stables. An antiquated flivver stood in front of the gate. There was a small door in the wall beside the near gatepost.

Sergeant Bigoury tried the door. It was locked. Turning, he perceived Mr. Treadgold, very red in the face, attempting to push the flivver back along the road. The car did not budge.

'Lend me a hand, will you?' Mr. Treadgold gasped, shoving harder than ever.

The detective chuckled. 'You put me in mind of this case, you and that car, Mr. Treadgold,' he remarked caustically. 'You can't move it. Why? Because you don't know what's holding it!' So saying he slipped an arm over the flivver's battered side and released the brake. The car rolled back. 'There you are!' said Bigoury, jumping clear. 'Find the motive for this murder and the investigation'll run as smoothly as that old tin Lizzie!'

Mr. Treadgold nodded understandingly as he mopped his brow.

'Take a look here a minute, will you?' he panted. 'Don't step on the sacking!' The sergeant then observed that in front of the car a ragged sack, held down by four stones, was spread out on the dusty road. 'The front wheels were just touching it,' Mr. Treadgold explained. He pointed at the sacking. 'When I came by here early this morning,' he said, 'the ground was soaked with the night's rain. The whole road was wet with the exception of the patch which you see here covered by this sack.'

'Your doing again?' queried the detective.

Mr. Treadgold nodded and went on: 'The patch was dry and dusty, and its edges, which were muddy like the rest of the road, displayed tyre-marks. It was evident that a car had stood here during the night's rain.'

'When did you say the shower was?' the detective asked.

'From ten-forty-five to eleven. And there's been no rain since.'

Bigoury nodded, jaws moving. 'I get you. You mean, this car parked here before the rain started and stayed till it was over, so that a dry patch remained on the road where it had stood.'

'Exactly! My point is that whoever was in this car must have reached the house about the same time as Adams.'

Arms akimbo, his head thrust forward like a cock sparrow, the little sergeant confronted him.

'And it's your idea that he was the murderer, eh?'

His companion furled his eyes. 'My ideas about this case are still entirely fluid. As I told you already, in my opinion the moment Gross speaks of has not yet arrived.' He stooped and pulled up the sacking. 'Let's see if the tyre-marks are still there.'

A faint pattern was visible in the dried mud. The centre of the patch was drier and dustier than the road surface surrounding it.

Bigoury went down on one knee. 'There's one thing about it,' he remarked, stooping over the marks. 'It's a straight-sided tyre!'

'I don't believe I know what a straight-sided tyre is,' Mr. Treadgold explained meekly.

His companion, who was dusting his trousers, straightened up and glanced over his shoulder.

'Like those there,' he said, pointing at the car behind him. 'All the early models of flivvers have them. The narrow tread's characteristic. Whose car is that, anyway?'

Mr. Treadgold shook his head. 'I can't say. It's been standing there quite a while. The radiator's almost cold.'

Bigoury poked his head in under the ragged canvas top. A leather portfolio was on the seat. He made no bones about lifting it out and unstrapping it. As he did so, some papers fluttered to the ground. One fell at Mr. Treadgold's feet. He picked it up. It was a letter addressed to 'Monsieur Marcel Boucheron, Notaire, à St. Florentin, P.Q.' He showed the envelope to the detective. But Bigoury had already read the name on one of the papers he had retrieved.

'Boucheron, eh?' he said, replacing the letters. 'I remember him – he's the St. Rémy family attorney, ain't he?' He buckled up the portfolio and tossed it back in the car. 'Then he's here, too!'

Mr. Treadgold had suddenly become tense – it was as though he had been wound up with a large spring. He pointed at the patch in the road where the sacking had been. 'Those tyre-marks,' he demanded abruptly. 'Would it be possible to identify them with any particular car?'

The sergeant gave him a long, enquiring look. With a casual air he turned back to the car, and, bending to the front wheel nearest to him, scrutinised the tyre. Then he examined the marks on the road again and indulged in a dubious head-shake.

'And if it were,' he said, 'what would it prove? There's no evidence that the car which sheltered those tyre-marks from the rain is the car that left them. Ninety per cent of the cars in these country districts are flivvers. One of them may have driven by here earlier in the day and any other vehicle – a buggy or even a farm cart – that happened to halt on the road during that shower could have kept the marks dry.'

'What should any vehicle be doing here at that hour of the night?' Mr. Treadgold demanded, but without much conviction – his spirits seemed dashed.

Bigoury shrugged. 'Search me! But when you suggest it was this car of Boucheron's...'

'I didn't suggest it,' Mr. Treadgold broke in indignantly. 'It was merely an idea that passed through my mind.'

'Okay. The theory's all right. Boucheron was the family lawyer and therefore on the old man's side against Adams. Besides, we know that the Seigneur sent for him. But Boucheron says he didn't get back from Trois-Ponts until late and Le Borgne corroborates him. Against this, all you have to show are the marks of a flivver on the road.'

'What about those footprints outside the window?'

'Is Boucheron the only guy to own a pair of rubbers in St. Florentin?'

'No, but...'

The detective laughed good-humouredly. 'You've been reading too many crime novels, Mr. Treadgold. This job of ours is a darned sight simpler than you think. You put three questions up to me: I'll give you only one in return. Who had the greatest interest in killing Adams? Find the right answer to that and then we'll look for the evidence. Any more clues?'

Mr. Treadgold shook his head and they made their way back to the house.

Chapter 20

A THIRD CAR HAD joined the two already waiting before the house. It appeared to belong to the coroner – through the open window of the salon they snatched a glimpse of his snowy locks as he stood in earnest conversation with Dr. Perronneau.

Ruffier met them in the hall, Maître Boucheron at his heels.

'Well, Inspector,' the mayor cried joyously, 'we're all ready for you. Dr. Côté, whom you know, is just going off with your colleague, Dr. Perronneau, to conduct the autopsy and this brave Constable Bissonnette is busy in the other room. At my suggestion he's examining the weapon of the crime which I brought along with me and also the little musket from which it was taken. I trust you had a comfortable trip?'

'The trip was all right,' said the detective, without amenity and, flinging a curt 'Bonjour!' to the lawyer, walked into the salon, the others trooping behind. The coroner's greeting was very deferential, but the sergeant paid as scant heed to him as he had to the mayor, standing in the centre of the gaunt apartment and letting his birdlike eyes travel round the walls.

'Eh bien, Messieurs,' he remarked at last, looking from the coroner to the mayor, 'you've lost no time, I hear. You've lodged your man in jail and the coroner's jury have returned a verdict against him. Quick work, quick work – my compliments! I've had my trip for nothing, it would appear!'

His cutting tone was not lost upon the coroner. Fumbling with his spectacles as he peered at the other, he said, rather indignantly, 'One acted for the best, Monsieur, and in accordance with the evidence...'

The little man sniffed. 'And was the man Lhermite, who keeps the Restaurant de la Gaieté, called at the inquest?' he enquired.

'Lhermite?' Uncomfortably the old doctor's glance appealed to the mayor.

'Or the guide Batisse, who's one of his customers, it would appear?' the detective persisted.

Ruffier spoke up suavely. 'If Monsieur l'Inspecteur would tell us the purport of these questions...'

Bigoury rounded on him. 'You know this bootlegger?'

'Very well. I also know the guide Batisse. I'd be glad to hear what he can tell us about Le Borgne...' He paused.

'Why?'

The mayor shrugged. 'I advise caution in dealing with that gentleman. He and Le Borgne are the worst characters in the parish...'

With an abstracted nod the sergeant turned to Dr. Perronneau.

'Better get on with the autopsy,' he said. 'I'll just have a word with Bissonnette, then I want to see the girl and the servant, Jacques...'

'Jacques is here,' Ruffier put in officiously, 'but the girl has gone to the camp with the American doctor...' He glanced towards Mr. Treadgold. 'Didn't you pass them on the road?'

'We went on to the village before coming here,' Mr. Treadgold explained. 'Sergeant Bigoury had to send a telegram announcing his arrival. What do they want at the camp?'

'It appears the young lady's going to stay there...'

Mr. Treadgold looked dismayed. 'Stay there?'

But the mayor was addressing Bigoury. 'Whenever you wish to drive to the camp, my car's at your disposal,' he said.

'I shouldn't dream of keeping you from your duties,' rejoined the detective, not without sarcasm. 'I've certain matters to see to here and I've no doubt that Mr. Treadgold will be good enough to give me a lift over to the camp. Later, should I require any help, I shan't fail to call on you.'

The mayor took his dismissal philosophically. 'Okay,' he remarked cheerfully. Nodding to the company, he went out and they heard him drive away.

The coroner, who had been bobbing about, trying to get a word with the sergeant, now pounced on him.

'We found the murdered man's pencil under him on the floor,' he announced. 'I brought it for you.' He fished the pencil out of his waistcoat pocket and placed it in the detective's palm. 'I believe you'll find we've neglected no clues, even the smallest,' he declared with pride.

'And pawed them all over first, like this pencil, I've no doubt,' Bigoury commented drily. He glanced at the pencil attentively before slipping it into his pocket.

The old doctor flushed. 'For the pencil, I admit, the question of fingerprints escaped us,' he conceded apologetically. 'But the lamp that stood beside the dead man's body, that, at least, hasn't been handled save with a silk handkerchief. The constable has it...'

'Where is he?' Bigoury demanded.

The constable was working in the room across the hall, Maître Boucheron explained. 'If you could spare me a few minutes, Inspector...' he added, his water-spaniel's eyes resting appealingly on the sergeant's face.

'Not now,' the detective snapped.

'It's a matter of some importance to the enquiry...'

'Later.' He paused. 'By the way, who has the keys of the house?'

'I have.'

'Got them with you?'

'Only the key of the side door.'

'Where your car's parked, do you mean?'

The lawyer nodded.

Bigoury put out his hand. 'Let me have it, please!' Taking the key from Boucheron, he turned to the coroner. 'I'll look in at your house later and go through your report on the inquest,' he told him. 'You can see me then,' he added to Boucheron. 'Au revoir, Messieurs!' He stormed out.

Boucheron slipped away.

The coroner gazed after the detective and up at the ceiling. 'What a savage!' he murmured.

Dr. Perronneau laughed. 'He's always like that. You'll get used to him. Coming?'

They went out together and Mr. Treadgold found himself alone.

He was vaguely conscious of the jarring noises of departing cars, as, pipe in mouth, he began to pace up and down. What the deuce did George Wood mean by planting the girl on them at the camp? The only hut available was Adams's, next to theirs – that meant she'd be continually in and out of their hut, damn it! It was devilish inconsiderate of George: he'd give the young man a piece of his mind.

But would he? Mr. Treadgold smiled to himself and shook his head. He was out of temper, exasperated by the blanket of fog in which they were all moving. Why take it out on George? – the young man was perfectly free to ask the girl over to the camp if he wanted to. It was sheer kindness of heart – well meant but not very discreet. Bigoury suspected the girl. And why not? Everything was so dark. Dejectedly he let his gaze roam round the naked walls. They knew what had taken place in that room: they had seen Adams slump to the floor: they could reveal whose hand had struck the fatal blow. Walls might have ears; but why the blazes didn't they have tongues?

A door creaked and he had a glimpse of the constable with flying feet flashing through the entrance hall towards the back of the house.

Bigoury poked his head in from the hall. 'Didn't you tell me you were present when the mayor interviewed Jacques about the bayonet?' he asked.

'Certainly.'

'He denied seeing anything of it, I think?'

'That's right. But I fancy he was lying.'

'You bet he was lying. His prints are all over that old musket.'

'Ah!' said Mr. Treadgold.

'Bissonnette had him fetch a glass of water – the old gag! – got his prints and compared 'em.'

'And the bayonet?'

'Wiped clean.'

'I thought as much. What about the lamp?'

'Only Adams handled it, Bissonnette says. I've sent for Jacques: I'd like you to be on hand when I talk to him. While he's with us, Bissonnette's going to run the rule over his quarters. Psst, here he is!'

Bigoury came into the salon and Mr. Treadgold saw that he had the bayonet in his hand. 'Par icitte!' he called into the hall.

The manservant appeared. He was scared. His sallow face was almost greenish in hue and the corners of his full lips drooped.

Bigoury held up the bayonet. 'What do you know about this?' he demanded.

The valet gulped, but did not speak.

'You lied about it before,' the detective reminded him. 'But now we'll have the truth!' And when the other still remained silent, 'Do you realise the position in which you find yourself?' he rasped. 'With the evidence I have against you I could arrest you for murder right away, do you know that?'

The man uttered a sharp cry. 'No, no, it isn't true.'

Bigoury pointed a denunciatory finger. The gesture was of the theatre. He was no longer the Chicago hotel detective, but a hundred per cent Frenchman.

'Speak!' he thundered.

'He was dead when I found him, I swear it,' Jacques burst forth. 'The little bayonet lay beside him on the floor. It was red with blood. I took it to my room and hid it before going to fetch this gentleman here.'

'Why?'

'It was to protect the Seigneur. He was a good master to me. I was starving when he found me in Quebec.'

'You mean you thought the Seigneur had killed Adams?'

Jacques averted his eyes. 'Who else should it have been?'

Mr. Treadgold interposed. 'He told me he didn't know Adams, that he had never seen him before,' he pointed out mildly.

'It was to shield Monsieur,' the valet broke in wildly. 'They were enemies. Besides, once before in Paris, Monsieur threatened to kill him.'

The detective snorted. 'Even so, you can't have believed that your master, a feeble old man suffering from heart disease, could have had the strength to stab anybody?'

The man did not reply, his eyes veiled and sullen.

'If it were Mademoiselle now...?' The sergeant's tone was casual, but his glance behind the big glasses was a rapier. Jacques was staring at the floor, wrapped in a non-committal silence. 'The Seigneur was dead, wasn't he? What did it matter about protecting him, as you call it?' Bigoury persisted.

'He wasn't dead when I found the bayonet – at least, if he was, we didn't know it.'

'Then why not come forward with it when you did know?'

The broad shoulders described an unwilling movement. 'It was to save Monsieur's good name.'

'You're lying. You were covering up the girl. You knew that she'd killed this man, isn't that it?'

From under heavy eyelids the man looked up quickly. 'You put things into my mouth I never said,' he muttered thickly. 'All I know is that the bayonet was on the floor, as I told you.'

'It was you who put it back on the musket, at any rate?'

'Yes.'

'When?'

'When they were in the other room – the dining room – examining Mathias...'

Mr. Treadgold nodded. 'That fits,' he remarked to the detective.

'After wiping it clean, eh?' Bigoury said to the servant.

'I washed it under the pump,' Jacques replied.

There was a tap at the door.

'Come in, Bissonnette,' said Bigoury.

Very smart in his blue tunic and straight as a ramrod, the constable marched up to him. 'I went through this man's things,' he announced. 'This was in his suitcase!' Opening his hand he displayed a small gold box.

It was a rococo snuffbox with scalloped edges and sides elaborately chased. Bigoury picked it up, at the same time flashing a rapid glance at Jacques.

Jacques was staring angrily at the constable. 'In my suitcase?' he exclaimed. 'I never set eyes on the thing before.'

Mr. Treadgold had unsnapped his pince-nez and was bending over the box as it rested on the sergeant's open palm. There was a crest on the lid – a pelican. 'That's the St. Rémy crest,' Mr. Treadgold pronounced and, turning sideways, pointed to the emblazoned shield hanging on the wall.

The detective's gaze shifted rapidly to the shield and then back to the box. Taking a magnifying-glass from his pocket, he scrutinised the crest.

'"Je tiendrai foy" – it's the same device,' he said, and raised his eyes to the valet. 'How did you come by this?' he demanded sternly.

With hands uplifted, the man protested shrilly. 'I know nothing about it. It's a plot to destroy me. I never saw that box in my life.'

The racket of a motorcycle engine outside the window drowned his words. Bissonnette glanced into the sunlit gardens.

'It's the Provincials,' he announced. The hammering of the engines died: two begoggled figures in khaki passed the window.

'Good,' said Bigoury. 'I asked for them. You can send them in, Bissonnette.'

'There's something else, patron,' the constable broke in while his hand dipped into his breeches pocket. 'I found this too.' He thrust out his hand. A small handkerchief, crumpled into a ball, lay there. It was stained with blood.

Bigoury frowned and his face set hard so that two deep furrows ran from nose to mouth.

'Was this in his box, too?' he questioned.

'No, patron. It was pushed away at the back of a drawer of the kitchen table. There's an initial on it – excuse me!'

Bissonnette unfolded the handkerchief. It was a tiny wisplike thing of fine linen. The constable turned it in his thick fingers until he found what he was looking for and held the handkerchief out. An 'A' was embroidered in the corner.

The detective's mouth closed with an audible snap. Lifting his eyes from the handkerchief, he glared at the valet.

'You never saw this handkerchief before, either, I suppose?' he growled. His glance whipped to Mr. Treadgold. 'What's her name?' he asked in English. 'Alice, Anne, Ada?'

'Adrienne,' said Mr. Treadgold.

Bigoury's eyes glistened and he gave Jacques, who was still staring stupidly at the handkerchief, a venomous look. Then he drew Mr. Treadgold aside.

'I'm going to leave one of the troopers in charge of the house and to keep an eye on our friend here, and when I'm through the other will take me down to the village in his side-car. Boucheron's going to meet me at the coroner's – he ought to be able to put us wise about this snuffbox.'

'If you'd like me to wait...'

'Not necessary. I'll be seeing you at the camp later on. And listen, if you speak to the girl, not a word about what you heard here this afternoon, savvy?'

The detective did not wait for the other's confirmatory nod, but bolted out into the hall. Mr. Treadgold, following at a more leisurely pace, found his car and drove back to the camp.

Chapter 21

As Mr. Treadgold entered Camp Number 3, his roommate, who was reclining on his bed, sprang up. 'Gosh, H. B.,' he exclaimed excitedly, 'you're certainly a sight for sore eyes. Man, I've a million things to tell you. The Angel said you'd driven the detective over to the Manor – I can't make out why we didn't meet you...'

'We went down to the village first,' Mr. Treadgold replied wearily, flinging down his Panama.

'I thought you were never coming back – I'd have followed you there, only I was afraid of butting in. I've been reading up on the classics in the interval.' He showed a book in his hand. It was Mr. Treadgold's calf-bound first edition of Tristram Shandy.

The gardien, burdened with a tray set out with sundry bottles, came sidling in. 'I see Mis' Treadgol' put hees char away,' he announced confidentially, depositing the tray on the table, 'so I breeng the dreenks. I don' forget nozzing, I guess, Doctor' – his finger ticked off the bottles one by one – 'veesky, gin, vermouth, French an' Italien, ice, orange' an' lemon' an'' – he touched a plate covered by a napkin – 'the sandveech' you order...'

'Is Batisse the guide anywhere about, Tremblay?' Mr. Treadgold enquired.

'Batisse, he go out with Mis' and Missus Montgomery after lunch. You lak' to spik with heem?'

'You might ask him to see me when he comes in.'

'Okay!' The gardien went out.

Mr. Treadgold turned to Wood. 'Are we throwing a party or what?' he demanded severely.

The young man flushed. 'Mademoiselle de St. Rémy's coming in around six o'clock for a conference,' he explained lightly. 'I thought, maybe, a cocktail would set her up. The Angel produced the fixings out of his hat, so to speak. Remarkable chap, the Angel!' He turned to his roommate, whisky bottle in hand. 'How about a little snort while we're waiting?'

'I don't mind!'

Wood waited until Mr. Treadgold, relaxed in a chair, his neatly lozenged legs stretched out in front of him, had taken a long drink from the glass the other handed him. Then he said, very offhand, 'By the way, I've arranged for Mademoiselle de St. Rémy to stay here for a bit.'

'In Adams's bungalow?'

The question had a faintly sarcastic inflection and the doctor reddened to the ears again.

'What do you take me for? The Angel let her have the spare room in his house. I sent her off to lie down. The poor kid was all in.'

Mr. Treadgold held his glass up to the light, contemplating its amber contents with an abstracted air.

'Wasn't that rather impulsive of you, George? I mean, we can't tell what's to be the outcome of this affair. And, believe me, things are beginning to move.'

The other laughed. 'You bet your sweet life they are. Wait till you hear what happened to us at the Manor this afternoon...'

'One moment. You must give me your word not to divulge to the young lady what I'm about to tell you.'

'Okay.'

'Not an hour ago the police found a blood-stained handkerchief of hers hidden in the kitchen.'

The young man stared. 'How do they know it's hers?' he demanded truculently.

'It has the initial "A" embroidered on it – it's the sort of flimsy thing a girl like her would carry, too.'

Wood shook his big frame restlessly. 'There must be some mistake, H. B.!'

'I don't think so. Another point – in Jacques's luggage they came across a gold snuffbox engraved with the St. Rémy crest!'

The American sprang towards him. 'I knew it! Then it was Jacques!' Hooking a chair with his foot he planted himself down in front of his companion. 'Light up your pipe, H. B., and listen to me!'

Breathlessly, incoherently, he told of the Seigneur's letter and its sequel.

His story of the attack upon him in the attic brought Mr. Treadgold to his feet in dismay.

'You were lucky, old man,' he said gravely, 'luckier, perhaps, than you and I can realise just now. Let's take a look at that hand of yours!'

Wood thrust the damaged member behind his back. 'It's nothing to get excited about. I gave it a dab of iodine and strapped it – the swelling will be gone in the morning. I'm much more concerned with what's behind all this. D'you know what I think?' He took a turn along the room while Mr. Treadgold, sitting down again, proceeded to relight his pipe. 'This is my theory. Adams goes to the Manor to investigate Shiner's story. There's nobody about when he arrives, but he hears something moving in the attic. He goes up and finds Jacques at that closet in the wall. Or perhaps he meets Jacques downstairs with the loot in his hands. Jacques loses his head and kills him; the Seigneur, aroused by the noise, comes out and finds the body, and dies of shock.'

Mr. Treadgold looked thoughtful: he did not speak for a moment.

'Plausible,' he commented at length. 'But it leaves two points unexplained. What brought Adams to St. Florentin in the first place?'

'What brought you here?' – Mr. Treadgold coughed rather uneasily – 'You came to fish, didn't you? Or, at least, to have a holiday. So did Adams!'

'The Seigneur returns to the home of his fathers after three years' exile and the man who drove him out is here waiting for him? No, old man, that's stretching the long arm of coincidence too far!'

Wood shrugged sulkily. 'What's your other point?'

'Those mysterious sounds at the Manor...'

'You haven't fallen for that bunk, have you?'

'Is it bunk? The robbing of the Seigneur's hoard would explain these noises and lights. Only remark, they were first reported long before Jacques appeared on the scene. Even before the miller was killed, a month back, people in the village were whispering about them – both Ruffier and the detective will confirm me. The girl heard something, too, didn't you say?'

'Yes. But she imagined it. Her nerves are shot to pieces.'

'She said that Jacques was with her at the time. Or so you told me.'

'That's so. You're right, she did...'

'That would appear to dispose of Jacques, then. Besides, nothing but the snuffbox was found. What became of the rest of the things?'

'What does Jacques say?'

'He says the box was planted on him. And I'm beginning to think he's telling the truth.'

'But who...' The young man broke off. 'Look here, H. B., if Jacques didn't rob the cache, then it obviously wasn't he who attacked us. In that case, who was it? The only other person around was the lawyer fellow...'

Mr. Treadgold took his pipe from his mouth and contemplated the speaker from under his shaggy eyebrows. 'Boucheron?'

'Yeah. He appeared just after we came down from the attic. Said he'd been walking down by the stream...' He paused. 'You agree with me, don't you? That the chap who attacked me is likely to have been the murderer.'

His companion started out of a brown study. 'It looks that way...'

The doctor leaned forward, his hands on the table. 'Could it possibly be Boucheron?' he demanded in awe-struck tones.

Mr. Treadgold did not reply at once. His pipe made sucking noises in the silence. 'Assuming that he wilfully misled us as to the time at which he returned from Trois-Ponts last night, it's possible,' he remarked at last. 'But believe me, George, old man, random accusations will get us nowhere in a case like this, and I'm not altogether without experience in such matters. Through my friend, Inspector Grote, of the New York police, it's been my privilege in the past to assist at the unravelling of certain knotty problems...'

The young man stared at him. 'You mean you go sleuthing? Like Sherlock Holmes or someone?'

'Inspector Grote is sometimes kind enough to take me along.'

'What cases were you on?'

'Remember the murder in the Jackson Building?'

'Where the man was found hanging in a closet and at first they thought it was suicide?'

Mr. Treadgold nodded. 'I'd the deuce of a job persuading Grote it wasn't...'

'What else?'

His companion shrugged. 'The Selby jewel robbery, the killing of Mortimer Brewster out at Hempstead Harbour...'

'You were on that, too? Do you mean to tell me that the police call you in?'

Mr. Treadgold knocked out his pipe carefully. 'Purely in a non-official capacity. You see, Grote and I have an interest in common. We both collect stamps!'

The doctor laughed incredulously. 'Well, I'll be jiggered! And here I've been thinking of you all along as a tailor!'

The other sipped his drink and set it down. 'Tailoring is just as much of an exact science as criminology. The only difference is that we cut from a pattern and sew the pieces into a composite whole, whereas the criminologist's job is the same process reversed. He's confronted by the finished garment – the crime: he has to unrip it in order to get at the component parts. One thing more: a tailor, let me tell you, is not only a student of anatomy, since, as you, as a doctor, must know, no two human beings are built alike: he's also a student of human nature. He has to be. Few of the vanities of human nature escape us' – he chuckled: 'no place like the fitting room for seeing Nature in the raw. One views a man, not only as Nature planned him, but also in the character he wishes his clothes to endow him with...'

The young man laughed. 'Darn it, H. B., you talk as though you fitted your customers yourself!'

'Of course, I fit our customers myself!'

Wood let his glance run over his companion's expensive-looking tweeds.

'I pictured you sitting in a luxurious President's office off Fifth Avenue punching bells and waited on by a flock of gorgeous lady secretaries.'

The blue eyes sparkled: Mr. Treadgold's healthy pink flush had deepened to a richer carmine.

'I'm a tradesman,' he said, suddenly irate, 'and I descend from a long line of tradesmen. I hope I shall never feel it beneath my dignity to wait upon a customer!' He drained his glass and, producing his pouch, proceeded to refill his pipe.

The action appeared to appease him, for presently, in his usual gentle tone, he went on:

'The successful investigation of crime, d'you see, George, is nothing but applied common sense. Read the great criminologists, especially the French, fellows like Locard or Lacassagne, and note the beautiful limpidity with which they write. If only one thinks clearly enough, there's no such thing as an unsolved crime. That's what's needed here – clear thinking!'

He put a match to his pipe and, tamping the bowl with his finger, went on:

'Every way I look at this case, I've the feeling that we're up against some sinister influence which, all through, has been bent on obscuring the truth. Unless I'm very much mistaken, the miller's death was no accident – he was killed because he knew, or it was feared he knew, what was going on at the Manor.'

'Those footsteps, do you mean?'

'I mean the looting of that cache. And you were attacked this afternoon for the same reason. Fortunately, we've only a relatively small number of suspects to take into account and, in view of this unseen influence I speak of, we shall do better to look for facts eliminating the innocent than dissipate our energies by trying to put a finger on the murderer straight away.'

The doctor nodded absently. 'Then the first thing we have to do is to establish the girl's innocence.' His gaze challenged his companion. But Mr. Treadgold's pipe was not drawing well and his whole attention appeared to be concentrated on it. The young man cleared his throat. 'You don't think she'd anything to do with it, do you?' he said huskily.

The briar gurgled. 'My dear fellow,' was the suave rejoinder, 'that's a question which at the present juncture I can't answer!'

'Then I can. I know Adrienne and you don't. She's fine, and... and loyal, and courageous, and the idea that she knows anything of the killing of this man is utterly grotesque. I'm not going to rest until she's cleared and you can tell this frog that if he starts any monkeying he'll have me to reckon with!'

His exuberance brought a smile to Mr. Treadgold's face. 'That's the spirit!' he murmured.

'I'm serious, H. B. Even if it means pinning the guilt on your friend the curé, I'll clear her. You don't know me. I may be bone-lazy and not so long on brains, but when I start anything I go through with it. Where's that book of yours I was reading? Here!' He snatched up Tristram Shandy from the bed and began feverishly to turn the leaves. 'Talk about common sense – your old Laurence Sterne has us moderns beaten to a frazzle. Here's what I was looking for – I was reading it just as you came in. It expresses my sentiments exactly.' He read out:

My father was a gentleman of many virtues, but he had a strong spice of that in his temper which might, or might not, add to the number. 'Tis known by the name of perseverance in a good cause – and obstinacy in a bad one...

Mr. Treadgold laughed. 'It's a famous quotation.'

'It's me!'

'Then let's persevere together, shall we?'

'You mean you do think she's innocent?'

Mr. Treadgold pointed at the book, his blue eyes twinkling. 'Read on!' he commanded, and Wood read out:

Of this my mother had so much knowledge, that she knew 'twas to no purpose to make any remonstrance – so she e'en resolved to sit down quietly, and make the most of it.

He cast the book aside. 'You're just stringing me!' he exclaimed bitterly.

Mr. Treadgold stood up and, going to him, clapped his hands on his shoulders. 'No, old man. To want to clear so charming a girl is a good cause, all right. But you must let me keep an open mind. You see, I can't help remembering what the French sage wrote, that "Probability isn't invariably on the side of truth."'

At that moment a shadow darkened the screen door and the frame was lightly tapped. A small man diffidently thrust a face as brown as a coffee bean into the room. He was in shirt-sleeves and waistcoat and a pair of stained and shabby khaki breeches clothed his legs, with heavy, woollen socks stuffed into well-greased boots that reached halfway up the calf. An old haversack was slung across him, a tin cup dangled from a button of his waistcoat, a hunting-knife was at his belt, and the ragged tweed cap he doffed sheepishly as he entered was stuck with an assortment of brightly coloured fishing-flies.

'Come in, Batisse,' said Mr. Treadgold.

The guide, smiling and complaisant, obeyed.

'Ah, Batisse,' Mr. Treadgold went on, 'this man, Le Borgne, was a friend of yours, wasn't he?'

So gnarled and sunburnt was the guide's face that it might have been whittled out of a peachstone. He had suddenly ceased to smile – his features had the unyielding impassivity of a redskin's.

'I know 'eem,' he agreed cautiously.

'He's in bad trouble: you'd like to help him, I dare say?' The man remaining silent, Mr. Treadgold proceeded: 'They tell me you sometimes go to Lhermite's place in the village. I was wondering whether you happened to see Le Borgne there last night?'

Batisse shook his head stubbornly. 'I no see 'eem!'

'Then why did you say that, if somebody cared to speak up, Le Borgne could be cleared?'

The man's movements were as lithe and quick as a wild animal's. The glance he flashed to right and left of him was of lightning rapidity.

Then he moistened his lips. 'Beeg meestak',' he murmured. 'I no spik lak' dees!'

'But you told the Rees boy.'

The wooden face creased into a compassionate smile. ''E ask what they spik in ze paroisse and I say lak' dees. But me, I know nozzing!'

'But why do they say these things, and who says them?'

Batisse shrugged. 'You lak' to know, you ask them at St. Florentin...'

'Ask whom?'

Another shrug. 'I don't know nozzing!'

Mr. Treadgold contemplated him severely. 'Were you at Lhermite's yourself last night?'

Gazing at him solemnly, Batisse shook his head. 'No, Monsieur!'

'But you go there sometimes?'

'Nevaire, Monsieur. Beeg meestak'!'

With a baffled air Mr. Treadgold clawed at the back of his head. 'All right, Batisse, that'll be all.'

Imperturbably the guide stumped out on his short legs.

Mr. Treadgold turned to Wood, dropping his hand to his side in a gesture of desperation. 'That's what I mean,' he declared tensely. 'Wherever one turns, obstruction.'

'It was a cinch, he was lying!'

The other nodded sombrely. 'He's been got at, of course. Well, we'll see what Sergeant Bigoury makes of him, this bootlegger, too!'

Wood had grown suddenly very quiet. Now he went to his suitcase that stood against the wall beside his bed and came back with a small burlap bag.

'I told you the fellow who slugged me wore a sack over his face. Well, there it is.' He put the bag in Mr. Treadgold's hands. The latter turned it over, inspected the holes torn in the fabric. 'Have you ever seen a bag like that before?' the doctor demanded.

His companion shrugged. 'I've had bottles of whisky delivered in New York in bags like this...'

'Exactly. It's a bootlegger's sack. They run the booze from St. Pierre Miquelon into the States and Canada in these bags...'

The blue eyes snapped. 'Ah!' said Mr. Treadgold softly. 'Lhermite, you mean?' He nodded approvingly. 'Very good, George – you were a jump ahead of me that time...' With precise movements he folded the bag into four and laid it under Tristram Shandy on the table. 'Bigoury must have this. I wonder if he saw Lhermite...'

There were footsteps on the verandah and the Angel's voice, pompous and deferential, 'C'est icitte, Monsieur l'Inspecteur!'

Like a tornado Bigoury burst in.

Chapter 22

THE LITTLE MAN WAS moist and breathless, and swearing to himself in French. 'Ah, the animal! Ah, the pig!' Then, catching sight of Mr. Treadgold, he cried in English, 'Have you been talking to Batisse?'

Mr. Treadgold looked somewhat shamefaced. 'As a matter of fact, he's just left here...'

There was disgust in the way the sergeant pitched his cap and overcoat on a chair. 'He has, has he? Then let me tell you you've properly gummed up the works. You questioned him, hein?'

'I merely asked him whether he'd seen Le Borgne at Lhermite's place last night.'

'Oh, yeah?'

'But he won't talk...'

'I'll say he won't talk! You gotta know these people – they're cagey like a lot of wildcats. Handle 'em right and they'll feed from the hand. I could have eased the truth out of the fellow – it would have cost me a pint of caribou and an hour or so of my time, but he'd have come clean.'

'He's probably still about, if you'd like to see him.'

'Hell! I've seen him. Directly I set eyes on the rat I knew I was all washed up. You scared the lights out of him!'

'I'm most fearfully sorry.'

Mr. Treadgold spoke so penitently that the sergeant became slightly mollified. Dejectedly he ran his fingers through his hair and sighed.

'You weren't to know – I should have warned you, on account of you're new to the country and all that. It don't make much difference, anyway – he had his orders, I guess...'

'His orders? From whom?'

Bigoury's shrug was eloquent. 'Old Côté – that big cheese, Ruffier, I dunno. Darn it,' he cried, bristling, 'it seems like I had the whole flaming parish up against me. It's a conspiracy, that's what it is!'

'A conspiracy, Sergeant?' Imperceptibly Mr. Treadgold's eye sought Wood's.

'That's what I said. To hang this murder on Le Borgne. Half of these people are tenants of the Seigneur, do you realise that? And they're not going to have mud slung at him or his family. They're out to block me, see? First, it's Lhermite, then it's Batisse.'

'Won't Lhermite talk, either?'

'Talk, hell! He's skipped!'

'Oh? When?'

'First thing this morning. The shop's padlocked and his wife swears she don't know what's become of him. But we'll see if they're going to stop me!' he went on ragingly. 'I'll rip the truth out of that bunch of hayseeds if it means spending the rest of my life in this dump!' He drew a deep breath and, glancing about him, barked out, 'Where's the girl?'

'Before you see her,' Mr. Treadgold put in, Dr. Wood here, whom I don't think you've met, has something rather important to tell you.'

The detective's keen glance challenged the doctor. He nodded indifferently. 'How are you, Doc?'

'Sit down,' Mr. Treadgold invited, 'and have a drink!'

'Thanks, I never touch it.'

The doctor held out a packet of cigarettes.

'I don't smoke, either!' He was tearing the wrapping off a strip of gum. 'Well, Doc,' he said brusquely, dropping into a chair and lifting an expectant face, 'what's your big surprise?' He popped his wad of gum into his mouth.

The sergeant was not a good audience. His eyes, like his jaws, were never still, and more than once he gave the impression that his attention was wandering. Somehow he contrived to suggest a certain incredulousness on his part towards the promised disclosure. Even when confronted with the sack, he displayed no excitement, but examined it with expressionless features preliminary to rolling it and stowing it away in a hip pocket. Nor did he vouchsafe any comment other than an inarticulate growl on Wood's theory linking the sack with the missing Lhermite.

But when the tale was done, the sergeant showed that he had not missed a single point of the narrative. Questions rained upon the American in a shower. Bigoury was particularly anxious to know, among other things, exactly where Wood had been standing, with relation to the girl, at the moment of the attack. A beam was between them when he was struck down – Wood was precise; and further agreed that, in the prevailing dimness of the attic, his assailant might not have noticed the girl.

On which Bigoury laughed rather stridently and shifted his gum. 'If he had, Doc,' he remarked, 'you wouldn't have got that swollen mit!'

'I don't see what Mademoiselle de St. Rémy has to do with it,' said Wood doggedly.

The sergeant cackled again. 'Oh, no? Well, stick around and maybe you will!'

The young man's face darkened. 'You're not seriously suggesting – ' he began heatedly; then, observing that Mr. Treadgold was shaking his head and frowning at him, he subsided.

A swath of bright sunlight behind them cutting the cool dimness of the bungalow brought the three of them to the right-about. Against the leafy background with the glitter of water between, the girl stood in the open doorway. She had changed her frock for a semi-evening one, black like the other, which left her neck and arms bare.

'You said six o'clock,' she explained demurely to the doctor, who had hurried forward. 'I hope I'm not too early!'

'Come in,' said Wood. His voice sounded dejected.

Catching its note, she paused, one bare arm propped against the door-post, and glanced past Wood at the two men, silent and expectant, behind him.

Mr. Treadgold sprang into the breach. 'Mademoiselle,' he said, 'this is Sergeant Bigoury, the detective from Quebec!'

Her formal 'Monsieur!' was unsmiling, even as the sergeant's no less austere 'Mademoiselle!'

She turned to Wood. 'You're busy now – I'll come back!'

But Bigoury took the door from the doctor and, with hand extended, ushered her in. 'On the contrary, Mademoiselle, we were waiting for you,' he said. 'Be good enough to sit down. I want a word with you!'

He left her to take the chair Mr. Treadgold drew up while, with a sternly absorbed air, he ran his eye over the pages of his bulky notebook.

She accepted a cigarette from Wood and busied herself with the lighting of it as though welcoming any pretext for filling in the disconcerting lull. The little, confidential smile with which she thanked Wood hovered across her face and was gone, leaving her mobile features grave and alert. Covertly, through a wreath of smoke, her eyes followed the detective's every movement.

'Mademoiselle,' Bigoury spoke at last, 'you're not obliged to answer my questions. But if you do, it's my duty to warn you that your replies may be used in evidence against you.'

A chilling silence fell. The girl was smoking her cigarette in short, nervous puffs. The detective uttered the time-honoured formula in English, bleakly, with a glibness that told of long practice. Wood made an impulsive movement. But, as though foreseeing it, Mr. Treadgold had sidled up to restrain him with a firm hand.

The girl took the cigarette away from her lips. 'I'll tell you anything I can,' she rejoined huskily.

'Thank you!' Bigoury referred to his book. 'You stated on oath at the inquest that you were the first to come upon the body of Adams?'

'That's so.'

'When Dr. Wood arrived, why didn't you tell him that a dead man was lying in the salon?'

'I was thinking only of my grandfather at the time. I...'

The detective made a clicking noise with his tongue. 'Please, Mademoiselle! We'll have no evasions...' He had stripped his speech of its slangy jauntiness, Mr. Treadgold noticed – his English was formal, precise. 'However sick the old gentleman was, you'd have found some way of telling the doctor, or the curé, or Mr. Treadgold here that a man had been murdered. Now wouldn't you?'

She ran her tongue over her lips nervously. 'I thought Grandpapa had killed him...'

Bigoury leaned forward. 'You were his nurse – the doctor had warned you that his heart was bad. How could you have imagined such a thing for a single instant?'

'I did, nevertheless,' she answered almost inaudibly.

'Why should you have thought it? The Seigneur and Adams were not on good terms, yes, but why should the Seigneur want to kill him?'

'Gideon Adams had driven Grandpapa out of the country. He...'

'I know all about that. What I'm asking you is whether you had any specific grounds for your belief...'

She paused. 'The last time they met my grandfather threatened to kill him...'

'Why?'

She hesitated. 'It was a private matter.'

'Tell me about it, please.'

She bent forward to shake the ash from her cigarette upon the tray of bottles on the table. The action was leisurely, an attempt to gain a moment's respite, as the detective was quick to perceive.

'Please!' he rapped out. 'I've no time to waste.'

'I'd prefer not to say,' she answered at length. 'It had nothing to do with this case, anyway...'

'Nothing to do with the case?' Bigoury echoed loudly. 'Didn't Adams want to marry you and offer to let your grandfather return to Canada if he'd give his consent?'

She had grown perfectly still, staring in front of her. Slowly the blood mounted to her face and, turning her head, she looked straight at Wood, then shifted her glance to the sergeant's angry countenance. With a faint shrug she said, 'It's true!'

'And did Adams renew his offer when you saw him last night?' asked Bigoury.

She drew back quickly. 'I never spoke to him. When I saw he was dead...'

'Why did he come to the Manor?'

She shook her head, her expression contemptuous. 'I don't know.'

'It wasn't to ask you or your grandfather what had become of certain valuables which had been unlawfully withdrawn from the jurisdiction of the courts?'

'I haven't the faintest idea. I didn't speak to him, I tell you!'

The detective had slipped a hand into his pocket. Now he withdrew it, holding up a small gold box. 'Ever seen that before?' She shook her head. 'Take it!' He thrust it at her. 'That's your crest, isn't it?'

She nodded, turning the box over in her hands. 'Yes.' She lifted her limpid gaze to his. 'Where does this come from?'

'It was hidden in your servant's suitcase. He'd like to know how it got there. And so would I! Your grandfather left you a letter. Let me see it, please!' Silently, she opened her bag and gave him the folded sheet. He snatched it from her and there was a moment of tense silence while he read it. With a frown he looked up. 'He speaks of a gold snuffbox presented to Seigneur Ignace by General Brock. Isn't this it?'

She moved her shoulders disdainfully. 'I know no more than you do!'

'There's a whole list of things catalogued here – what's become of the rest of them?'

'Since you seem to know so much about me and my affairs,' she answered coldly, 'you've probably heard that when we went to the attic, Dr. Wood and I, to look for these heirlooms in the hiding-place my grandfather indicated, they were gone.' She handed him back the box.

Her calmness appeared to exasperate the sergeant. 'I'm giving you every chance,' he retorted sharply, 'but I warn you, I mean to have the truth. Come, come, Mademoiselle, you may as well own up. It was you who received Adams when he called at the Manor last night. He threatened your granddad, but offered to lay off of the old gentleman, if you'd agree to marry him, isn't that right?'

With a firm gesture she crushed out her cigarette on the tray. 'The last time I spoke to Gideon Adams was that day in Paris,' she said, enunciating clearly and deliberately. 'The next time I saw him he was dead. It's no use your trying to make me say I spoke to him last night because I didn't!'

Bigoury reddened. 'He was dead when you found him, is that it?' he rasped.

'Yes, yes, yes!' At last her composure had given way. She had sprung to her feet and faced him angrily.

Her outburst seemed to relax the sergeant's nerves. 'And that's your last word?' he demanded quietly.

'It's the truth!'

He nodded significantly. 'Okay!' He paused. 'Where did you lose your pencil, Mademoiselle?' he asked, his large glasses boring into her face.

As though by instinct her hand stole to the thin gold chain she wore about her neck. 'My pencil?' There was a puzzled look in the blue-grey eyes. She shook her head. 'I can't tell you that, I'm afraid. I noticed I'd lost it only today...'

Wood struck in. 'That's right,' he said eagerly. 'At the Manor this afternoon I asked Mademoiselle for a pencil and she said she'd lost hers...' His voice trailed off as he became aware of a portentous hush in the room. The girl was staring at the detective in perplexity; but Mr. Treadgold's eyes, the doctor noted, were clouded with dismay, while as for Bigoury, his face was a stone mask.

A small gold pencil was displayed as the detective unclenched the fingers of his outstretched hand.

'Is that yours, Mademoiselle?'

She inclined her head. 'Yes. Where did you find it?'

He snapped his fingers. 'Let's see that chain, please!'

Without speaking, she slipped the chain from her neck and trickled it into his palm. He bent over it, scrutinising it, link by link, and the circular clasp uniting the two ends, then turned his attention to the pencil and its split ring. After that he drew a magnifying-glass from his waistcoat pocket and, crossing to the daylight at the door, began his examination all over again.

A leaden silence rested over the room. Wood would have spoken to the girl. But she had no eyes for him, standing apart, her features proud and unrevealing, staring down at her clasped hands.

Bigoury came back. He dangled the pencil at the girl 'You admit it's yours?'

'Certainly!' Her tone was icy.

'It was found under Adams's dead body. How did it get there?'

She had gone very white. Her lips stirred, but no sound came forth. She cleared her throat.

'I can't tell you,' she said at last. 'I missed it only today.'

The sergeant thrust the chain at her. 'The clasp's buckled. It looks as if this pencil had been violently torn from it. What have you to say?'

'Nothing. I lost that pencil – how or where' – she shrugged – 'I can't tell you. That's all I know about it!'

His brow darkened: his mouth made a bitter line; but his voice ran on in an even, official key. 'Denials won't help you. I'm willing to believe you killed him in self-defence. He got fresh with you, you snatched that bayonet from the rack to defend yourself, in the rough-and-tumble he was stabbed and you lost the pencil off your chain. Wasn't that the way of it?'

'No!' she cried, and stamped her foot. 'No, no, no, and a thousand times no!' She wrung her hands desperately. 'Oh, what's the use of my talking? None of you believe me!'

Elbowing aside his roommate, who vainly tried to hold him back, Wood thrust himself forward. He was boiling with anger.

'Look here,' he shouted at the detective, 'this has gone far enough!'

'Will you stay out of this?' Bigoury rapped back, dangerously calm. 'If you didn't kill Adams, why did you clean that bayonet and make Jacques put it back?' he asked the girl.

'I didn't!' she cried, plaintively indignant.

'Oh, no?' He held out a wisp of linen. 'Isn't that your handkerchief?'

Her face contracted. She nodded without speaking.

'How does this blood come to be on it?' the detective demanded, shaking the handkerchief at her. 'And why was it hidden in the kitchen drawer?'

She fluttered her hands helplessly. 'I can explain everything, if you'll only give me time. You confuse me with all your questions!'

'You don't want time to speak the truth, Mademoiselle. You wiped the bayonet on this handkerchief, didn't you?'

'No!' Her voice rang through the quiet hut. 'There was blood on one of Grandfather's slippers – he must have dragged himself to where Adams was lying just inside the door and collapsed in the vestibule as he went to get help. I wiped the blood off with my handkerchief. It was just after I had found the body, when I still believed that Grandpapa – that Grandpapa had killed him. I put that handkerchief in the kitchen drawer, meaning to wash it out, and then forgot about it. Please, you must believe me! Honestly, I never saw the bayonet. If anyone picked it up and cleaned it, it must have been Jacques. I suppose, like me, he thought that Grandpapa...'

'Oh, for God's sake, Adrienne,' Wood now struck in, 'why try and shield the fellow? You know darn well it was Jacques who killed Adams. He cleaned the bayonet and put it back, simply to save his own skin!'

She addressed her answer to Bigoury. 'Dr. Wood knows nothing about it,' she said, with cold dignity. 'If Jacques were guilty, he'd never have let them arrest poor Mathias.'

The detective laughed unpleasantly. 'Oh, wouldn't he? Shall I tell you why he's been lying all through? It's to cover up for you.'

She drew back, one hand over her heart. 'Me?'

'You heard me! He suspected you from the first of killing Adams and, when he saw them find that pencil, he was sure of it!'

'Bunk!' cried the doctor ragingly. 'Why, you poor sap, don't you know he's only throwing dust in your eyes? Adams caught him with the goods on him and he killed Adams, just as he tried to kill me this afternoon. Now he's trying to hang it on Mademoiselle and you fall for it. You make me tired!'

The sergeant kept his temper. 'You're wrong,' he told him evenly. 'To the last he did his best to shield her. He wouldn't have admitted that the pencil was hers if I hadn't bluffed him into it. You see, that was just a lucky guess of mine – that pencil was bought in Paris: it's stamped with the maker's name. Jacques tried to slug you in the attic because he thought you were alone, I guess. He and Mademoiselle between them had moved those valuables to a safe place and he was taking no chances on your discovering their secret. Once you were on to those heirlooms, you were on to the motive of the crime!'

'You're crazy!' Wood flared back. 'If what you say is true, why did Mademoiselle show me that letter and ask me to go with her to the attic, will you answer me that?'

Bigoury shrugged, his gaze fastened meaningly on the girl. 'A number of Mademoiselle's actions have yet to be accounted for.'

The screen door flapped back, revealing Constable Bissonnette standing smartly at attention on the threshold.

'The police at Trois-Ponts are on the telephone, patron,' he announced in French.

'Take a message, Bissonnette! I'm busy.'

The constable did not budge. 'It's urgent, patron. Le Borgne broke jail this afternoon!'

Chapter 23

THROWING UP HIS HANDS, Bigoury rolled infuriated eyes to the ceiling. 'Ça, par exemple!' He swung to Mr. Treadgold. 'If that isn't the pay-off!' he burst out in English. 'First they arrest the wrong man, who's probably an important witness, and then, before I get a chance at him, they let him slip through their fingers. These country jails, ah, maudit! Is that motorcyclist still there?' he barked at the constable.

'Yes, patron.'

'Tell him to go as fast as he can to Le Borgne's shack and stay there – these animals always work their way back to their holes. If he doesn't know the way, someone in the village will show him. Stop!' His eye sought out the girl. 'Your baggage is here, Mademoiselle?' She nodded. 'I'll have to go through it. Any objection?' She shrugged her indifference. 'Give the officer the keys, please!'

'My things aren't locked. The gardien will show him my room.'

He turned to the constable. 'See to it, Bissonnette! Wait! I'm coming with you.' He bent his stern gaze on the girl. 'We'll resume this conversation later, Mademoiselle.' Snatching up his cap and overcoat, he hurried out in the constable's wake.

'Can you tie that for gall?' Wood exploded, the moment he was gone. He swung to the girl. 'Damn it, he treated you like a criminal! Your explanation about that handkerchief was perfectly reasonable, and as for the pencil, you might easily have caught that chain of yours on something...'

The girl had not moved from her place by the table. She was touching up her face in a small mirror she had taken from her bag.

'Can't you try and remember about that pencil?' he asked anxiously. 'Mightn't you have dropped it in the salon – I mean, before ever Adams appeared on the scene? Here's an idea! Perhaps your chain snapped as you were helping your grandfather to his room. How about it?' He gazed at her eagerly.

She paid no attention to him. With set features she replaced her mirror and puff in her bag. Then she glanced interrogatively at Mr. Treadgold, who, with a brooding air, was filling his pipe.

'I wonder,' she said rather quaveringly, 'whether you'd do me a favour? You have a car, haven't you? Would you mind running me over to the convent?'

'The convent?' said Wood, in surprise. 'What do you want at the convent?'

But she was gazing at Mr. Treadgold, waiting for his answer.

'Of course,' Mr. Treadgold replied. He glanced at his watch. 'The only thing,' he went on, 'is that we dine at the ungodly hour of six-thirty. Did you want to go at once, because...'

'I shan't be dining,' she said, in a suffocating voice, 'I've changed my mind about staying here.'

'Adrienne!' cried the doctor in dismay.

She still ignored him. 'Will you take me?' she asked Mr. Treadgold.

'Of course, my dear. What I was going to say, you'll have to wait a little for your luggage, won't you?'

'I don't want to wait! I don't want to stay in this place another minute!' Her voice vibrated with sudden passion.

'But, Adrienne,' Wood protested, 'what's the matter? What's happened?'

With a glance at his roommate, Mr. Treadgold crossed to where she stood.

'Come, come, my dear,' he said gently, 'you mustn't take the sergeant too seriously. Let's sit down, the three of us, and see if we can't get some sense into this business.'

'No,' she cried, 'no! I've said too much already. Oh, why should you pretend with me? You believe I killed this man.'

Mr. Treadgold shook his head. 'No, my dear young lady! I believe nothing that cannot be proved. In any case, if you're determined to leave us, you'll have to wait for your luggage. And, frankly, I'm not sure the constable will let you go – I'll have a word with him presently. In the meantime, I don't see why we shouldn't have a drink, do you? George,' he called out over his shoulder, 'what about those cocktails?' He advanced a chair. 'Sit down,' he bade the girl. 'We don't have to go in to dinner, you know. There are sandwiches on that tray – we'll have a bite here, and later on, if you still wish it and the officer's agreeable, I'll drive you down to the village. Right?'

His tone was so gentle and understanding, there was such a kindly twinkle in the turquoise eyes, that she capitulated, albeit with a hurt and distrustful face. Obediently the doctor had betaken himself to the table – there was the tinkle of bottles and presently the rattle of the shaker. Pipe in mouth, hands folded behind his back, Mr. Treadgold mouched over to the door and remained for a spell gazing forth into the golden evening. When he turned round, Wood was pouring the cocktails. The girl would have refused hers, but Mr. Treadgold made her take it and help herself to a sandwich.

'America's gift to the Old World,' he commented, glancing approvingly at the drink which the doctor handed him. 'I've the instinctive feeling that our young friend is an expert at this sort of thing. Well, here we go!' He drank testingly, set his glass aside and wiped his moustache. 'George, George,' he said solemnly, 'a cocktail as good as this is a sure sign of a misspent youth!' Carefully nursing his drink, he crooked his foot round a chair and sat down opposite the girl. 'Tell me about Boucheron!' he said gently.

She gave him a questioning look. 'What about him?'

'I was wondering just why the Seigneur sent for him last night.'

'It was about our rents, I imagine. Boucheron used to collect them. He hadn't forwarded any money for six months. And he didn't answer letters...'

'Why?'

'Grandpapa said it was the depression – he thought the censitaires, the tenants, were in arrears. But I think it was Adams.'

'You mean that Boucheron was working in with him?'

She shrugged. 'All I can tell you is that, as long as my aunt was alive, she insisted on Grandpapa receiving his rents: as soon as she died, they stopped.'

Mr. Treadgold nodded bleakly, puffing at his pipe.

'Why did your grandfather send for Boucheron in such a hurry? Le Borgne told us that the Seigneur's order was urgent – Boucheron was to come that very night. Why? This rent business had been going on for six months – what was the rush?'

Blankly she shook her head. 'I don't know.'

Mr. Treadgold was staring at her. But it was evident he did not see her – his gaze was remote.

'Your grandfather was up and dressed: you and Jacques were in your rooms. Mightn't he have decided it was a good time to go to the attic and see if those heirlooms were safe? Finding them gone, whom would he send for? For Boucheron, his man of confidence, for Boucheron, who had the keys of the house! Am I right?'

She nodded fearfully. 'I never thought of that.'

'You suggest that Boucheron was hand and glove with Adams? But was he? If he had been, wouldn't he have known that Adams was at St. Florentin and have looked him up?'

'How do you know he didn't?' she asked point-blank.

'I spent an hour or so in his company at the curé's the night I arrived. Boucheron knew I was stopping at the camp – it would have been only natural if he'd asked me whether I'd met

Adams. It was pure chance that I didn't mention Adams myself. Do you see what I'm driving at? Why didn't Boucheron know that Adams was here? Because Adams didn't tell him! And why didn't Adams tell him? Because he didn't trust him.'

Wood broke his long silence. 'You mean that Boucheron was double-crossing him?'

Mr. Treadgold hoisted his shoulders. 'Mademoiselle suggests they were confederates; but there's nothing to show it. He may have withheld those rents on his own account – dishonest solicitors do it every day. The obvious explanation is usually the most likely. Boucheron was the family lawyer and therefore on the other side. If Adams smelt a rat and came down here to investigate, Boucheron is the last person he'd communicate with...'

A bell clanged out of the distance. 'If we're not going in to dinner,' said Mr. Treadgold, looking at the doctor, 'I think we'd better let Madeleine know!'

'I'll tell her.'

'And see if Bissonnette's through,' Mr. Treadgold added as the other moved to the door.

'Okay.'

A silence fell in the hut. Mr. Treadgold sat down and instinctively felt for his tobacco-pouch. He glanced up to see the girl standing before him. It was plain that he had forgotten all about her, for, with a hasty exclamation, he attempted to scramble to his feet. But her hand stayed him.

'Please don't move!' she said. 'I want you to answer me a question. Will you?'

He stuck his pipe back in his mouth, eyeing her closely from under his shaggy eyebrows. 'If I can...'

'Do you believe I killed this man?'

He shook his head. 'No, my dear.'

She uttered a little sigh. 'Thank you. I wanted to be sure.'

'But I realise,' he added, still regarding her intently, 'that you've yet to prove it. Make no mistake – out of these three clues, the pencil, the handkerchief, and the box, to say nothing of Adams's offer of marriage, Bigoury's in a position to build up a pretty strong case against you and Jacques. Especially Jacques. The only fingerprints we have are his, you know – they're all over that musket. He might have left them taking the bayonet down just as well as putting it back, don't forget that.'

Her head-shake was very positive. 'He put the bayonet back to shield me and then only because of Grandpapa. He idolised Grandpapa. Jacques used to work in the hotel where Grandpapa and all the St. Rémys stayed when they came to Quebec, a funny, old-fashioned place in the oldest part of the town. It changed hands and Jacques lost his job. He came up to Grandpapa in the street one day – he was out of work, ragged and penniless. Grandpapa was just leaving for Europe and took him along as valet, although he couldn't afford it, poor darling! We owe Jacques a lot of money – his wages haven't been paid for months.'

'When Bigoury discovers this, he'll say it explains the snuff-box.'

'Jacques didn't steal those things, whatever Bigoury or any-one else cares to think.' She spoke in a tone of suppressed indignation. 'He didn't kill Adams, either. He was fast asleep when I went to his room – I'd quite a business to rouse him. Besides, if he were guilty, he'd never have let them arrest poor Mathias, as I told the detective.'

The blue eyes smiled indulgently at her insistence. 'I know, my dear, I know. None the less, you're in a tough spot, the pair of you.'

She gazed at him appealingly – she had the wide-open regard of a child. 'Won't you help us?' she said huskily.

He shrugged. 'It's not easy for me to interfere.'

'Dr. Wood told me you were a very clever criminologist.'

His laugh had a modest ring. 'Like all Americans, dear old George has a tremendous capacity for hero-worship.'

'But you have made a study of crime, haven't you?'

He scratched a match and laid it to his pipe, cupping his hands about the bowl.

'Merely as a hobby,' he mumbled, puffing. 'I happen to be cursed with a fatal curiosity, that's all – I like to know the why and wherefore of things. Crime offers an irresistible temptation to this craving of mine. A great English author wrote that "Desire of knowledge, like the thirst of riches, increases ever with the acquisition of it!" It's the case with me!'

'That's from Tristram Shandy, isn't it?'

He snatched the pipe from his lips to survey her with incredulous delight.

'Shades of Sterne!' he almost shouted. 'You know it!'

She blushed becomingly and made a little, disdainful grimace. 'Pooh, I thought everybody had heard of Uncle Toby and Corporal What-do-you-call-him...'

Dolefully he wagged his head. 'George hasn't – at least, he hadn't,' he remarked, replacing his pipe. 'But then the way he shakes a cocktail shows that his education's been neglected. If you don't mind my saying so, my dear, you're a highly intelligent young woman as well as a very pretty one.' He beamed at her.

Fleetingly, with a flash of white teeth, she gave him back his smile, then, with features grave, held out her hands to him.

'Please, you won't refuse me. It's for poor Jacques I ask as much as for myself. If anybody can clear us, you can!'

The light died out of his face. 'That's easier said than done!' He said nothing for a spell, sturdily smoking his pipe. 'You know, I was born and brought up in London,' he remarked at last. 'Well, this case puts me in mind of going out to post a letter in a London fog. You stumble along to the letter-box at the corner of the square and when you look for your house again, hey, presto! It's gone. Dim figures loom up – you stop one and find it's somebody who's lost his bearings the same as you. You step aside to avoid a lamppost and lo and behold! It's a policeman trying to locate his surroundings; you politely address a tall shape suddenly confronting you and it's a tree. Still you struggle forward because you know your house is somewhere there, solid and substantial in the swirling, yellow haze. Now I'm groping in the fog again. All you people – you and Jacques, Mathias, Lhermite, Batisse – you're like figures that suddenly appear out of the gloom – I've the impression that if I accost one, it'll only be to discover somebody as befogged as I. But all the time I've the sensation that somewhere close at hand, towering through the fog, is a presence, unseen but fully realised, as real and as concrete as that London mansion of my boyhood days!'

He broke off, staring sombrely into the gathering dusk. She did not venture to intrude upon his thoughts. 'Years ago in England,' he resumed presently, 'I read an inscription on an ancient sundial – "Life's but a walking shadow!" it said. A walking shadow – it has an eerie ring! Shall I tell you that there's a shadow stalking in the background of this case, elusive, unsubstantial, but omnipresent and full of resource, obliterating clues, blocking the investigation from stage to stage?' He pursed his lips glumly. 'And the background's still so dark! If I could discern but a single ray of light to pierce the gloom!'

He raised his head to contemplate her sternly.

'If I'm to help you, you'll have to follow my advice.'

'Indeed I will. Anything you say.'

His hand pointed downward to the spot on which they stood.

'Stay here! Don't go down to the village!'

She glanced at him timidly. 'But why?'

'Because you're safer here where I can look after you. Everyone involved in this affair is in danger.'

She shrank away from him. 'You're not serious?'

'I was never more serious in my life,' he assured her unsmilingly. 'You'll stay?'

She bowed her head. 'Very well.'

The curtest of nods was her only acknowledgement. He had fallen silent again, his jaws firmly clamped upon his large and blackened briar. Once more she had the impression that he was oblivious of her presence. So she took a chair and, folding her hands in her lap, composed herself to wait.

When after a moment he spoke, this impression was confirmed. It was not to her that he addressed himself, but to the ceiling.

'What did he want here?' he muttered in an agonised voice. 'Ye gods, why did he come?' With a sudden air of resolve he hauled himself out of his chair.

Wood, coming back at this juncture, saw him planted in the centre of the floor, plucking at his grey moustache with a harried and indecisive air.

'The officer's through,' the young man announced and glanced somewhat reproachfully at the girl. 'I asked him about you,' he informed her. 'He says he has no orders to detain you.'

'She's staying here,' Mr. Treadgold broke in curtly.

Wood smiled expansively at the girl. 'That's better.'

'Is the constable still around?' Mr. Treadgold cut him off impatiently.

'He went down to the village.'

'And Bigoury?'

'Gone to Trois-Ponts. But he'll be back!'

The florid face cleared. 'Will you do something for me, George? Hang about the verandah for a bit and keep an eye on the Angel's quarters. If you see him or Bigoury or anyone else approaching, whistle! I'm going to slip into Adams's hut next door for a minute.'

'The place is locked up and Bigoury has the key, so the Angel told me...'

'There are windows, aren't there?'

'Sure. But what's Bigoury going to say?'

'To hell with Bigoury!'

The screen door fell to with a bang.

Chapter 24

WOOD WAGGED HIS HEAD admiringly. 'What a grand old boy!' he remarked to the girl. 'Don't you think so?' He opened the door and held it for her. 'Come out on the porch and watch me put on my Sister Anne act.'

Head in the air, she swept by him. He caught her on the verandah steps. 'Where are you going?' he demanded.

'To my room.'

'Nonsense! Sit down and let's talk.'

She kept her gaze averted. 'Thanks, but I prefer to be alone.'

She sought to pass him, but he blocked the way. 'What's the matter with you?'

'I'd rather not discuss it.'

'But that's silly. Have I done anything wrong?' And when she remained obstinately mute, 'Is that why you wanted to go back to the convent?' he questioned.

'Please let me go to my room,' she said.

He did not move. 'Not until you tell me what I've done.'

She flashed an angry glance at him. 'Why be hypocritical?'

'About what?'

She struck the balustrade with her hand. 'I don't care if you do suspect me! But don't think you deceived me, pretending to take my part against that odious detective!'

He gazed at her steadily. 'That wasn't pretending, Adrienne.'

'Then why set this man on to me?'

He had gone rather white. 'What in God's name are you talking about?'

She shook herself impatiently. 'It wasn't you, I suppose, who told him about that scene with Gideon Adams in Paris?'

'It certainly was not.'

'Then how did he know?'

'Detectives have their own ways of finding out things – it's their business!'

Her foot tapped nervously. 'You know nothing about me – you're entitled to believe what you like. But if you had any decent instincts, at least you'd have respected a confidence.'

'Are you suggesting that I went and repeated this story about you to Bigoury?' he demanded hotly.

Her face flamed. 'Oh, you're impossible! Except Grandpapa and I no one ever knew that Gideon Adams wanted to marry me...'

'You said yourself that Jacques was there.'

'He didn't hear the discussion. He came in after it was all over.'

'The Seigneur may have told him about it.'

Her glance froze him. 'My grandfather was not in the habit of taking servants into his confidence – certainly not where I was concerned!'

'I give you my solemn word of honour I never mentioned it to a soul, not even to old Treadgold!'

She moved an indifferent shoulder.

'You don't believe me?' His eyes rested challengingly on her face.

She looked away. 'I tell you again, it could have been no one else but you.' She spoke with less conviction, and for a fleeting moment her glance, half-veiled by long lashes, flickered to his flushed and hostile face.

'Have it your own way!' he said, and turned his back on her, staring through the twilight to where the first lights of the camp were twinkling through the trees.

When he looked round, she was gone and Mr. Treadgold was standing there.

'All serene?' the latter enquired.

'All serene,' Wood rejoined listlessly, and added, 'Well, did you make it?'

Mr. Treadgold nodded. 'Yes. Where's the Mademoiselle?'

'Gone to her room.'

'Good. Listen, I'm going down to the village. I don't know how long I shall be away. But when Bigoury comes back, he's got to wait for me, do you understand? Make any excuse you like, but hold him. I must see him tonight!' So saying, with a hasty stride Mr. Treadgold disappeared into the bungalow.

The doctor followed him inside. Mr. Treadgold was on the far side of the room, rummaging in his dressing-case.

'What's the programme now, H. B.?' Wood asked casually.

His companion did not reply, but came forward to the table. He had an automatic in one hand, a loaded charger in the other. With an absorbed air he slipped the charger home, clicked a cartridge into the breech, and slid the weapon into his pocket.

'A gun?' Wood exclaimed in surprise. 'What's the idea?'

He was now aware of a subtle change in his roommate's demeanour. Mr. Treadgold's habitual air of mild complacence had vanished. His expression was grimly resolute: his eyes had a hard glitter; and his speech was of an uncompromising brusqueness.

'Where are you off to, H. B.?' said Wood.

'I told you, to the village.' He had snatched up his cloak and was glancing about for his cap.

'But why the gun?'

He had found his cap and was pulling it on. 'A mere precaution! So long, George! Hold Bigoury for me, won't you?' He made for the door.

'Hold Bigoury, nothing! I don't know where you're going, but I'm coming, too.'

'No! I want you here.'

'Then tell me at least what you're up to.'

'Not now.' He paused. 'And keep an eye on that nice girl of yours, do you hear? I don't care whether she sits in her own room or in ours, but she's not to wander alone about the camp after dark. And that goes for you, too.'

'You mean, she's in danger?'

'We're all in danger, so long as the murderer's running loose. Why the deuce couldn't you have kept her with you?'

The young man laughed ruefully. 'Better ask her that. She accuses me of running to Bigoury with a tale about her...' With an injured air he told of the scene the girl had made with him.

Mr. Treadgold was not much impressed – he was obviously itching to be off.

'Bah!' he growled, 'Bigoury can always clear you. I wonder how he got on to it...'

'She swears that, apart from herself, no living person knew about it but me.'

'Odd!' He shifted his cape to his shoulder. 'If your conversation hadn't taken place out-of-doors, I'd have said someone had been eavesdropping...'

The doctor's jaw dropped. 'Holy cats!' he ejaculated, 'what was I thinking of? There was something moving in the bushes while we were talking. At first we thought it was a wild animal, but then, as we drove out, I noticed a flivver parked off the trail and I assumed it was a lumberman or forest guard we'd heard.'

Suddenly alert, Mr. Treadgold laid his cape down on a chair. 'A flivver?' he echoed in a curiously strained voice. 'Not a dark blue, very battered-looking machine, was it?' His voice was suddenly shaking with excitement. 'You didn't take the number, by any chance?'

Dejectedly Wood shook his head. 'It looked like any other tin Lizzie to me, with a dark body – whether blue or black, I can't say. And I didn't take the number. It never occurred to me that anybody could have wanted to spy on us. Now, of course, I realise it was Bigoury!'

Mr. Treadgold nodded absently, murmuring, 'Quite, quite.' With the same slow and abstracted air he gathered up his cape, while gazing bleakly at Wood. 'Boucheron drives a dark blue flivver,' he remarked.

'Boucheron?' The name cracked like a pistol-shot. 'Gosh, H. B., it was he – he must have followed us to the woods!'

The older man gave him a jaundiced look. 'It's only a shot in the dark. There are probably a dozen cars like that in the village.'

'A shot in the dark be damned, it's a bull's-eye!' Wood was wildly excited. 'When Boucheron was at the Manor this afternoon, he knew something – something about Adrienne, I mean. He was definitely hostile. He tried to stop her leaving with me. He wanted the mayor to interfere – said she'd have to wait and see the detective.'

Mr. Treadgold's eyes flashed. 'Hostile, was he? What did he say?'

Wood shrugged. 'They spoke in French – you know what my French is. But I gathered he was insinuating that she'd told a string of lies – he was vaguely threatening. It didn't go so well with me and I let him know it pretty plainly. And your friend, the mayor, bless him, backed me up!'

His companion nodded darkly. 'This explains a lot. After you two had left, when Bigoury and I arrived, Boucheron tried to buttonhole him – said he'd something of importance to communicate. Bigoury told him he'd see him later, at the coroner's. It's plain to me now that Bigoury came straight from that interview to the camp to have it out with the girl.'

With a resounding bang the doctor's fist came down on the table. 'By Gad, I believe you've hit it!' His face blazed with anger. 'The rat! He overheard our conversation and repeated it to Bigoury, just to put her in Dutch with the police. But why should he want to incriminate her?' He broke off, dumbfounded. 'Good grief, H. B., do you realise what this means?'

But Mr. Treadgold was already halfway through the door. 'Keep it till I'm back,' he called over his shoulder.

Spoke and went clattering down the verandah steps into the falling night.

Chapter 25

THE SUN HAD GONE to bed under a quilt of angry purple which, with the waning of the light, had turned to an inky black. Darkness had closed in early for the season and there was thunder about and summer lightning flashing behind the hills. Lamps already gleamed in windows as Mr. Treadgold drove up the village street. But at the lawyer's, where he stopped the car and got out, there was no sign of life, and the front door remained obstinately closed to the whirr of the bell.

A lad who was putting up the shutters at Evariste Laliberté's, the butcher's, across the street, told the caller that the notary had accompanied 'Monsieur le Détective' and the coroner to Trois-Ponts. With a vexed air, Mr. Treadgold drove slowly on. The space in front of Ruffier's store at the end of the village was the first available spot to turn. Perceiving a light in the shop window, although the door was shut, Mr. Treadgold left the car and went inside.

A woman who was sewing at the cash desk glanced up at the 'ting' of the doorbell and, laying down her work, came slowly forward. Mr. Treadgold recognised the faded blue gingham dress – it was Madame Ruffier.

He lifted his cap. 'Monsieur Ruffier?'

She pinched tight lips. 'He's not at the garage?'

'The garage, Madame?'

'Beside the house, at the back.' She returned to the desk.

There seemed to be quite a lot of land behind the store. A wooden gate led from the street into a yard enclosed by a number of crazy-looking sheds, with a passage between them giving access to the dwelling-house set in its little garden. One of the sheds disclosed through a sliding door ajar a glimpse of boxes piled up – a warehouse, evidently. Five generations of merchants in Mr. Treadgold were impressed. Sensible people, the French. No money frittered away on show. If all these tumbledown shacks were warehouses, the fellow must carry pretty considerable stocks. Well, his old-fashioned store notwithstanding, he probably did a thriving business round the farms. Worth a packet, most likely, even if he did live and look like a peasant – what they call in Yorkshire 'a warm man.' Bigoury – Mr. Treadgold smiled to himself – might rail against the mayor as a hick and a hayseed; but he could doubtless buy and sell a poor devil like the sergeant ten times over. Not such a hick, at that!

A voice called sharply, 'Qu'est-ce que c'est?' Attired in grimy overalls Ruffier appeared from the passage leading to the house. Mr. Treadgold went to meet him and saw, beyond the passage, the tall doors of a barn folded back and on the ground between them a pilot light, lying where it had been dropped, with a car or two and all the litter of a farm garage behind.

'Té, it's Monsieur Treadgol'!' cried Ruffier, as he recognised his visitor. 'You wished to see me?'

'Not if you're busy. I was just passing – I thought I'd look in and see if you had any more stamps for me.'

'But yes, Monsieur. I managed to collect a few. I meant to let you know, only with all this upset... Have the kindness to wait for me in the store a little instant while I clean up and I'm at your service.'

They had crossed the yard together. Ruffier opened a door in the wall. 'This way, Monsieur! I shan't be a moment.'

It was the back door of the store. Beyond raising her head on his entry, Madame Ruffier paid no attention to the visitor. After a little the mayor appeared, brisk and bright as ever, in his dark suit and blue béret. He had a small brown-paper parcel in his hand. He looked at Mr. Treadgold and then at the woman and placed his finger significantly on his lips.

'You may leave us, my love,' he told her ingratiatingly. Without looking round, she went out.

Ruffier planked his package down on the counter and opened it. 'Voilà!' A mass of stamps came to view. Each had been neatly clipped from its cover.

'Oh, dear,' said Mr. Treadgold plaintively, 'and I told you to leave them on their envelopes!'

The mayor shrugged his shoulders. 'These were some I had by me: I regret, but they were cut already. I shall know for another time. Nice stamps, hein? You like them, no?'

'Would you mind if I took them away to examine them at my leisure? Then I'll make you an offer for the lot.'

'But, of course. As Monsieur wishes!'

'How many are there here?'

He smiled agreeably. 'For that, my dear Monsieur, I've no idea!'

'We'll count them.'

'As you will.'

Raking the stamps over with his finger, Mr. Treadgold started on his task.

'Three hundred and seventy-one!' he announced at length. 'You'd better check it!'

Ruffier laughed. 'I'll take your word!'

'In any case, I'll just jot the figure down.' He produced a pencil and began to feel in his pockets for a piece of paper. The storekeeper made a move towards the counter. 'It's all right,' said the other, 'this'll do.'

A torn envelope lay on the floor. Mr. Treadgold picked it up, made a note on the back, and slipped the envelope into his pocket.

Ruffier had turned to the counter and was rewrapping the stamps. 'Voilà,' he remarked, putting the parcel down beside the visitor. 'And now, may I offer the gentleman something to drink?'

'Thanks, no!'

'A glass of caribou? It's well aged.'

'Caribou? I thought caribou was an animal?'

The storekeeper chuckled. 'It's also a drink. You shall see!' He disappeared behind the counter and returned with a bottle and two glasses, which he filled from the bottle with a ruby liquor, not unlike burgundy in appearance. 'Try that!' He handed Mr. Treadgold a glass and took one himself.

Mr. Treadgold sipped, licked appraising lips, and tried again. 'Pretty strong, isn't it? What's it made of?'

'Pure alcohol with lemon steeped in it and burnt sugar added for colouring – it's an old habitant drink. This is five or six years old – caribou improves with keeping.'

His visitor risked another sip. 'The flavour grows on one, certainly.' He glanced tentatively at the other. 'Bootleg, I suppose?'

Ruffier's black eyes glinted waggishly. 'You wouldn't suspect the mayor of breaking the law?'

Mr. Treadgold could not restrain a chuckle – the alert face quizzed him with such a roguish, impudent air.

'Someone in Quebec was telling me,' he pointed out, 'that hardly any of the liquor consumed in your French Canadian villages has paid duty.'

The storekeeper met his eye with an expression of the most delicate irony.

'I don't remember even hearing the question raised,' he observed drily.

'That reminds me,' Mr. Treadgold went on,' I suppose there's no news of Lhermite?'

His companion made a deprecatory gesture. 'He's out of the country by this!'

'Did you know that Le Borgne had escaped?'

The mayor looked glum. 'Yes. The trooper came to me for a guide. They're watching his shack.'

'It makes no odds. I fancy Bigoury had made up his mind to release him, anyway.'

The other looked up quickly. 'Indeed?'

'It's merely my impression. Do you think Lhermite could have cleared him?'

Ruffier shook his head. 'For that, I can't tell you!'

'Lhermite's disappearance is difficult to explain. Unless he had something to do with the murder...'

'Lhermite? That frightened rabbit! All he's thinking of is his licence. He's been fined already for selling liquor and it's jail for him the next time. He'll just stay under cover in Buffalo or Detroit until the fuss has blown over.'

'All that may be true. But I think he was got at. And so does Bigoury.'

The mayor's lip curled. 'An ugly suggestion, Monsieur, and worthy of the man!'

Mr. Treadgold shook his head. 'I'm sorry, but I'm afraid I agree with him. You see, Batisse, the guide, who also apparently knows something, won't talk, either...'

The other seemed to prick up his ears.

'Batisse, did you say?'

'Yes. The guide at the fishing camp. What do you know about him?'

'Nothing.' He raised his tumbler and drank.

'Please explain yourself.'

Ruffier hesitated. 'It's merely that I happened to see him going into Maître Boucheron's house this morning.'

Mr. Treadgold laughed. 'Is that all? They were probably arranging a fishing excursion.'

The storekeeper shrugged his shoulders. 'If our friend's a fisherman. I wasn't aware of it.'

His visitor said nothing, but producing his cigar-case, extended it to Ruffier, who declined. Mr. Treadgold selected a cigar and, snipping the end between thumb and first finger, said casually, 'I suppose Maître Boucheron has a pretty good practice, hasn't he?'

'He had' – the mayor was pouring himself another drink. 'Things are not going so well in that quarter, they tell me. He lost a lot of money at the time of the Wall Street crash' – with an absent air he held his glass against the candlelight. 'Between ourselves, he was round here the other day to ask me to lend him five hundred dollars.' He drank thoughtfully.

Mr. Treadgold was silent. He had lit his cigar and, having savoured the first two or three puffs, was meditatively studying the tip. Suddenly a window blew open and a hayfork clattered to the floor. They heard the wind go whistling down the village street and from the far distance the low growl of thunder. Ruffier went and closed the window.

'Well,' said Mr. Treadgold, picking up his parcel of stamps, 'I think I'll be on my way before the rain starts.'

He took his cap and cape from the counter and turned to find the storekeeper gazing at him fixedly.

'One moment, Monsieur!' The mayor's manner was faintly embarrassed. 'I'm in need of advice. Something has come to my knowledge – I'd approach Bigoury if I had any confidence in that gentleman – it concerns Maître Boucheron!'

Mr. Treadgold stopped dead in the act of slipping on his cape. 'What about him, Mayor?'

Ruffier spread his hands. 'You remember he told us that he was not back from Trois-Ponts last night until past eleven?'

'Yes...'

'Eh bien, Monsieur, that statement is inexact. Laframboise, the baker, who works all night at his ovens, saw Boucheron's car outside his house at half-past ten. Five minutes later it was gone!'

'Did the baker see Maître Boucheron?'

'No. But if his car was there, he was there. He drives himself.'

'Have you spoken to Maître Boucheron about this?'

The storekeeper squeezed his hands together uneasily.

'It's not easy to suggest to a man, especially an old friend and neighbour, that he's lying.'

Mr. Treadgold nodded briskly. 'Then say nothing to him, but leave it to me!'

Ruffier's gaze was charged with anxiety. 'It may be an honest mistake. I don't want him to think...'

'He won't know where the information comes from, I promise you.'

'And Bigoury? The man has no discretion. What guarantee have I...'

'It may not be necessary to tell him. Not until I've verified the statement, anyway.'

'You verify it?'

Mr. Treadgold coughed. 'Between ourselves, the sergeant and I don't see absolutely eye to eye on this case. So I'm doing a little hunting on my own.'

The other looked bewildered. 'You talk as if you were of the police, too!'

'I've probably had as much practical experience as our friend Bigoury, and in a city where criminals are criminals.'

Ruffier gasped – he appeared dumbfounded. 'A detective!'

Mr. Treadgold laughed as he buttoned on his cape. 'Only in my leisure moments and when I come across a case as puzzling as this one.'

The mayor was impressed – there was no doubt about it: it seemed as though he could not take his eyes off his visitor.

'You are a detective, as you collect stamps, pour le sport, hein?' he said, craning his neck at him. Then he looked the other squarely in the face. 'And are you confident of finding the answer to this puzzle?' he demanded.

Mr. Treadgold pulled on his cap and gave the mayor his hand. 'I don't despair,' he answered cryptically and, tucking the stamps under his arm, went out to the car.

The rain still held off, but the night was dank with the promise of it and pitch-black. Lights among the trees and the jingle of the radio from the central hut were a welcome relief from the darkness of the road as he drove into camp. Heavy drops pattering on the leaves sent him at a blundering lope along the duckboards, and as he entered the bungalow the rain began to fall in earnest.

Save for the reading-lamp beside the doctor's bed, the hut was in darkness. Wood, fully dressed, knees up to his chin, sprawled on the bed engrossed in Tristram Shandy. He moved his head a fraction of an inch as Mr. Treadgold switched on the centre light.

'Well?' he questioned.

His roommate heaved his cape on a chair. 'Any sign of Bigoury?'

'Not yet. Bissonnette's back. He's promised to give him your message. Well, what have you been up to?'

There was no reply. Glancing round, the doctor had a glimpse of Mr. Treadgold in his shirt-sleeves. The jacket he had taken off was hung across his arm and he had apparently been emptying the pockets, for his pipe and pouch and bunch of keys were on the dressing table. At that moment, however, he was engaged in scrutinising a scrap of paper which he held under the light.

'Hey, H. B.,' the young man called out, 'I'm talking to you!'

The other started. 'No questions, George, do you mind?' His voice sounded weary. 'I'm not fit for human society tonight!' He laid his piece of paper aside and put on his dressing-gown.

'Okay,' his companion retorted with perfect good-humour. 'Drink?'

'No, thanks!'

The doctor wriggled himself into a more comfortable pose and returned to his book. 'This Uncle Toby of yours is the grandest person,' he murmured.

For a long interval perfect silence reigned in the hut, the steady hiss of the rain the only sound. Then, as he reached for a cigarette, Wood perceived Mr. Treadgold seated at the table. With the aid of a magnifying-glass he was poring over a mass of stamps spread out on a sheet of brown paper.

The young man chortled. '"The President likes nothing better than to spend a quiet evening arranging his stamp collection,"' he quoted unctuously. And when the other ignored this sally, 'H. B.?'

'What?'

'You'll really have to talk to that young woman tomorrow!'

'What about?'

The doctor hoisted himself into an upright position. 'You tell her it must have been that rat, Boucheron, who gave her away. If she don't believe you, we'll have Bigoury up. Not that I give a damn, but she can't call me a liar to my face!' He punched a pillow viciously. 'And talking about Boucheron...'

'George,' Mr. Treadgold broke in firmly.

'What?'

'Will you please shut up?'

'But surely I can...'

'Shut up!'

As he swung in sudden exasperation towards the bed, Mr. Treadgold remarked that the doctor was staring past him and had swung his legs to the floor. Swiftly the older man whipped round.

Sergeant Bigoury stood just inside the door. He had no look or word for either of them, but, with a curiously mechanical action, was shaking the rain from his hat. His fleecy overcoat was soaked through and his whole attitude was one of profound dejection. On seeing the look on his face, Mr. Treadgold rose precipitately to his feet.

In a voice raw from fatigue Bigoury uttered a single word: 'Lhermite...'

'Well?' The question exploded like a shell on Mr. Treadgold's lips.

With an air of utter lassitude the detective dashed the moisture from his brow.

'Strangled,' he said. 'They found him in the woods tonight.'

Chapter 26

It seemed to Wood, speechless and horror-struck in the background, that an unseen hand was suddenly passed over Mr. Treadgold's face, wiping from it the last trace of that expression of benevolent tolerance which was its salient characteristic. Under their bushy brows the eyes were as cold and hard and blue as an arc-light, the features stamped with stern majesty. Like a rock he stood, gazing down from his full height upon the insignificant figure of the detective.

'Where?' he asked stolidly.

Bigoury was loosening his sopping overcoat.

'Two miles on the other side of the village, on the main road to Trois-Ponts,' he replied listlessly. 'The body was lying in the undergrowth just off the highway. It was pure chance they discovered him – a farmhand going home sent his dog in after a rabbit.'

'When did it happen?'

'Early this morning, apparently. That's to say he'd been dead for at least twelve hours, old Côté says, when he was found around seven o'clock this evening.'

'Any clues?'

'His wife says that soon after daylight gravel was thrown up at the bedroom window and he pulled on his clothes and went out, without saying where he was going. The troopers are on the job, but as far as we know nobody saw anything of him or the murderer.'

'How was it done?'

'With a noose flung from the back, I'd say. The rope's missing, of course.'

'Of course.' Mr. Treadgold nodded darkly. 'Another witness gone,' he said, as though speaking to himself, 'because he knew too much...' He paused. 'What news of Le Borgne?'

'Still at large. He's not been near his shack.' He broke off to shoot the other a quick glance from between his lashes. 'But Le Borgne didn't pull this job, Mr. Treadgold. He didn't make his breakaway until late this afternoon.'

Mr. Treadgold nodded again. 'Quite. That's why Lhermite was killed!'

The sergeant's hand stopped halfway to his mouth with a wad of gum. 'I don't get that...'

'Lhermite was killed because Le Borgne was still in jail...'

'And Lhermite could have cleared him, is that what you mean?'

'Precisely. You hadn't yet appeared on the scene and at that time there was apparently no doubt about Le Borgne's guilt. Lhermite was an inconvenient witness who had to be removed.' He paused. 'But Batisse is still alive, isn't he?'

Bigoury glowered, jaws moving. 'He'll be sorry he is before I'm through with him, if he don't come clean...'

'Are you aware that he called on Maître Boucheron first thing this morning?'

Once more the beady eyes ferreted in Mr. Treadgold's impassive face.

'Is zat so?' He made a long pause. 'I've been thinking about that guy, Mr. Treadgold. After you left the Manor this afternoon, I took another gander at them tyre-marks – with the glass, this time. Well, the off front tyre's badly worn.' He looked hard at the other. 'And so's the off front tyre on that buggy of Boucheron's!'

'Ah!' said Mr. Treadgold in a toneless voice.

'He was over to Trois-Ponts with us in it this evening. While he was in the police station, I nipped out and had a quick look. The tread on that tyre's shot to pieces!'

'I can tell you something else,' said Mr. Treadgold quietly. 'Maître Boucheron told us he didn't return from Trois-Ponts until past eleven last night. I think he should explain what his car was doing outside his house at ten-thirty.'

Bigoury glared. 'Where did you get this?'

'Laframboise, the baker, saw it standing there. Five minutes later it had disappeared.'

'Ten-thirty-five!' said the detective, rubbing his chin. 'And the rain started at a quarter of eleven. If your theory about those tyre-marks is good for anything, he must have gone straight to the Manor.' He went on rubbing. 'Could the three of them, the girl, the lawyer, and the servant, have been in this together?' His gaze wandered to Mr. Treadgold's attentive face. 'It was he who gave me the dope about the girl, you know. Why?'

'I can tell you that,' Wood broke in suddenly. 'It was for the same reason that he murdered the miller and now this poor devil, Lhermite. To divert the suspicion from himself!'

Bigoury took this outburst quite phlegmatically. 'It may be,' he remarked, chewing briskly. 'But why did he kill Adams?'

'It's as plain as the nose on your face,' the young man returned to the charge. 'It was he who'd robbed that cache – he had the keys of the house, hadn't he? He and Adams had a turn-up about the things being missing and Boucheron killed him. It's easy!'

'It would explain those mysterious footsteps,' the sergeant agreed meditatively. 'But why did he go to the Manor last night?' He glanced rather fretfully at Mr. Treadgold. 'You were quite right,' he observed, 'we shan't get anywhere until we know what brought Gideon Adams to St. Florentin. I wired his office at Toronto for a report on it this afternoon.'

Mr. Treadgold had taken his wallet from the dressing table. 'Perhaps I can throw some light on that question,' he said. He opened the wallet and extracted a letter. 'During your absence at Trois-Ponts, Sergeant,' he said, 'I took a liberty of looking round Adams's hut, next door to this.'

Bigoury frowned olympically. 'I told that fat gardien to lock it – I have the key in my pocket.' He tapped his waistcoat.

'Don't blame Tremblay,' the other rejoined quickly. 'I'm not as slim as I was, but I can still squeeze through a bathroom window. And none of these windows fasten properly. Anyhow...' He unfolded the letter. 'This letter was in the pocket of Adams's dressing-case. It's addressed to Adams at Toronto from a firm of antique dealers in Quebec – Roy and Michaud, in the rue St. Louis. It's dated the 17th of July – three weeks ago. I'll read it, shall I?'

And to the accompaniment of the rain beating pitilessly upon the roof, he read out:

Dear Sir, With reference to the Stafford cups and plates you recently purchased from us, the assistant who bought the articles on our behalf has now returned from her holidays. She states that to the best of her belief this china was offered to us, some time in June, by a woman who was not known to her. This person, who refused to give her name, was unquestionably a French Canadian and by her speech and general appearance evidently came from a country district. We note to reserve for your inspection any further articles bearing the St. Rémy crest which may come into our possession and will notify you promptly in that event. Thanking you for past patronage...

'... and so on and so forth,' Mr. Treadgold wound up. 'You have that letter of the Seigneur's, I think?' he said to the detective. 'Might I see it, please?'

Bigoury's hand went to his pocket and the two letters were exchanged.

'Listen to this,' Mr. Treadgold bade the detective tensely, looking up from the Seigneur's letter. 'He speaks here of' – his eye dropped to the sheet and he read out – "'*Your great-grandmother's Stafford tea-service inscribed with the family crest...*'" His finger tapped the letter. 'Adams must have seen portions of that service offered for sale – probably in the window of this antique shop – and instituted enquiries...' He tapped the sheet once more. 'This is what brought him to St. Florentin – he was determined to find out how these family possessions had come into the market.'

The sergeant was eagerly scanning the other letter. "'...*unquestionably a French Canadian and by her speech and general appearance evidently came from a country district,*'" he read out slowly, then raised his eyes to Mr. Treadgold. 'Boucheron has a housekeeper,' he said bleakly. 'She opened the door to me this afternoon. The description's vague, but it would fit her to a T!' He glanced at his wrist. 'Ten-twenty! Boucheron's likely to be home now – I'll see him at once!'

'Wouldn't it be better to have a word with Batisse first?' Mr. Treadgold hazarded mildly.

'I asked the coroner to have him at his house at ten. But your idea's a good one – the more we know, the more likely Boucheron will be to talk. I'll go down to the coroner's right away.'

'Then leave Boucheron until tomorrow, will you?' Mr. Treadgold's air was grave and pleading. 'We're up against an able and dangerous adversary, Sergeant, and if we leave the tiniest chink unstopped, he'll wriggle through. The picture's still far from complete. See Batisse, see Laframboise, if you will, gather every scrap of evidence you can, but hold off Boucheron until you have him thrown and tied!'

The detective frowned, but it was evident that he was impressed by this logic.

'I don't like delay...' he grumbled. 'Play a fish too long and it's apt to slip off the hook. However...' He cocked his head at the other. 'You're on to something, aren't you? Well, how much time do you want?'

Mr. Treadgold paused to consider.

'Twenty-four hours,' he said tentatively.

The sergeant nodded. 'Okay. Boucheron'll keep that long, I guess. But, get this straight, I'll be tailing him.'

Mr. Treadgold gave a little sigh. 'I understand. But for God's sake get Batisse under cover, now – tonight, or he'll be the next one to go!'

Bigoury nodded again, and again referred to his watch.

'Is the girl about?'

'She went to her room hours ago,' said Wood.

'I'll have to have her out of bed,' was the blunt rejoinder.

The doctor shrugged sulkily. 'I'll fetch her!'

'She don't have to turn out in all this rain,' the sergeant remarked not ungraciously. 'Bring her down to the dining room – I'll talk to her there!'

The young man nodded and turned towards the door.

'You'll want an umbrella or something,' Mr. Treadgold called to him. 'Here, take my cape!' He threw the long tweed cloak across to Wood, who wrapped it about him and bareheaded, darted out.

'It's about Le Borgne,' the detective confided to Mr. Treadgold when they were alone. 'He decided to talk this afternoon, it seems, but he told the Assistant District Attorney he'd talk only to the girl. They were trying to locate her when the bird hopped the nest.'

Mr. Treadgold's eyes snapped. 'Then we shall have to find Le Borgne,' he declared with emphasis.

The sergeant nodded carelessly and opened the door to discard his gum. 'We'll get him!'

'By the way,' Mr. Treadgold added ingratiatingly, 'when you see the young woman, you might make it clear to her that it isn't Wood who's been running to you with tales about her. It appears that...'

The words died away on his lips as, with an ear-splitting roar, a shot crashed out of the dripping night.

Chapter 27

For one paralysing fraction of a second the two men exchanged glances. Bigoury was the first to find his tongue. 'Holy smoke,' he squealed, 'they've got the doctor! Ah, bong jee de bong jee! Ah, zut!' He was still holding the door and he was through it like a shot from a gun. Mr. Treadgold, vaguely comprehending that it was pouring in torrents, paused only long enough to snatch his umbrella from its corner and, opening it, set off after the detective.

The path-lights had been extinguished, but the lantern on the dock dimly revealed the sergeant, hatless under the beating rain, running at full tilt along the duckboards. The shot had aroused the camp. Voices were already raised in alarm, there was the banging of doors, lights waved in and out of the dripping branches. Dashing along, umbrella down, Mr. Treadgold collided with a solid mass. Lifting his umbrella, he found himself confronted with a startling apparition in a flowing robe surmounted by a dark garment with a pointed cowl drawn over the head like a burnous. It was Tisserand, bare-legged in a long white nightshirt under a hooded raincoat of the French type.

He caught Mr. Treadgold by the arm. 'There was a shot!' he clamoured, his teeth chattering with the damp. 'Are we all to be massacred in our beds?'

'What the devil's going on?' came in an irascible shout out of the darkness under the trees, and General Rees in British warm over pink-striped pyjamas stepped onto the duckboards.

Lights appeared on verandahs and a woman's voice – Madame Tisserand's apparently – kept calling fearfully, 'Papa! Papa!' Above it Bigoury's stentorian shout rang out from the dark, 'Doctor, Doctor! Are you all right?'

Thrusting the others out of his way, Mr. Treadgold rushed on. The sergeant had disappeared, but there was a crashing in the brake and the sound of his voice calling for the doctor. Now came an answering hail, and the next moment Wood, breathless, his face streaming with water and Mr. Treadgold's cape flapping behind him, stumbled out of the thicket almost into his roommate's arms.

Mr. Treadgold caught him, held him. 'My dear fellow,' he murmured solicitously, 'thank God, we've found you! What happened?' Then, as the young man staggered, clutching at his side, 'Merciful Heaven, George, you're wounded?'

But the doctor shook his head. 'Only winded,' he wheezed. 'Fellow took a pot at me – I chased him. Gosh – I'm properly blown! Give me a moment until I get rid of this infernal stitch, will you?' He leaned back against a tree and panted.

Mr. Treadgold had a brief glimpse of Bigoury at Wood's side, then the whole pack of guests was about them. There were Tisserand and the General and Lady Gwendolyn, the last in a curious attire consisting of gum boots, blue kimono, and umbrella, Montgomery in an undervest and breeches dropping down his legs, his wife in two blankets, and one of the Misses Tisserand in sou'wester and oilskins. The last to join the group was the Angel, babbling with excitement, his shirt hanging outside his trousers like a Russian peasant's. Everybody talked at once: only Mr. Treadgold, his large umbrella held over the doctor, was content to say nothing – the doctor, doubled up against his tree, coughing and puffing, seemed glad of the respite.

'Whew!' he gasped, 'I must have run a mile!'

'But what happened, dammit?' the General broke in. 'Were you attacked or what? And who fired?'

The young man mopped his face. 'I was walking down the path on the way to the main hut,' he said. 'The lights were out and the path, as you see, is pretty dark. I was just about here or a few yards farther on when suddenly, without any warning, a shot was fired. It was quite close – I heard the bullet zip past my ear and saw the flash.'

'Where did it come from?' the General demanded.

Wood pointed to the left of the path where the ground, thickly wooded, sloped up from the lake. 'From between those trees. I flung myself flat on my face – I fancy this bird lost sight of me because he didn't fire again. Then I heard a rustling in the bushes and I jumped in after him.'

'Did you see the feller?' Rees wanted to know.

'No,' said Wood. 'But I could hear him in the undergrowth in front of me. I went after him as best I could, but I never stood a chance – it's as dark as pitch in there and the going's terrible...' He grinned round the circle of concerned faces, dimly discernible in the reflected light from the landing-stage. 'Well, I don't know how you people feel about it,' he remarked. 'But I'm getting wet!' He turned to Mr. Treadgold. 'Come on, H. B., let's go to bed!'

But the General was not to be appeased.

'This is a nice state of things, I must say, Tremblay,' he declared sternly to the gardien. 'One of our number murdered and another the victim of a deliberate and... and dastardly attempt on his life. What's become of the police who were here this afternoon? Why don't they protect us?'

'Gently, gently, my friend,' said Tisserand in French. 'Might not the doctor have failed to hear the challenge of one of Sergeant Bigoury's men, posted for our safety? For, enfin, it was dark and everybody had gone to bed.'

'He suggests that it was one of the police who fired at you because you didn't halt when challenged,' the General said to Wood.

'Rubbish,' was the uncompromising reply. 'Nobody challenged me. There was just the shot and that's all!'

Bigoury's voice came out of the darkness in the direction of the main hut. 'Is the gardien there?' A torch shone whitely and the detective came striding along the duckboards. At the sight of Tremblay, who had advanced to meet him, he stopped. 'Where's Mademoiselle de St. Rémy?' he barked.

Chapter 28

OWLISHLY TREMBLAY BLINKED AT him through his spectacles. 'Pardon?'

The sergeant seemed to choke with exasperation. 'I said, where's Mademoiselle de St. Rémy?'

'Isn't she in her room?'

'No!'

With one accord Mr. Treadgold and Wood sprang forward.

'She tol' me two hour ago she go to bed,' the gardien explained tremulously to the detective.

'Her room's empty and the bed hasn't been slept in,' was the savage rejoinder. 'You didn't see her go out?'

With a bewildered air the gardien shook his head. 'No, Monsieur!'

The detective smote his palm with his fist. 'Ah, maudit!' Then, as though for the first time aware of the grotesquely attired group behind the gardien, 'What do all these people want?' he trumpeted. 'Let them go to bed!'

With that, signalling to Mr. Treadgold and the doctor to follow them, he pounded off along the path and did not stop until they were at the central hut and out of earshot of the others. There, forestalling all questions, he abruptly asked his two companions, 'What's become of the girl?'

Both shook their heads, but it was the doctor who answered. 'She left me, just after you were called to the telephone, to go to her room.' He flashed a glance at Mr. Treadgold. 'Maybe she went to the convent after all.'

'She's not at the convent,' the sergeant snapped. 'I telephoned them just now. Besides, how would she go? She hasn't a car, has she?'

Mr. Treadgold struck in. 'I persuaded her not to go to the convent. She gave me her word to stay here.' In the ray of the naked electric bulb burning over the hut door his face was very disturbed. 'I hope to God nothing's happened to her.'

Bigoury's glasses glittered in the light as he slowly turned his head. 'Does either of you know whether she had a gun?' he asked.

'A gun?' said Wood. He caught the sergeant's arm suddenly. 'You're not suggesting she's committed suicide?'

Bigoury shook his head. 'I was thinking of that shot just now.' he rejoined quietly.

'You mean...' the doctor began, and broke off on rather a shrill laugh. 'You're screwy,' he declared angrily. 'Why on earth should she want to shoot me?'

The detective looked at Mr. Treadgold. 'Didn't you tell me just now that she accused the doctor of bringing a tale about her to me?'

'And suppose she did?' Wood broke in furiously. 'Is that to say...'

Shirt flying, the gardien came whizzing round the side of the hut. 'Docteur! Docteur!' he cried breathlessly, 'your auto!' Doubling like a hare in its tracks he ran back in the direction from which he had come. Helter-skelter they followed after, a fantastic cortège, the sergeant like a drowned rat in his sodden overcoat, Mr. Treadgold in his dressing-gown clutching his umbrella, and Wood in the tweed cape. The garage lights were on and one of the doors stood wide. 'Your char, you leave heem outside, hein?' the Angel declaimed to Wood dramatically. 'Eh bien!...' His arm described a wide arc about the empty space before the garage doors. 'And he ees not eenside!'

The sergeant pounced on Wood. 'Did you give her leave to take it?' he demanded fiercely.

'No, I did not!' the American replied with equal emphasis. 'She didn't have to ask me, anyway – she knew I wouldn't mind. But where would she be going on a night like this?'

With an authoritative air Bigoury snapped his fingers at Mr. Treadgold. 'Bissonnette went away with the car that brought me. I shall want yours. Drive me or I'll drive myself; but let's waste no time.'

Officiously the gardien fell to sliding the doors back.

'I'll drive you with pleasure,' Mr. Treadgold replied, 'but I'd like to get rid of this dressing gown...'

'No time!' Bigoury was pushing him to where, within the garage, the coupé was standing.

'But where are we going?' the other enquired mildly, closing his umbrella.

'To the Manor!'

'*The Manor?*'

'That's where she's making for. Hurry, please. Start up that engine!' They were at the coupé now – he hustled Mr. Treadgold, dressing-gown, umbrella, and all, into the driving-seat.

'But why should she go there at this time of night?' the latter persisted, his foot groping for the starter.

'Because she realises that Boucheron has double-crossed her,' was the firm reply, 'and she means to beat him to the loot they've hidden there.'

The purr of the engine drowned his voice. Bigoury sprang into the car. The Angel and Wood were raising the hood. Mr. Treadgold paused an instant while this operation was completed, then the doctor, uninvited, squeezed himself in beside the two men on the driving-seat and the car glided out into the rain.

There were a police car and two motorcycles under tarpaulins outside the Manor and from the salon windows the flicker of firelight. The front door was barred, but almost simultaneously with Bigoury's knock there was the clank of a bolt and a trooper stood before them, staring in astonishment at the extraordinary spectacle the three visitors presented.

'Mademoiselle de St. Rémy, has she been here?' the detective snapped.

A stolid head-shake. No one had been near the Manor all the evening, except the guard from Le Borgne's shack whom Corporal Thibault had relieved an hour before. Impatiently Bigoury pushed the man aside and went into the salon. An enormous log fire blazed on the hearth. Before it Jacques and a second trooper sat round an upturned crate playing cards.

'Has this man been outside tonight?' the detective demanded, indicating the servant.

He had not been out of his sight the entire evening, the first trooper replied. He had got them some food and after they had played cards together.

In response to a further question from Bigoury, the second trooper declared that Le Borgne had not reappeared at his shack.

'Go back there at once,' the detective ordered, 'and if the girl appears, bring her to me at Dr. Côté's house in the village where I'm staying!'

With rather a sullen glance at the streaming windows the trooper clumped out.

Bigoury swung to the first trooper again. 'Are all the doors and windows locked as I ordered?' he rasped.

'Yes, Sergeant!' From his tunic pocket the trooper produced a collection of keys.

'Show me!' said the detective. He turned to Jacques. 'You come with us.' The three men went into the vestibule together.

It was then that Wood, looking round for Mr. Treadgold, discovered that the latter had disappeared. Thinking that his roommate was at the car, the young man strolled as far as the front door. But the car, its headlights cutting through the steady drizzle with their glare, stood as they had left it on the avenue. From the gardens mounted, above the gurgle of gutters and the patter of the rain, the melancholy murmur of the mill-stream.

A wave of depression engulfed him. For the first time he found himself squarely facing the inference to be drawn from the girl's disappearance. Old Treadgold was no scaremonger, yet he had warned her that she was in danger – had she met the fate of the miller, of Lhermite, because she knew too much? Was she even then lying dead under some bush in the woods and would her poor, battered body, too, be ultimately dragged to the light of day?

Bitterly he blamed himself. He should never have let her leave the hut. She had misjudged him, but she had gone through a grim ordeal – her grandfather dead, the horror of that murdered man lying at her feet, and then to be hounded by this infernal detective. He should have made allowances, pocketed his pride. And now it was too late!

Behind him, on the uncarpeted boards the measured tramp of Bigoury and his companions going the rounds rang ominous. Fear gripped him, the unmanning fear of the unknown: like the chill of the dismantled house it struck to his very marrow. He closed his eyes against the vista of tossing branches framed in the doorway and the girl's face, luminous and serene, was before him: and when he gazed forth once more her face was still there, blended with the black, wet night. The thought was suddenly vivid in his mind that life for him would be as empty as those gardens under the rain were he to lose her now. A man might say a prayer – God was good to lovers. He shut his eyes and joined his hands...

So presently Mr. Treadgold, entering soft-footed from the vestibule, a lighted candle in his hand, came upon him.

At the sound of his step Wood sprang about. 'What are we doing to find her?' he exclaimed in a voice raucous with emotion. 'Are we going to let this damned detective waste precious time when perhaps – perhaps...' He broke off short, staring wildly at the other.

Without speaking Mr. Treadgold bore his candle into the salon, deposited it with others that stood in a row on the high mantelpiece, and returned.

'Where's this man Bigoury?' the doctor apostrophised him fiercely. 'Isn't he going to do anything about it?'

'Just at present he's tapping about in the attic, looking for those heirlooms,' was the toneless answer.

'He's crazy. She knows no more of them than of that shot tonight. You don't think it was she who fired at me, do you?'

The other's expression softened. 'No, George, and for a very good reason. That bullet was meant for me!'

'For you?'

A gently deprecatory smile played about the firm lips. 'Have you forgotten you were wearing my cape?'

Thunderstruck the young man glanced down at himself, then lifted a startled face. 'God!' he murmured. 'And Adrienne?' he said brokenly. 'H. B., what's happened to her?'

A look of pain crept into the kindly eyes. Mr. Treadgold shook his head. 'I can't tell you, old man – we can only hope and wait.' Then his face hardened and he squared his jaw so that his mouth under the trim moustache was a hair-line. 'But I can tell you,' he added grimly, 'that at last I know who's at the back of all this!'

Before Wood could frame the question that sprang to his lips, Bigoury swept in from the vestibule.

'To the village!' he commanded. 'We're going to call on Boucheron!'

Mr. Treadgold frowned. 'Boucheron?' He shrugged his shoulders. 'If it's to enquire about the girl, all right. But you won't let him see you suspect him?'

The sergeant faced him doggedly. 'I don't know why not!'

'You promised me twenty-four hours,' cried the other – his manner was strangely agitated. 'I hold you to your word, Sergeant. Ask him if he's seen the girl, by all means, but no third-degree stuff, do you hear? We mustn't put him on his guard!'

The detective's look was long and lingering. 'Okay,' he said drily, and added, 'Let's go!'

The rain had ceased and the stars were shining in the puddles as they threaded the sleeping village street. A light still burned above the lawyer's door. Boucheron himself opened to their ring. The sight of the trio in their odd garb clearly startled him, for he seemed to shrink back.

Mastering himself with an effort, he said to the sergeant, 'Did you wish to speak to me? Won't you come in?'

'That's all right, Maître,' Bigoury replied easily. 'It was merely to enquire whether you'd seen Mademoiselle de St. Rémy this evening.'

The notary's eyes narrowed. 'Mademoiselle de St. Rémy? No. Why?'

'She's missing from the camp. As she took the doctor's car I thought she might have gone down to the village.'

He shook his head quickly. 'She hasn't been here.'

'Have you been at home all the evening?'

'Ever since you left me before supper – I've been working on a brief. The mayor looked in for a chat – he's only just gone!'

The sergeant grunted. 'What did he want?'

'He was anxious to know if there were any news of Le Borgne. Is there?'

Bigoury shook his head. 'He hadn't seen anything of the young lady, had he?'

'No – if he had, he'd have told me. As it happens we were speaking of her.' He was growing more and more nervous under the detective's steady scrutiny. 'What should have become of her?' he demanded sharply.

The sergeant humped an indifferent shoulder. 'That's what I'm trying to find out. You can't help me, then?'

All of a sudden Boucheron seemed to lose patience. 'What makes you think I can?' he asked in a voice shrill with anger. 'I've told you all I know about this girl and I – I resent your coming here like this, pestering me with questions about something that doesn't concern me. Will you kindly understand that I've nothing to do with Mademoiselle de St. Rémy or she with me? I've not exchanged a dozen words with her, as I informed you this afternoon!'

Bigoury received this explosion with characteristic phlegm. 'Okay,' he remarked dispassionately. 'In that case, I won't keep you longer from your bed. Good night, Maître!'

'Good night!' The door closed with a bang.

'And now what?' Wood demanded feverishly of the detective.

Bigoury prodded him in the chest with his finger. 'Bed for you two gentlemen. There's nothing more you can do tonight.'

'But the girl, man, the girl! We've got to find her.'

The sergeant grunted. 'We'll find her all right. By the way, what's the number of that car of yours?' The doctor gave it and Bigoury jotted it down in his book. 'Once this number's circulated,' he remarked, tapping the book as he put it away, 'she won't go far!'

'You mean you think she's bolted?'

'Yeah. And halfway to Quebec by this. Well, Bissonnette?'

The constable had materialised out of the shadows of the street. 'Batisse, Sergeant,' he said in a low voice. 'He's waiting!'

'Okay. Where are those two plain-clothes men who came with us from Trois-Ponts?'

'At the coroner's, Sergeant!'

The detective pointed at the notary's house. 'From now on I want a report on his movements. He's not to be interfered with nor must he suspect that he's under observation, but I wish to know where he goes and whom he sees. Put those two on to it and listen, tell them to keep out of sight – we don't want the entire village talking!'

'Very good, Sergeant!' As the man vanished into the darkness, Bigoury turned to Mr. Treadgold. 'I'm taking one hell of a risk laying off this guy. I suppose you realise that?' he said crossly.

The other shrugged. 'As long as he feels himself safe, I don't think you have to worry. But I appreciate it all the same.'

'Your twenty-four hours expires at nine tomorrow night. I don't hold off a minute after that.'

Mr. Treadgold sighed. 'Very good.' His air was careworn.

'Okay. I'll have him at the Manor at nine. You'll be there, of course, and the doc, if he likes, but no one else – I'm not going to have the village elders gumming things up again. In the meantime, I can use the delay – I'd like to have Le Borgne and the girl on hand when we get down to business. No, don't trouble,' as Mr. Treadgold opened the car door, 'it's only just up the street.' Saluting the two men with his hand, he set off briskly towards the coroner's house.

By this time Wood was almost frantic. Mr. Treadgold had considerable difficulty in persuading him to enter the car.

'The fact that she borrowed your bus, George,' he remarked as they drove back to camp, 'suggests to me that she went off on some deliberate errand. What this could be I've no idea, unless...' He broke off abruptly.

'Like this comic detective of theirs, I suppose you think she's lit out, is that it?' the young man exclaimed angrily. 'Well, I tell you, you're all wet! She's not the sort that runs away. If she's missing, it's because she's been kidnapped, and they used my car for the job!'

'Let's hope you're both wrong,' observed his companion placidly. 'For myself I shouldn't be surprised to see her back tonight!' The doctor's questioning could draw no further word from him and presently they reached the camp. The first thing they perceived, held in the glare of the headlights, was the missing roadster, heavily mud-splashed, standing before the garage.

Almost before they had stopped, the gardien's fat face appeared at Mr. Treadgold's elbow.

'Mademoiselle ees return a leetle after you leave,' he announced confidentially. 'She say she take doctor's auto, go leetle drive...'

Wood was already out of the car. 'Where is she?' he shouted.

'She ask for Mis' Treadgold,' was the ingratiating reply. 'She say she go to your camp, wait for 'eem!'

With an incoherent exclamation the American dashed away into the darkness.

As he burst into the hut, the girl rose up quickly. She had a coloured scarf bound gipsy fashion about her hair and wore a heavy black-and-white travelling ulster over her evening frock. At the sight of him her face brightened, and she seemed about to speak when his first words silenced her.

'What's the idea of disappearing like this?' he stormed. 'Are you aware that we've been ransacking the countryside for you? Why couldn't you have told someone you were going out?'

With a little air of perplexity she gazed at him. 'Oh, dear,' she sighed, 'I was afraid you'd be annoyed. I shouldn't have taken your car without asking you. But I was afraid…'

'Damn the car! Here I've been thinking you were kidnapped or dead or something and all the time you were just joy-riding! You're a selfish, inconsiderate person and – darn it, didn't it ever occur to you that I'd be half-crazy with anxiety?'

Her look was penitent. 'I'm sorry…'

'Like hell you're sorry,' he retorted mockingly. 'First you call me a liar to my face and then you go and do a thing like this…'

'I couldn't help myself,' she answered with spirit. 'I had to have a car, so I took yours. If I'd asked your permission, you'd have wanted to go with me or you'd have told Mr. Treadgold and he'd have stopped it. I didn't damage the car – I drive quite well…'

'Why must you keep harping on the car?' he cried in exasperation. 'It's you I mean, you, can't you understand? Do you realise what I've been through tonight, believing you were dead, murdered like the others?'

She was staring at him dumbfounded, her eyes starry, her lips parted in a little smile.

'Oh, Georges,' she murmured. Seeing that he was looking sullenly away, she went to him and put her hands on his coat. 'I can realise very well,' she said simply, 'for I felt the same about you when the gardien told me how they'd tried to kill you tonight...'

He caught at her hands. But she snatched them away, covering her face.

'I treated you so badly,' she whispered, 'and I'm so ashamed!'

He put his arms about her, resting his cheek against one of the hands imprisoning her face.

'I thought I'd lost you,' he murmured. 'Adrienne, sweetness, I can scarcely believe that I've found you again...'

The touch of her hand was cool on his forehead as her fingers lightly caressed his hair.

'Georges, dear Georges,' she sighed.

Then she slipped out of his arms. Wood, veering about, saw Mr. Treadgold in the doorway.

'Gosh,' he declared disgustedly, 'if it isn't Uncle Toby himself.' And before his roommate could speak, he went on, 'How'd you care to go take a little jump in the lake, H. B.?'

Mr. Treadgold laughed good-humouredly. 'I see that you young people have composed your differences,' he remarked. 'I should be delighted to take the hint, my dear George, but Mademoiselle Adrienne and I have to have a little chat. As for you,' he went on, with a whimsical glance at his roommate, 'how would you like to ring up Bigoury and let him know that Mademoiselle's back?'

'Not at all,' was the prompt reply. 'Mademoiselle and I have one or two very important matters to discuss ourselves.'

Mr. Treadgold smiled. 'Listen, George. Bigoury has to be told and at once. If this is handled right, we can head him off until tomorrow evening. Otherwise... Now, pay attention! You'll say that Mademoiselle in a fit of panic took your car and drove off, intending to disappear. When she came to her senses she returned and is now in a state of collapse.'

'Right. But why shouldn't you tell him?'

'Because I'm not a doctor, you juggins – you are. Say you've ordered her to bed for a complete rest and you won't be responsible for her reason if she's disturbed. Call it what you like, give him the Greek and Latin for nervous prostration, stun him with the whole pharmacopoeia, but head him off the Mademoiselle at least until tomorrow evening. Do you get the idea?'

'Sure. But won't he think...'

'I don't care a damn what he thinks, as long as he keeps away from her. Besides, for the time being, the only place where she's in safety is in her room with the door locked.'

The young man nodded sagely. 'I get you.' He turned to the girl. 'You'll see me as far as the verandah at least?'

She followed him outside. There he gathered her into his arms and kissed her.

'It would have saved a lot of misunderstanding if I'd done that before,' he remarked, and kissed her again. 'And by the way,' he remarked, 'I believe I can explain...'

Leaning back in his arms, she put her hand on his mouth. 'No explanations!' she said softly. 'Let's forget everything but this!'

So saying she drew his face down to hers and kissed him tenderly on the lips. Then she ran into the hut.

Mr. Treadgold was standing at the table, waiting for her. For a moment the kindly eyes rested shrewdly on her flushed face.

'About tonight,' he said at length, 'you found him, eh?'

She uttered a little gasp of wonder. 'How did you know?'

He smiled. 'The old recipe – clear thinking. For the rest, you asked for me, so I conclude you've something to report.' He pointed to a chair. 'Sit down there and tell me what Le Borgne said!'

Chapter 29

THE BATS WERE SKIMMING about the village street next evening when, towards the hour of half-past eight, George Wood drove up to Ruffier's store. It was the close of a day which had proved sheerly unbearable for the doctor. His nerves were on edge. The gentle melancholy of sundown only had the effect of increasing the impatience with which he awaited the fall of night. With a jaundiced eye he contemplated the leisurely pageantry of the dying sun – the fading splendour of the western sky, the growing sombreness of the woods laid in a frieze against the lemon glow, seemed to heighten the sense of foreboding which had haunted him all day.

In the twilit store, the mayor was a dim figure at the shelves, stacking cans, in shirt-sleeves and tweed cap. Close-by, a gangling individual in a mackinaw shirt smoked his pipe on an upturned box – it was Laframboise, the baker, who had discovered Le Borgne's blood-stained brogues.

'Ah, Docteur...'

Deferential and smiling, Ruffier bustled forward. Wood had a letter in his hand.

'From Mr. Treadgold,' he announced, tendering the letter. 'I was to give it to you personally.'

The storekeeper wiggled a disclaiming finger. 'No spik English,' he intoned protestingly. But he took the letter, turning it over dubiously in his strong hands. Then his look appealed to the baker, who, pausing only to spit with unerring aim into a box of sawdust three feet away, proceeded to translate the doctor's remark into French.

'Ah!' said the mayor, his face lighting up. 'Excusez, Messieurs!' He broke the seal, read with unrevealing features the few lines the note contained, and slipped it into his pocket. 'Et Mademoiselle,' he enquired of the visitor solicitously, 'comment va-t-elle ce soir?'

Wood was not unprepared for the question. Since the girl was supposedly confined to her room, it had been found necessary to postpone the Seigneur's funeral for twenty-four hours, with the result that the story of her collapse was common property in the village. She was sleeping, he replied. Mademoiselle dort – that, at least, was one French phrase he had learnt.

His tone was dispirited. Actually, he had not set eyes on her since that unforgettable moment on the verandah the previous night. Every time he had gone to the gardien's house to try to see her, Madame Tremblay had interposed her ample bulk between him and the stairs with the same, unvarying announcement, 'Mademoiselle dort!' As the girl's doctor he might have insisted on going to her room, but he was restrained by the suspicion that Mr. Treadgold was responsible for keeping her out of sight. As for Mr. Treadgold, he had already disappeared when his roommate opened his eyes that morning. He was absent all day until, supper past, he had stormed into the hut, typed off this note on his portable, and requested the doctor to deliver it personally into Ruffier's hands without delay – no answer was required. George could come on to the Manor from the village – they were to meet Bigoury there at nine o'clock, Mr. Treadgold reminded him.

Wood was sore with his roommate. He had still to learn where the girl had been in his car on the previous night, for, on returning from a long and exhausting session on the telephone with Bigoury, he had found the girl gone and Mr. Treadgold already in bed and to all appearances asleep. He was anxious, too. The rendezvous at the Manor weighed heavy on his mind. He had not seen Bigoury all day. But that, he told himself, was merely because he had impressed the detective with the belief that the girl was really ill: he had the feeling that Bigoury still regarded her as Boucheron's accomplice. Did Mr. Treadgold think so, too? And was his solicitude for her safety just a ruse to separate her from the only person who had believed in her innocence from the start? As the day waned and the hour of the meeting drew nearer, the young man found himself obsessed with a growing concern.

He was aware that Ruffier was saying something to him in French. Once more the baker came to the rescue.

'Mis' Ruffier, he say investigation go on very nice now...'

'Sure,' said Wood absently.

Another flood of French from the mayor and Laframboise went on, 'Mis' Ruffier say, pretty good thing Batisse talk...'

The doctor was startled out of his lethargy.

'You don't mean to say he's confessed to these murders?' he asked.

'No,' the baker replied stolidly. 'But he tell Inspector he take letter from Mis' Adams to Mis' Boucheron the day Mis' Adams arrive, let Mis' Boucheron know Mis' Adams at the camp, I guess, only Mis' Boucheron away to Quebec when Batisse bring letter and he don't get heem for two, t'ree day!'

He rolled this off at top speed in his broken English, then looked towards the mayor and repeated the statement in French.

'But if this is true,' Wood struck in, 'why didn't Maître Boucheron mention it?'

The baker laughed knowingly. 'Lawyers ver' careful – no tell much!' He chuckled at his joke.

Ruffier had resumed stacking his cans. Bidding the two men good night, the doctor went out to his car.

At the Manor the detective's voice was audible in the salon. Wood's first glance was for the girl. He was struck by her tense air. But her face was eagerly turned towards the door by which he entered and his heart leaped, for he knew she had been watching for his arrival. At the sight of her all the cares of the day seemed to slip away – the smile she had for him, brief yet full of secret understanding, told him so surely that the old intimacy was re-established between them.

By this time it was almost dark outside and a row of candles on the mantelpiece cast a lurid light round the bare room. A table had been fetched from somewhere and an oil lamp placed upon it threw into relief the detective's hairy and sinewy hands planted palms downwards as, standing, he leaned towards Maître Boucheron, who confronted him, arms folded, in a chair. Mr. Treadgold sat apart, nursing his knee with an aloof air. He looked up on Wood's entry – his glance questioned, 'Well?'

Someone brought the doctor a chair. It was Jacques, tight-lipped and pallid. Wood signalled to him to put it next to Mr. Treadgold. As the young man sat down, he whispered to his roommate, 'Okay!' Mr. Treadgold said nothing, but his face glowed with satisfaction. It was only for a moment, then he reverted to his attitude of studied detachment.

Constable Bissonnette closed the door. The atmosphere was taut with suspense. The detective's voice grated on the stillness.

Chapter 30

'You admit, then, Maître, that these rents were paid?'

Gravely Boucheron inclined his head. 'Yes.'

'As the result of the death of the Seigneur's sister, you say, the legal position was unclear and you therefore decided to withhold this money? Was this at Adams's request?'

'No.'

'But you knew Mr. Adams?'

'I'd met him...'

'But you were not aware of his presence at St. Florentin?'

The lawyer cleared his throat. 'I've already told you I was absent in Quebec at the time of his arrival. Mr. Adams, I believe, reached the camp last Sunday and I didn't get home until Tuesday afternoon.'

Wood caught his breath. He was following the conversation sufficiently to perceive that Boucheron evaded the question. What about that note of Adams the baker had spoken of? Bigoury must know all about it, for it was he who had wormed this fact out of Batisse, hadn't Laframboise said? Yet the detective's manner betrayed nothing, and Boucheron evinced no trace of embarrassment. The notary's air was cool – condescending, even – his pose relaxed. This was not the Boucheron they had seen on the night of the murder, flamboyant, mercurial, restless. The man was on his guard, summoning all his wit and energy to the task of controlling his nerves.

The sergeant did not press the point, but proceeded evenly:

'What were you doing in Quebec, Maître?'

'I had to attend at the Palais de Justice in connection with a succession case.'

Bigoury consulted a slip of paper. 'Know a firm there called Roy and Michaud?'

'A legal firm?'

'No. Antique dealers.'

Boucheron shook his head. 'I don't know any antique dealers in Quebec.'

The detective paused. 'You were acquainted with the contents of the Manor, were you?'

'Generally speaking, yes.'

'Certain family treasures didn't appear at the auction...' He referred to his notes again. 'Among them a gold snuffbox, some silver and porcelain. Why not?'

Boucheron shrugged. 'We assumed that the Seigneur had taken them with him to France.'

'You didn't know that he'd concealed them in the attic?'

The olive face was impassive. 'I certainly did not.'

'Adams knew – that's what brought him to St. Florentin!'

The lawyer raised his shoulders again. 'Then he was better informed than I...'

'You were not aware, then, that these valuables had been stolen from their hiding-place at the Manor...'

'I was not.'

The sergeant's expression hardened. 'Surely it was your business to know these things? You were the Seigneur's representative, you had the keys of the house. Hasn't it occurred to you that the Seigneur sent for you last night because he had discovered the theft and intended to call you to account?'

'I don't know why he sent for me.'

Bigoury nodded stonily. 'At what time did you get back from Trois-Ponts last night?'

'I can't say to a minute. It was after eleven, anyway.'

'Then what was your car doing outside your house at half-past ten?' Seeing that Boucheron was in the act of shaking his head, the sergeant shot out a warning finger. 'Mind how you answer, Maître Boucheron,' he cried sharply. 'I've a witness!'

For the first time the notary changed colour. Unfolding his arms he slowly rubbed his palms together.

'It's possible I may have been mistaken in the time,' he replied, with a slightly offended air.

'Then you might have been back by ten-thirty?' the sergeant insisted.

'If you say so!'

Bigoury adjusted his glasses. 'Thank you!' He picked up his notes once more. 'Why did you send for the guide Batisse this morning?'

Boucheron had regained his composure. He laughed easily. 'I'd heard a rumour that he could clear Le Borgne. I thought I'd question him.'

'It wasn't to give him a hundred dollars to keep his mouth shut about those notes from Adams he left at your house – one on Sunday and another last night?'

The lawyer sprang to his feet angrily. 'It's a lie!'

'It's the truth!'

'I know this drunken ne'er-do-well and I know police methods, too. I don't suppose you sat up until dawn pumping this ruffian for nothing. Suborning witnesses will do your case no good, Inspector. I stand for something in these parts, let me tell you and...'

'What were you doing up at the Manor on the night of the murder?'

The detective's question exploded like a firecracker.

The angry voice fell silent. Boucheron cleared his throat.

'These gentlemen will bear me out,' he said, looking from the doctor to Mr. Treadgold. 'I went there with the coroner.'

'I mean before that – before these gentlemen or anybody appeared on the scene?'

'I was nowhere near the Manor – I was at Trois-Ponts.'

'Not at half-past ten, I think? And if you were in the village at half-past ten you could have been up here at a quarter to eleven, I believe you'll agree?'

The dark eyes blazed: the man's face was livid. 'It's preposterous! Are you suggesting that it was I who...'

Unexpectedly Mr. Treadgold's calm voice struck in. 'If I might be permitted to say a word?' he remarked in his deliberate French. He turned to the notary. 'Maître Boucheron,' he said, 'Sergeant Bigoury's suspicions are based on certain footprints which were discovered in the grounds.'

The detective flushed with anger. 'I must really ask you, Monsieur, to leave this matter to me.'

But, without heeding him, Mr. Treadgold went on, staring hard at the lawyer's feet: 'You see, Maître, these footprints are narrow and pointed. They correspond fairly closely to the pattern of the shoes you're wearing.'

Bigoury's face was a study. Open-mouthed he was staring at the persistent rebel.

'Eh bien,' Boucheron broke in triumphantly, 'I give you your answer. I was wearing goloshes last night and the girl who keeps the garderobe at the Gerbe d'Or Hotel at Trois-Ponts can prove it, because, when leaving last night, I forgot them and had to go back.'

His words fell on a strange silence. Mr. Treadgold had resumed his air of careful aloofness while the detective was turning over his papers.

'Far from reproving this gentleman,' the notary concluded severely, 'you should thank him for preventing you from making a fool of yourself!'

'And yet,' Bigoury declared impassively, 'you were here at the hour I say!' He made a deliberate break. 'You see, those footprints were left by someone wearing goloshes, someone who stood outside the linen room window. I can give you almost the exact time – it was just before the rain stopped at eleven.'

The notary was trembling. In the fitful light the sweat made gleaming patches on his forehead and cheeks. He glanced about him wildly.

'It's a lie!' he screamed suddenly. 'It's a plot to ruin me!'

'You were here before eleven,' the detective flung back at him in a voice deep with menace. 'From ten-forty-five until after the rain stopped, your car stood at the side door – the marks of your tyres are there to prove it. You went to meet Adams who'd sent you word by Batisse that he was going to the Manor – you found the note when you got home. Don't trouble to deny it – I've got sworn statements from Batisse and from Laframboise who saw your car outside your house. You were broke and desperate. Those rents you were embezzling were virtually all you had to live on, and if the Seigneur should find out that it was you who'd robbed the cache and that you were selling the things to dealers in Quebec, it was ruin for you. You killed Adams to prevent him denouncing you, just as you killed the miller who'd probably seen you carting the stuff away, and Lhermite because he could have cleared Le Borgne whom your friends in the village had obligingly framed for you. And when things began to look bad for you, you tried to switch the guilt onto Mademoiselle de St. Rémy, your accomplice. Where did she go last night? To meet you, wasn't it? Come on,' he trumpeted, 'let's have the truth!'

Boucheron had sunk down on his chair. 'All right,' he said in a hollow voice, 'I'll tell you. But let someone fetch me a glass of water!'

Wood was looking at Adrienne. He had not followed Bigoury very well, but he had heard the girl's name, and the sergeant's angry tone told him the rest. Her serene expression, however, reassured him. She sat with her hands in her lap, her bright gaze fastened on the figure slumped in the chair.

Jacques brought water and stood by while Boucheron wet his lips. Then, casting back a dank, black lock from his forehead, the lawyer began to speak, staring on the ground with head sunk.

'When Mrs. Adams died six months ago,' he said miserably,' I began to keep back those rents. I was hard-pressed for money and I calculated that the Seigneur would think Adams had ordered me to withhold them. But I know nothing about those heirlooms and I didn't kill Adams or the others.'

Bigoury snorted irascibly. 'I've no time to waste on your denials,' he rasped. 'You're guilty and you know it!'

Mr. Treadgold leaned to the detective's ear. Bigoury shrugged and, taking out a piece of gum, started to strip it. But he allowed the lawyer to proceed.

'If it hadn't been for those rents, I'd have spoken up before,' Boucheron resumed in the same despairing tone. 'But I could see that here was a motive for the murder directly incriminating me and...' He shrugged. 'Adams did write to me last Sunday that he was at the camp and wished to see me,' he went on. 'But on getting in from Quebec on Tuesday afternoon, I found a mass of work awaiting me at the office and I did not have a chance to open my mail until I came back from the presbytery where I spent the evening in company with this gentleman.' His hand indicated Mr. Treadgold. 'Adams's note was among my letters. It was too late to do anything that night and next day I had to be in court at Trois-Ponts. So I let the matter lie for then. But on reaching home from Trois-Ponts on the following night, I found another note from Adams pushed under the door.'

'You have that note?' Mr. Treadgold asked.

The notary shook his head. 'I destroyed it. But I can tell you what was in it. He wrote angrily. He said that lights had been seen that night in the Manor and that he was going over to investigate; that it was of no use my trying to avoid him – I'd better meet him there with the keys and explain myself.'

'So you went?' said Mr. Treadgold.

Boucheron nodded, 'I had a presentiment that the Seigneur had returned – he'd threatened to do so in one of the letters he wrote me about the rents...' He stopped.

'Go on!' Bigoury snapped.

'I had the key of the stables entrance,' said Boucheron, 'but I decided to investigate before entering the house. So I left my car at the side entrance and crept round to the front. There was a light at the side and going along the path I saw that it came from the linen room. The shutter was ajar, but the window beyond was flung back and there were voices in the room. I peered through. Adams and the Seigneur were there, standing up, facing one another across the table. The Seigneur was crying out in a voice terrible with rage, "I've been robbed! I've been robbed!" And I realised that he'd told Adams about the rents.'

'Why shouldn't he have been speaking about the things he'd hidden in the attic?'

'It was the rents. Adams had a pencil in his hand – that gold pencil of his which was found under the body – and a piece of paper. There was an hotel bill in his pocket, do you remember? With some figures pencilled on the back. Well, those were the totals of the rents, reckoned yearly, half-yearly, and quarterly. They'd evidently been discussing it!'

Bigoury had turned his eyes away from the speaker to look at the girl. He said nothing, but the glance he gave her was faintly quizzical. His regard swung back to Boucheron.

'And then?' he barked.

'Some remarks were exchanged which I couldn't catch,' the notary replied. 'Then, suddenly, Monsieur de St. Rémy pushed Adams aside and ran out into the vestibule. Adams snatched up the lamp from the table and followed after. And I fled back to the car.'

'And that's all you know about it, eh?' the sergeant said drily.

With flashing eye the notary raised his hand aloft. 'As God is my witness, it is the truth!'

Bigoury was gathering up his papers. 'I shall detain you on suspicion,' he announced crisply. 'A summary of your statement will be prepared for you to sign. We start for Trois-Ponts at once...' He broke off impatiently. 'Well, what is it?'

Mr. Treadgold, watch in hand, stood beside him. 'One moment,' said Mr. Treadgold.

Taking the detective aside he spoke lengthily in his ear. Boucheron, with his head between his hands, was an image of despair.

Wood went over to the girl. 'Well,' he said cheerfully, 'if my French isn't all at sea, you're cleared! Didn't I understand him to say he'd seen Adams with that gold pencil of yours in his hand before ever he was killed?'

She nodded. 'I must have caught it on something and Grandpapa found it, perhaps on the linen room floor. Either he lent it to Adams or it was lying on the table...'

He was looking at her intently. 'But, honey, you're trembling,' he exclaimed. He caught her hands. 'And your hands are as cold as ice!'

Her teeth were chattering, her eyes bleak with fear. 'I can't help it,' she said in a low voice. 'Something terrible is going to happen. Mr. Treadgold...'

Bigoury's voice rang through the room. 'Thibault – Laflamme' – the two troopers sprang to attention – 'I leave this man in your custody. Search him and see that he's not armed. Bissonnette, you come with me!' He glanced round the salon. 'See that no one leaves the house until I return. Wait a minute – where's Jacques?' he asked the constable.

'He took the tray back to the kitchen, Sergeant,' Bissonnette replied.

'I want him here where we can keep an eye on him. Thibault will attend to it. Come on!' He strode to where Mr. Treadgold was waiting at the door.

Without a word the doctor had left the girl's side. Seeing him approach, Mr. Treadgold stopped short in the act of following Bigoury and the constable into the hall. His look was sour, his eyes were pin-points of steel.

'No, George,' he said peremptorily, 'you keep out of this.'

'I've been kept out of things long enough, it seems to me,' retorted the young man, bristling. 'I don't know where you're going, but I'm coming, too.'

The blue eyes softened. 'You've had one narrow escape, old man. Leave this to us, will you?'

Wood laughed. 'You wouldn't do that to your faithful Corporal Trim, would you? Lead on, Uncle Toby! I'm with you!'

He clapped his arm about Mr. Treadgold's shoulder and, glancing round for the girl, saw her, with her thin hands folded across her breast, gazing at him beseechingly. He waved his hand at her, then, perceiving that Mr. Treadgold had gone on, hurried out after him.

Chapter 31

THE AIR WAS LIKE velvet, the night ablaze with stars. The moon had not yet risen and the darkness vibrated with the chorus of crickets and frogs. Under a tree across the gravel space before the house, out of reach of the glow from the salon windows, Mr. Treadgold was haranguing the sergeant in an undertone.

'This job has to be done in the dark,' he was saying as Wood joined the group. 'Therefore, no lights and, above all, no talking, once we start.' He held his watch to a glimmer of light from the porch. 'We shall have to wait a little, but not for long. Psst, who's that?'

A trooper was silhouetted against the lighted doorway. 'Are you there, Sergeant?' he called softly.

Bigoury stepped out from under the tree.

The man was breathless and rather agitated. 'It's Jacques, Sergeant. He's not in the house!'

'Not in the house?' Bigoury swore under his breath, and turned to Mr. Treadgold. 'Do you hear that? Now Jacques has disappeared.'

'No matter,' the other struck in irritably. 'Let's get going – we've no time to lose. And listen, Sergeant – keep those men of yours in the house, do you mind?'

Bigoury whispered the order. The trooper was about to retire when Mr. Treadgold said: 'Wait! Has that man a gun? Let the doctor have it, will you?' On a word from Bigoury the trooper passed his automatic across: then he returned to the house. 'You brought a gun as I told you?' Mr. Treadgold asked the detective. Bigoury patted his pocket. 'You, too, constable?' The officer nodded. 'All right,' said Mr. Treadgold. 'Then follow me! And not a sound, do you hear?'

Their way led through the gardens down a path which, after skirting the trout pool, dropped steeply between high banks towards the road. A little and they were out of sight of the house, under the hillside, moving in Indian file in the obscurity of overspreading branches. Here the sound of running water was much louder: the gardens smelled sweet in the night air. Presently they brushed through a gap in a hedge and the rough grass of a paddock was under their feet. Now that they were clear of the trees, the darkness had lifted a trifle and they made out the line of a building black against the sky. 'The old mill!' whispered Bigoury, pointing, to Wood, who was behind him. Mr. Treadgold angrily motioned him to silence.

It immediately became evident that it was for the mill they were heading. They followed a high, blank wall round the angle of the building and thereafter some palings which brought them to a rickety wooden gate. Here Mr. Treadgold left them and, noiselessly forcing his way between two loose timbers of the gate, disappeared. It was several minutes before his low 'Hist!' summoned them to join him.

He was waiting for them in a small yard sunk below the level of the highway, the guard-rails of which, gleaming whitely in the dark, were visible above the lattice fence enclosing the far side of the yard. By this their eyes were growing used to the obscurity, and they could see that a door in the side of the mill-house was partly open. A wooden ramp led up to it – evidently it was the entrance at which the grain was delivered.

Mr. Treadgold's whisper rustled sibilantly. 'Sergeant?'

'Here!'

'I'd like Bissonnette to stay outside the gate – there are some bushes outside where he can take cover. He's not to interfere with anyone going in, but he must stop anyone who tries to leave. Will you tell him, please?'

'Okay!' The constable tiptoed away. 'You and I and the doctor,' Mr. Treadgold said to Bigoury, 'will post ourselves behind that cart there.' The glare of a torch revealed a farm cart standing in a corner of the yard. 'But one thing I beg,' he added, switching off his light, 'whatever you see, do nothing until I give the signal. From now on, not a sound, on your life!'

In that hollow, overshadowed on one side by the oblong mass of the mill, on the other by a screen of tall trees with branches overhanging the containing wall, the darkness was Stygian. From where they stood they could only just distinguish the outline of the mill door and the ramp that led up to it. Only in the centre of the yard a faint reflection in the night sky relieved the obscurity.

Out of the silence that succeeded to their whispers and the stealthy creaking of the sergeant's shoes all manner of little sounds, the noises of the countryside at night, began to mount. Far away a train whistled mournfully above the crescendo rattle of flying wheels; down in the village a dog howled; and from time to time the distant clatter of a buggy was wafted over the stillness. Now it was an owl that flew across the yard hooting; now a crane uttering its strident call in the marshes by the river; or some other eerie cry echoing back from the surrounding woods.

At their observation post the three men were motionless. So quiet was it in the yard that Wood could hear the ticking of his watch. The detective was at one end of the cart, peering round the tail of it at the dim door, Wood at the other, Mr. Treadgold between, crouched down, gazing through the spokes of the tall wheels. Suddenly Wood saw him stiffen, straighten up. Someone was passing on the road.

The footsteps were clearly audible, coming from the direction of the crossroads. Then they ceased abruptly as though the unseen pedestrian had left the hard macadam and taken to the roadside grass. With bated breath the three men waited, their faces lifted to the highway above the lattice fence – the line of white posts must surely show up anyone who passed the mill. But the road remained deserted: once more the yard was plunged in silence.

And then a faint sound. Someone was at the lattice fence. They heard it creak, saw it move. Behind it, below the highway, the shadows were inky black; but a darker shadow seemed to hover there. The fence shivered and shook; a lath snapped; the shadow had melted away.

Wood felt Mr. Treadgold behind him. He turned and tried to peer into the other's face. But Mr. Treadgold was staring into the darkness and gave no sign.

There was a movement in the shadow under the house. A dark shape was sidling stealthily towards the ramp. It made no sound; it was no more than a ripple on the surface of the night.

The ramp was faintly grey against the surrounding gloom. It seemed to Wood, straining his eyes into the darkness, that some unfamiliar outline obtruded itself upon that lighter background. He caught his breath and touched Mr. Treadgold's arm, silently pointing. Dimly silhouetted against the ramp was a hooded head furtively craned towards the open door. Still Mr. Treadgold made no move, and when the doctor looked again, the ramp was once more a smooth grey patch.

Once more the yard lay dark and deserted before them. Wood's heart was thumping against his ribs. This shadow that came and went, it was like the trout he loved to watch, lying motionless in the holes under the riverbank; noiseless and elusive, it seemed able to merge itself into its surroundings and disappear, even as they. There was still no sound and no further movement was discernible. Yet somewhere in the darkness about them that hooded figure lurked.

The distant stroke of a bell was wafted through the stillness. It was the church clock. Wood counted. Ten o'clock! He wondered how much longer they were to wait there. His throat tickled: he was seized by an irresistible desire to cough.

A board creaked and he was aware that the door at the top of the ramp had opened. A dim shape was outlined on the threshold, looking out. There was a long pause, then a match was scratched. The tiny flame, carefully cupped against the air, lit up a savage, hairy face. It was Le Borgne. The flame rose and fell to the accompaniment of a sucking noise as he lit his pipe. Then the match went out and once more the doorway was a black void – the man had disappeared inside the mill.

Something brushed Wood's face. It was Bigoury's sleeve as the detective, leaning across him, silently touched Mr. Treadgold's arm. But Mr. Treadgold raised his hand in a gesture that said 'Wait!'

The shadows under the house seemed to tremble. The hooded figure had appeared again. They had only a momentary glimpse of it, for the next second it had flashed up the ramp and vanished through the door. Mr. Treadgold's tense 'Now!' as, pistol in hand, he sprang out from their hiding-place was answered by a muffled cry from the house.

Within the mill a wild hubbub had broken out. Mr. Treadgold had disappeared inside. A cloud of prickly chaff dust caught his companions by the throat as they burst across the threshold and found themselves in a stifling, stagnant darkness that was all alive with the slither of feet and the sounds of hard breathing. Wood heard Mr. Treadgold's warning cry, 'Guard the door!' and almost simultaneously a heavy body struck him and sent him reeling backwards against some rigid obstacle.

The door slammed. Gathering himself up, Wood remembered the flashlight in his hand and switched it on. The scuffling had abruptly ceased. All about him were huge beams, upright and transverse, and a welter of ancient, clumsy mill machinery – he had crashed into the timber framework enclosing the millstones. Not three feet away Le Borgne was standing with the blood running down his stubbly cheeks and Bigoury, brandishing his gun, was close by. Then a torch glared in the back of the room and Mr. Treadgold's voice, sharp and commanding, rang out in French, 'Put down that knife! I have you covered!' With one accord the three men rushed towards the sound.

Pistol in one hand, torch in the other, Mr. Treadgold faced an angle of the wall. It was an instant before they were aware of the strange apparition which, partly concealed by a corn-bin, confronted him, for its unfamiliar outline was all but merged in its dim and dusty background. It was an eerie-looking figure, faceless by reason of the burlap bag drawn over the head, with two holes for the eyes. The hands were gloved and one grasped a long, gleaming butcher's knife. The figure did not move.

'Put down that knife!' Mr. Treadgold ordered again. A pause, then the knife pitched tinkling on the planking at their feet.

Bigoury's dry laugh rang hollow under the low roof. 'So, it was friend Jacques, after all!' he said mockingly. 'Hold him there,' he bade Mr. Treadgold, 'while I summon the good Bissonnette with the darbies for the gentleman!' So saying, he clapped a whistle to his lips and, turning towards the door, blew a succession of piercing blasts. He had switched on his torch and its beam, cleaving the darkness, revealed the burly form of Jacques planted before the entrance.

With a muttered exclamation the detective veered about. From Mr. Treadgold's sternly impassive countenance his glance whisked incredulously to the muffled form before them.

'Then who's this, bong jee?' he murmured. Springing forward, he snatched the bag from the hooded face.

It was the mayor, Joseph Ruffier.

Chapter 32

AT THE SAME INSTANT Le Borgne leaped.

Cackling in a cracked voice, 'Ah, misérable, then it was you in the salon that night!' he sprang at Ruffier, launching himself through the air with the force and ferocity of a wildcat, face all bloody, fingers outstretched and clawing. The corn-bin was between him and his quarry, but he disregarded it, landing doubled up on the ridged top, yet unerringly finding his mark. Lapping his powerful fingers about that bull neck, he drove his victim's head back with a crash against the solid masonry of the wall. Ruffier screamed out in terror, his eyes agonised in the relentless glare of the torches, while, heedless of the levelled guns, his hands tore at the grip encircling his throat.

The sergeant was the first to regain his presence of mind. Dropping his pistol, he hurled himself upon Le Borgne, seizing his wrists and driving his knee into his back. In a writhing mass the three men fell on the floor. By this Mr. Treadgold and the doctor had come into action, and Jacques joining them from the door, the four of them at length contrived to drag Le Borgne off. Panting, his solitary orb rolling defiance, the scrub on his face matted with blood, he remained in Jacques's grasp.

'Imbécile,' gasped the detective, settling his glasses, 'would you take the bread out of the hangman's mouth? Té,' he added, glancing at Le Borgne more closely, 'he's wounded!'

'A little slash with this snicker,' said Jacques, picking up the knife from the floor. 'I was waiting for him' – he jerked his head in Ruffier's direction – 'as Monsieur here' – now he indicated Mr. Treadgold – 'bade me. But he was too quick for me, this animal. I grabbed him, but it was dark and he broke away. *Dame!*' he added with a sage head-shake, 'a scratch in the face is better than a knife in the kidneys. Or so it seems to me!'

Then Bissonnette whirled in. The sergeant pointed at Ruffier. 'Handcuffs!' he barked.

The mayor had risen to his feet. He was a pitiable sight. There was blood on his face – it was from Le Borgne, they realised – his collar was torn, his dark suit powdered with dust. With a purely mechanical action he was brushing himself when the constable stepped up to him. There was a moment's pause. Then Ruffier presented his wrists.

For the officer he did not have as much as a glance. His gaze was rivetted on Mr. Treadgold, whose pistol again covered him. Despite his deplorable appearance, his pose was not without a certain dignity and even under its coat of blood and grime the swarthy face retained its air of unshakeable self-reliance. But the latent humour of the eyes had banished. Their expression was terrible in its basilisk hardness as he addressed Mr. Treadgold.

'So, that note of yours tonight was a trap?' he said while the constable was affixing the handcuffs.

Mr. Treadgold shrugged. 'Call it rather a test.'

The olive countenance remained impassive. 'Trap or test, if the light had been better last night, you'd have set none for me, my friend.'

The other shook his head. 'You're wrong, Ruffier. It would have made no difference. That was the doctor wearing my cape.'

Ruffier scowled. 'My compliments, Monsieur le Policier,' he said with a hard laugh. 'It was cleverly planned.'

Mr. Treadgold moved his shoulders indifferently. 'As a matter of fact, it was an accident.'

The strongly marked eyebrows came down farther, the eyes were suddenly veiled. 'When a man's luck forsakes him,' he muttered, 'the end is near!' He looked down and spoke no more.

One of the troopers from the Manor was at the door. Bigoury gave Bissonnette a whispered order and between the two men the mayor was led away. Jacques had produced a candle from his pocket and by its light the doctor was bathing Le Borgne's face with water which the servant had brought from somewhere. Hands behind his back, jaws moving, the detective stopped to watch the operation. 'It's only a surface wound – there's no real harm done,' said Wood in answer to the sergeant's unspoken question. Bigoury nodded and, clapping Le Borgne encouragingly on the shoulder, drifted to where Mr. Treadgold, having put his pistol up, with a brooding look on his face was filling his pipe.

The sergeant appeared to be deeply interested in this familiar performance, staring through his glasses at the deftly moving fingers with an air of rapt attention. He waited to speak until the pink countenance before him was enveloped in a blue wreath. Then, with an upward cant of the chin, he said curtly, 'And Mademoiselle?'

Mr. Treadgold's eyes shone. 'It's mainly owing to her pluck and intelligence that we've laid this dangerous criminal by the heels,' he remarked with feeling.

Bigoury was not impressed. 'How come?' he questioned impassively.

'She knew that Le Borgne was continually in and out of the mill during the miller's lifetime. On hearing of his escape from jail, she immediately jumped to the conclusion that it'd be the mill he'd make for, since, of course, he couldn't return to his shack.'

The sergeant scratched his head. 'I could have thought of that myself! So that's where she went that night! And she found Le Borgne here, did she?'

Mr. Treadgold nodded. 'Indeed she did and extracted from him the fact that someone was in the salon when he went back to the Manor on the night of the murder. You see, drunk though he was, he seems to have had the feeling he should let the Seigneur know that he hadn't been able to get hold of Boucheron. He reached here after the girl had taken the old gentleman to his room and despatched Jacques for the doctor.'

'That's right,' the detective broke in. 'Le Borgne left Lhermite's eleven striking, Batisse told me. That would have brought him to the Manor by a quarter past.'

'You'll hear the story from Le Borgne himself, only he's a bit upset just now, I fancy. At any rate, he told the girl that he entered the house through the kitchen, as usual, and went through to the linen room to look for the Seigneur. The linen room was dark, but there was a light in the salon. Adams was dead on the floor with the lighted lamp beside him. Believing that it was the Seigneur who had had another seizure, Le Borgne went closer to look. As he did so, he says, something seemed to move in the shadow by the door and he heard a heavy footstep go creaking through the hall. He didn't stop to investigate, for at that moment he discovered that it was not the old gentleman, but Adams who was lying there, and he fled in a panic by the linen room window.'

The sergeant was listening attentively. 'But how did you know it wasn't Boucheron? After all...'

'I didn't know, except that Boucheron was wearing goloshes, and goloshes don't creak. But it was Ruffier himself who finally settled the question...'

'By attacking Le Borgne here tonight, do you mean?'

'Precisely. You see,' Mr. Treadgold went on rather diffidently, 'in that note of mine I told him that Le Borgne had got in touch with the girl, that she'd wormed out of him the fact that he'd actually seen the murderer of Adams and that, on condition she came to the rendezvous alone, Le Borgne had arranged to meet her at the mill at ten o'clock tonight when she hoped to persuade him to reveal the murderer's identity...'

'Just a minute!' drawled Bigoury. 'I didn't understand that Le Borgne actually saw the murderer – so that he'd recognise him again, I mean...'

'He didn't. But Ruffier was not to know this. I arranged with Jacques to slip away to the mill here an hour ahead of time as a protection for Le Borgne in case Ruffier stole a march on us. Ruffier had no idea that Le Borgne was hiding here and I calculated – rightly, as it happened – that he'd wait outside for his quarry to appear. Le Borgne and Jacques concealed themselves inside and Le Borgne's instructions were to lie low until ten o'clock, and then come out and show himself ostentatiously, with Jacques close at hand in anticipation of an attack.'

The detective wagged his head dubiously. 'And supposing Ruffier had taken a shot at Le Borgne as he stood there in the doorway?'

'He wouldn't have risked it,' was the prompt reply. 'There were police at the Manor, in the grounds, too, for aught he knew to the contrary. The knife was silent, and just as sure...'

The sergeant nodded, nibbling a finger. 'Answer me this: If Ruffier was the murderer, what was he doing in the salon a quarter of an hour after he'd done the job?'

'The same thought occurred to me,' said Mr. Treadgold. 'Only our friend the mayor can answer that question with any certainty, for the two persons who could have told us exactly how the tragedy happened are dead. For me, I believe he went back to retrieve that bayonet. Ruffier isn't the man to leave a clue like that lying about – if he did it's because he was disturbed in the act of stabbing Adams – by the Seigneur, most probably.'

Bigoury frowned. 'We've yet to learn what he was doing up at the Manor that night,' he said rather peevishly. 'Everybody's movements except his are accounted for...'

Mr. Treadgold's smile was tinged with mischief. 'I'm afraid I was responsible for sending him there.'

The sergeant stared. 'You?'

Mr. Treadgold laughed and slipped his arm in Bigoury's. 'It's a long story and I discern marked signs of impatience in the doctor. Suppose we postpone it until your day's work is done? You'll hand our friend over to the police at Trois-Ponts, I suppose?'

'The troopers will attend to that when I'm through with him. Not that I'm hopeful that he'll talk – I know his type. I thought I'd take him over to his store and question him there – I want to have a look round, anyway. Coming along?'

The other shook his head. 'It's your bird, Sergeant,' he said urbanely. 'This is where I gracefully retire. If I might offer a word of advice, however, I believe I'd take a peep in those barns of his behind the store.'

'For these heirlooms, do you mean?'

Mr. Treadgold laughed. 'Bah, those have long since been disposed of. No! For liquor!'

Bigoury nodded darkly. 'I get you!' He glanced at his watch. 'Ten-thirty – I could be at the camp in an hour's time, if that's not too late for you...'

'For the love of Heaven, H. B.,' the doctor now broke in tempestuously, 'do we stay here all night? I want to get back to the Manor. Mademoiselle de St. Rémy...'

'Dear me,' said Mr. Treadgold mildly, 'I declare I'd forgotten all about her.'

'She'll be wondering what on earth has happened to us. Come on if you're coming...'

Composedly the other tamped down his pipe with his finger. 'I don't know if you remember, George,' he remarked, 'the passage in Tristram Shandy where Uncle Toby...'

'Oh, damn your Uncle Toby!' Wood hustled his roommate out.

Chapter 33

MIDNIGHT WAS LONG PAST and still Bigoury did not appear. In Camp Number 3 Mr. Treadgold and Bigoury's friend Tisserand waited for the detective. For perhaps the tenth time Tisserand had waddled to the door to look for him. Outside the hut a great yellow moon, low down on the horizon, flooded the woods with light.

In dressing-gown and pyjamas of a chaste blue, pipe in mouth, glass in hand, Mr. Treadgold took his ease in a long chair.

'No sign of him?' he asked the clerk.

'Not yet,' Tisserand wheezed. 'What keeps the man, diable?' He swung round to the room. 'The young people are still out there,' he remarked, lowering his voice.

'Ah!' said the other blandly.

'It's already two hours they sit there in the dark,' Tisserand observed. 'I ask myself what they find to talk about!'

His companion smiled secretively. 'Plenty,' he returned.

The clerk threw up his hand. 'Bigoury!' he cried joyfully.

The little sergeant came bounding in. Whirling up to Mr. Treadgold, who had heaved himself to his feet, he flung his arms about him and kissed him resonantly on the cheek.

'Ah, sapri!' he exclaimed in French, springing back to beam at his astonished vis-à-vis, 'Monsieur Treadgold, you're a great man!'

Mr. Treadgold chuckled. 'I've had all manner of odd experiences in my life,' he observed humorously, 'but I cannot recall ever having been kissed by a policeman before!' He smiled engagingly at Bigoury. 'Are we to infer from this demonstration that our friend the mayor has confessed?'

The question seemed to sober the sergeant. 'I wouldn't say that,' he admitted, ruefully scratching his head. 'And he ain't the kind that responds to treatment. But,' he added, perking up, 'we've got plenty on him without that. Back of the store, in that yard of his, tucked away in rear of the garage under a lot of drums of oil, we found a crate full of silver and china stamped with the St. Rémy crest!'

Mr. Treadgold was radiant. 'Aha,' he cried, 'this is better than I hoped for!'

'You were right about them barns of his, too,' the detective went on. 'They're stacked with liquor – that guy must have supplied the countryside for miles around – cases of it, done up in gunny bags sim'lar to the one the doc picked up in the attic and what Ruffier wore as a mask at the mill. He and Lhermite ran that blind pig in the village between 'em, I guess, and the old flivver they had for collecting and distributing the stuff is the one Ruffier used tonight – he showed my men where he'd left it, hidden up under a hedge about a quarter of a mile from the mill. As for Lhermite, it was the old story, I reckon – when they had it all set to railroad Le Borgne he got rattled and threatened to blab. Ruffier killed him in the garage, I believe, and dropped the body out of the car where it was found. Where Ruffier made his mistake was not knocking off Batisse as well – the little runt was smarter than Lhermite in keeping out of his way, I guess. Are those sandwiches I see there?'

'Help yourself!' said Mr. Treadgold.

'It's the first bite I've had since lunch.' He took a sandwich from the tray. 'It's just a question now of gathering up the threads of evidence against our friend. The first point is, what took him to the Manor the night of Adams's murder? And what do you mean by saying that you were responsible for sending him there? Come on, sir, spill it!'

Mr. Treadgold asked for nothing better. He liked an audience. Besides, the quiet room with the moonlit woods outside seemed to invite confidences, his pipe was drawing well, and after the excitement of the evening he was finding his three fingers of Scotch uncommonly stimulating. Without speaking he went to his dressing-case and, returning with the two lots of stamps he had obtained from Ruffier, laid them on the table.

'My friends,' he said, 'I've a confession to make. Hitherto I've left you in ignorance of the real business which brought me to this remote part of the country. You, my dear Bigoury, are entitled to feel that I was remiss in not mentioning earlier a circumstance which, as I'm about to show, had an important bearing on the case. In mitigation I can only say that my failure to have done so is on all fours with the singular obtuseness I've displayed throughout!'

With that he told them of his friend Hunter's experience at St. Florentin and of his own determination to investigate Ruffier and his stamps. 'I won't pretend,' he declared, after narrating his first meeting with the mayor at the store, 'that he didn't hoodwink me, as he seems to have hoodwinked everybody in the village, from the curé down. I don't know whether you appreciate it, Sergeant, but our friend the mayor is an extraordinarily able person. With greater opportunities than his surroundings afford, he might have been a great captain of industry – I'm not alluding to his singular ruthlessness,' he added drily, 'but rather to his ability to make decisions with lightning rapidity and to look ahead. Clever as he is, however, even at that first interview between us, there were certain circumstances which left, as it were, a query mark in my mind against him. Take his wife, for instance...' He glanced sharply at the detective. 'You've questioned her, I suppose?'

Bigoury shook his head, stolidly munching. 'She flew the coop this evening. She knew all about his goings-on, I guess, though whether she approved of them... She was seen at the station tonight, her eyes red with weeping – I wouldn't wonder, she tried to stop him from going to the mill. By the way, I wired those antique dealers for a full description of the woman who sold them that porcelain.'

Mr. Treadgold indulged in a sage nod. 'You'll find it was she, I make no doubt. The afternoon I arrived, soon after I'd met Ruffier for the first time and seen him and the wife together, I happened to notice her praying in the church. I was struck by her face and the thought passed through my mind, "There's an unhappy woman!" It was perfectly evident that her husband cowed her. Yet, in binding me to secrecy about these stamps of his, Ruffier didn't hesitate to represent himself as henpecked. In my excitement over my find, the incongruity of the thing didn't strike me at the time. But it recurred to me later.'

'But what have the stamps to do with the murder?' the sergeant asked, standing up to help himself to another sandwich.

'I'm coming to that...' Delicately Mr. Treadgold sipped his drink. 'At my time of life, you know,' he pursued, 'one takes no man at face value. Ruffier said that those stamps came from letters belonging to Madame Ruffier's deceased mother. The fact that they'd been cut from their envelopes made it impossible for me to verify this assertion. But Madame Ruffier was clearly, like her husband, of a peasant type, her mother, presumably, the same, and I remember wondering idly how it was that a woman of this class should have had people writing to her from the United States, France, England, Australia, the Cape – for the most part, on expensive-looking stationery, too. But, having no suspicion of Ruffier at the moment, I didn't follow up this line of reasoning to its logical conclusion. It was only last night, on examining a torn envelope I'd chanced to pick up from the floor of Ruffier's shop, that suddenly a pent-up flood of subconscious doubts and suspicions was released and I saw the truth staring me in the face!'

While speaking he had drawn his wallet from his pocket. Extracting a creased fragment of paper from it, he spread it out upon the table while the two men drew near to examine it over his shoulder.

'If you'll look at this envelope,' said Mr. Treadgold, 'you'll notice that an irregular wedge has been roughly scissored out of it, going right through from front to back, where the stamp has been cut away...'

He turned the mutilated envelope over and, taking a folding magnifying-glass from his pocket, straightened it out and handed it to Bigoury.

'There's a seal, or at least part of one, impressed in relief on the flap,' he pointed out to him. 'Would you mind telling us what you make of it, Sergeant?'

The detective applied the lens to the paper. 'It seems to be a bird, what's left of it,' he remarked at length. 'And there's some lettering underneath. It's French. I can read Je and t-I-e-n...'

'It's Je tiendrai foy and the bird's a pelican,' Mr. Treadgold broke in quickly. 'It's the St. Rémy crest, in short. And on the front' – he reversed the envelope once more – 'while the name of the recipient has been cut away, the "Madame" survives and on the next line, look! The "Man" of the word "Manoir," meaning the Manoir de Mort Homme, and below that again a capital "S," the first letter of "St. Florentin"!'

Tisserand spoke up. 'You mean, Monsieur, that this letter was written by a member of the St. Rémy to someone at the Manor, perhaps by one of the seigneurs to his wife?'

The blue eyes flamed. 'I mean that Ruffier lied to me,' said Mr. Treadgold sternly. 'I mean that all the letters from which these stamps were clipped are the property of the St. Rémy family, as is very easily demonstrated by comparing the paper adhering to certain of the stamps I obtained from Ruffier with the texture of this envelope...'

'I begin to follow now,' Bigoury put in. 'I wondered what you'd been up to at the Manor last night when I met you coming down from the attic. I noticed those old trunks of letters and papers...'

'Old letters, and bills, and leases, and even old newspapers and farm catalogues,' Mr. Treadgold replied. 'The Seigneurs de Mort Homme seem to have had a rooted objection to throwing anything away. If you'll forgive my saying so, my friends, it's a characteristic French trait!'

The detective grinned and winked at Tisserand. 'And Ruffier plundered those trunks of their letters at the same time as he cleared out the Seigneur's cache, is that your idea?'

Mr. Treadgold blew a cloud of smoke. 'I'm not so sure. The fact that mysterious noises were heard over a period of weeks suggests that he made repeated visits to the attic. There's no evidence that anybody at St. Florentin, even Boucheron, knew that those heirlooms were concealed in the house and it's my belief that Ruffier stumbled upon their hiding-place more or less by chance.'

'But, in that case, what was he doing up in the attic?'

Mr. Treadgold shrugged. 'He had this liquor business, hadn't he? The Manor, with its reputation of being haunted, would have made a safe storehouse. However that may be, I fancy that, having removed these valuables, he returned, either to fossick around for more or perhaps merely to see what else he could pick up. It was undoubtedly on one of these expeditions that the miller surprised him, probably as he was carting the stuff away — to shift all that china and glass must have required more than one trip. Rummaging in those trunks, he came across some letters in their original envelopes and, having heard vaguely of people collecting stamps, took them along with him on the chance of being able to dispose of them.

'He was certainly in the attic last Sunday night, the day the old gentleman and the girl arrived,' he went on, 'for that evening they heard sounds in the house — a sort of heavy, scraping noise, the girl called it in describing it to the doctor: clearly, the sound of a trunk being dragged across the floor. Now do you realise what took our friend to the Manor on the night of the murder? He'd seen me the evening before and found that I was willing, as he thought, to pay blindly any price he cared to ask for the stamps. Those trunks must have seemed to him a veritable gold mine and he lost no time in returning to the attic on the first available opportunity which was the next evening.' Mr. Treadgold laid his hand on the larger of the two packets of stamps. 'And here's the harvest of that night of blood!' he added gravely.

His pipe had gone out and he made a break to relight it.

'The discovery of the St. Rémy crest on the flap of that envelope,' the placid voice proceeded, 'was like a beacon shining through the fog in which we had all been groping. I began to think back. I was already conscious of a certain rhythm in the sequence of events, imposed by some unseen force which, quietly and firmly, controlled and guided them. As a start-off, Le Borgne is arrested and the coroner's jury dragooned into entering a verdict against him. There's talk of an alibi and immediately, of the two men who might have cleared the accused, one vanishes and the other refuses to speak. The case against Le Borgne continues to crumble and Jacques's fingerprints are found on the musket. Forthwith, that gold box is discovered in his suitcase and, on top of this, the doctor, exploring in the attic, is the victim of a murderous attack. Finally, there was that shot at the doctor last night.'

'That was Ruffier, all right,' the sergeant growled. 'You remember he was from home, paying a late call on Boucheron?'

'I don't mind confessing,' said Mr. Treadgold, 'that until the incident of the shot, following immediately upon my discovery regarding the stamps, my suspicion was focussed on Boucheron. But that shot hardened into virtual certainty my growing belief that Ruffier was the author of these murders. Old Côté was putty in his hands – until your appearance on the scene, Sergeant, he ran the whole investigation, profiting by my impulsive zeal in outlining a case against Le Borgne to deflect suspicion from himself. Thereafter, as I discovered on looking back, he was invariably to be found hovering on the fringe of each successive event. At the Manor yesterday afternoon you questioned him about Batisse, and thereafter Batisse is dumb: you let him see that you're suspicious of Jacques, and within the half-hour Bissonnette, going through Jacques's things, comes across the gold box. We don't know that he was in the Manor when the doctor was slugged, but a minute or two afterwards he turned up in his car and there was plenty of time for him to have attacked the doctor, regained his car, parked somewhere out of sight but close at hand, and driven up to the house, as though he were just arriving. But it was that shot at the doctor which finally opened my eyes.'

'How?' the sergeant questioned.

'It was meant for me – the doctor was wearing my cape. Not an hour before Ruffier had seen me in it when I called on him at the store and I realised at once that he must have followed me back to the camp.'

'But why should he have wanted to shoot you?'

Mr. Treadgold sighed. 'That was my vanity, I'm afraid. You see I told him I was an amateur criminologist – I also let him see that you were convinced of Le Borgne's innocence. That was enough for him – he knew that the chase was open. With his type of mind, thought and action are one. I was gambling on that when I wrote him that note tonight.'

'Then you still had no suspicion of him when you saw him at the store last evening?'

'Yes – and no. I happened to notice something rather curious on arriving at the store. It worried me all through our talk...' He paused. 'You told me that, yesterday afternoon, after I left the Manor you had another look at those tyre-marks of Boucheron's. I suppose Ruffier didn't happen to see you?'

The detective adjusted his glasses to peer at the other. 'As a matter of fact, he did. He came over from the coroner's to fetch the bayonet – Perronneau wanted it – and Bissonnette sent him out to me...'

'Did you tell him that one of those treads was worn?'

Bigoury looked rather uncomfortable. 'Now that I come to think of it, I believe I did!'

Mr. Treadgold nodded. 'Just as I suspected. When I reached the store Ruffier was out in the garage. Do you know what he was doing? He was changing a tyre on an old flivver.'

'Boucheron's?'

'No. Boucheron's is a roadster. This was a sedan.'

'That's the car he was out in tonight – I guess he used it on all his nocturnal excursions. What was the idea?'

'Nothing, except that he was playing safe. That car had straight-sided tyres, the same as Boucheron's, and one was probably defective. He realised that he, too, might have left tracks that night which you might have picked up, and he was taking no chances. It could be a coincidence, I told myself – he might have had a puncture. But I couldn't get rid of the feeling that chance had given me a glimpse of the man we were looking for – this shadowy figure that forestalled every move, obliterated every clue. And then, when I got back to camp and discovered that the piece of paper I'd picked up off the floor was an envelope with the stamp cut off it and that it bore the St. Rémy crest, I began to see the light. That shot at the doctor told me the rest!' He wagged his head. 'When a brain of that type turns to crime, the combination's as lethal as dynamite! To catch him red-handed was the only way. If he'd had as much as a sniff of the trap I laid for him, you might have whistled for your evidence. That's the only reason I left you in the dark, old man. You didn't take it amiss, I hope?'

The detective laughed. 'That's quite all right. We've nailed our man, that's the main thing. But tell me this, how did Adams meet his death?'

The blue eyes were suddenly dreamy. 'I doubt if we shall ever know. He and the Seigneur may have talked about the rents, as Boucheron alleges, but I think that when the old gentleman cried out, "I've been robbed!" he was referring to his cache in the attic. And the proof is that, almost directly after, he ran out of the linen room towards the front of the house where the staircase was, presumably to show Adams the empty hiding-place: at any rate, as we know, Adams followed with the lamp.'

'And Ruffier?'

'Ruffier's movements are less easy to reconstruct. He seems to have had no idea that the Seigneur and the girl were living in the house which suggests that he had some direct access to the attic, without going through the lower rooms. There's a shed at the side of the house, from the roof of which an active man might scramble in at one of the windows of that first-floor landing. Furthermore, he doesn't seem to have been familiar with the geography of the house or he'd have been able to find a way out without having had to kill Adams. What I think happened is that, attracted by the sound of angry voices below, he crept down from the attic and was listening at the linen room door when the Seigneur burst out upon him. Whether because the old gentleman recognised him and knew him for the thief or from sheer excitement, the Seigneur collapsed in the vestibule and Ruffier bolted into the dark salon. From the fact that only Adams's fingerprints were on the lamp and that it was found intact and still alight on the floor, I infer that, perhaps on some frantic gesture of the Seigneur's death agony, Adams went straight on into the salon and put the lamp down to look about. The only possible place of concealment in that barren room is behind the door and I believe Ruffier drew back there. As Adams entered with the lighted lamp, Ruffier recognised him and, not knowing which way to escape, silently drew the bayonet in his gloved hands from the musket and waited for the other to turn.' He shrugged. 'There's the picture as I see it and for what it's worth. Your guess is as good as mine. Only Ruffier can tell us the truth!'

The door fell back. Bissonnette looked in. 'Your call to Quebec, Sergeant!'

The detective sprang about. 'I'm coming!' He whirled to Mr. Treadgold. 'We'll speak of this again tomorrow. Bonne nuit et merci, ami!' Fluttering his hand at Tisserand, he scurried out into the moonlight.

In an impressive silence the clerk contemplated Mr. Treadgold. 'Good work,' he said at length. 'Our little Napoléon will earn fresh laurels and they'll print his picture in L'Evènement. He should be grateful to you, Monsieur. Eh bien, I leave you to your slumbers!'

He went to the door, peering cautiously out. 'Psst!' he called to Mr. Treadgold.

'What now, my friend?'

'The little Mademoiselle, she's crying!'

Composedly Mr. Treadgold joined him and, an arm about the other's unwieldy shoulders, glanced along the dark verandah.

He chuckled softly. 'She has her head on his shoulder, anyway!'

The fat man gurgled. 'How droll are women! When you expect them to smile, they weep! Love should be gay, maudit! Bonne nuit!' Still gurgling happily, he stumped out.

Left alone Mr. Treadgold went to the dressing table and, gathering up a leather-bound volume lying there, bore it to the light. Having found the passage he wanted, he read aloud to himself in his gentle voice: '*I thought love had been a joyous thing, quoth my uncle Toby. 'Tis the most serious thing, an' please your honour, that is in the world, said the corporal.*'

With that he closed the book and turned his face, kindly and wise, towards the dark verandah.

THE END

Visit our website to explore the list of great Golden Age books and sign up to our new titles newsletter:

www.oleanderpress.com/golden-age-crime

OREON titles in this series

The Man in the Dark
John Ferguson – 9781915475220

The Dressing Room Murder
J.S. Fletcher – 9781915475213

Glory Adair and the Twenty-First Burr
Victor Lauriston – 9781915475206

The Tunnel Mystery
J.C. Lenehan – 9781915475190

Murder on the Marsh
John Ferguson – 9781915475183

The Fatal Five Minutes
R.A.J. Walling – 9781915475176

The Crime of a Christmas Toy
Henry Herman – 9781915475169

Death of an Editor
Vernon Loder – 9781915475152

Death on May Morning
Max Dalman – 9781915475145

The Hymn Tune Mystery
George A. Birmingham – 9781915475091

The Essex Murders
by Vernon Loder – 9781915475053

The Middle of Things
J.S. Fletcher – 9781915475060

The Boat Race Murder
R. E. Swartwout – 9781915475039

Murder at the College
Victor L. Whitechurch – 9781999900489

The Charing Cross Mystery
by J.S. Fletcher – 9781909349711

The Doctor of Pimlico
William Le Queux – 9781909349735

Who Killed Alfred Snowe?
by J. S. Fletcher – 9781915475015

The Yorkshire Moorland Mystery
by J. S. Fletcher – 9781999900472

Fatality in Fleet Street *
Christopher St John Sprigg – 9781909349759

* Free ePub & PDF on sign-up to the
OREON newsletter:

www.oleanderpress.com/golden-age-crime